# Murder Most Confederate

# Murder Most Confederate

## Tales of Crimes Quite Uncivil

Edited by Martin H. Greenberg

Cumberland House
Nashville, Tennessee

Published by Cumberland House Publishing, Inc., 431 Harding Industrial Drive, Nashville, Tennessee 37211

Cover design by Gore Studio, Inc.
Page design by Mike Towle

Library of Congress Cataloging-in-Publication Data
Murder most Confederate : tales of crimes quite uncivil / edited by Martin H. Greenberg.
    p. cm
  ISBN 1-58182-120-4 (hardcover : alk. paper)
    1. United States–History–Civil War, 1861–1865–Fiction. 2. Detective and mystery stories, American–Southern States. 3. Historical fiction, American–Southern States. 4. Southern States–Fiction. I. Greenberg, Martin Harry.

PS648.C54 M87 2000
813'.087208358–dc21

                                                                    00-055487

Printed in the United States of America
1 2 3 4 5 6 7 8 9 — 05 04 03 02 01 00

# Contents

# Introduction

The War Between the States. The War of the Rebellion. The War of Northern Aggression. The North versus the South. A conflict fought by one-half of a nation against the other more than a century ago, and a conflict that inspires close examination and deep passion even today.

With a higher casualty rate than any other war involving our nation, the Civil War threatened to tear a relatively young United States apart just when it was on the cusp of becoming a powerful nineteenth-century force. Divided by economic, political, and social issues such as individual states' sovereign rights, industrial vs. agrarian economies, and slavery, the nation was a powder keg of dissent waiting for a fateful match. On December 20, 1860, South Carolina voted to repeal the U.S. Constitution. They were followed by Mississippi, Florida, Alabama, Georgia, Louisiana, Texas, Virginia, Arkansas, Tennessee, and North Carolina. Thousands of men flocked together to rally behind their respective banners. In the South the conflict was seen as a call to arms to preserve their continued way of life and states' rights. For the North this, too, was a war of great importance, as they saw themselves battling to hold a young nation together.

Actual hostilities didn't commence until April 12, 1861, when General P. G. T. Beauregard exercised orders to fire upon Fort Sumter in South Carolina, then held by Union troops. The Confederates unleashed a firestorm that would rage from the Pennsylvania valleys of Gettysburg to the twisted wreckage of Georgia in the wake of General Sherman's infamous march to the sea. More than three million men donned either Union blue or Rebel gray and marched into a war that lasted four and a half years. When the cannons finally fell silent, almost half a million men lay dead, and America was still one nation, but at a terrible price.

The South began the war seemingly outmanned, outsupplied, and outgunned, but what they lacked in men, materials, and equipment they made up for in the brilliance of their military leaders—men like Robert E. Lee, Thomas "Stonewall" Jackson, and Nathan Bedford Forrest—and the tenacity and spirit of the men they commanded. The courage and honor of the men who fought for the Confederacy still exist in the men and women of the region, and the ideals the South fought for, especially the sovereign rights of the state, are still upheld, although now more as a tribute to what had been lost after the war.

Of course, when a nation's attention is turned toward something as significant as war, opportunities for other crimes present themselves. Against the backdrop of brother fighting brother and cities and states under siege, civilians and soldiers alike could use the cover of conflict to steal, cheat, spy, and even murder, for whatever reason, whether it be for the honor of their cause or pure personal gain. Sometimes, the crimes committed because of war can be the most terrible of all.

With that in mind, we've assembled this all-new anthology of crime and mystery stories set in the Confederacy. From the war-torn city of Richmond, Virginia, where a husband and wife run an unusual boarding house, to the story of two brothers fighting on opposite sides of the war, and of the terrible price one of them pays for happiness. From men and women doing their duty for their country to rogues and criminals committing crimes obscured by the ongoing horrors of the Civil War, the savage side of war is revealed is these stories of murder most Confederate.

*—John Helfers*

# Murder Most Confederate

# The Hessian

## Doug Allyn

Horsemen drifted out of the dawn mist like wolves, strung out loosely across the hillside in a ragged line. Two outriders on the flanks, seven more in the main body. Polly guessed they'd already put riflemen in position at the stone fence beyond her barn, ready to cut down anyone who tried to run.

Her son was sitting on the corner of the porch, whetting the scythe, daydreaming.

"Jason," Polly said quietly. "Riders are coming. Get to the barn. And walk! All the way."

Without a word the ten-year-old rose and sauntered across the yard as he'd been taught, toting a hay blade longer than he was tall. He disappeared inside. A moment later the upper loading loft door opened a crack.

Picking up a besom broom, Polly casually swept her way across the porch to the front door of the farmhouse. She opened it to sweep off the sill, leaving it ajar as she turned to face the riders coming across the stubbled fields to the house.

Federals. Of a sort. Only one rider was in full uniform—a Union cavalry captain; tall, hollow-eyed, and gaunt as a vulture, with a thin mustache and goatee. His men were irregulars, dressed in a mix of work clothes and uniform coats or pants. Farmers and tradesmen from the look of them. Definitely Union, though. Their mounts were sleek and well fed. She'd heard Forrest's men were slaughtering their horses for food.

The riders sized her up as they filed into the yard. A farm wife, square as a stump in a man's flannel shirt, canvas trousers, and pebble-leg boots; handsome once, but careworn now, auburn hair awry in the November wind, her hands reddened and rough from field work.

Polly scanned their faces, desperately hoping to recognize someone—damn. Aaron Meachum was with them, slouch hat down over his eyes, stubbled cheek distorted by a plug of chaw. Trouble. Casually, she sidled half a step closer to the door.

"Good day to you, ma'am," their leader said softly. "I am Captain Charles Gilliaume, of the Eighth Missouri. My men and I—"

"These men aren't Eighth Missouri," Polly said coldly. "They're militia. Hessians, most likely."

"Hessians?"

"It's what these Rebs call the kraut-heads," Meachum said. "Like them German mercenaries back in the revolution? Most of Sigel's troops was Germans from Saint Louis when they raided through here in '62."

"I see," The captain nodded. "You're quite right, ma'am. My men are a militia unit from Jefferson City, and many of them are of German heritage. But they're as American as you or I now. May we step down?"

"Captain, there is a creek on the far side of my garden. You're welcome to water your animals. I have nothing more to offer you. We've been picked clean by both sides. Hospitality in southern Missouri is runnin' a little thin these days, hard to come by as seed corn."

"She'd find grain quick enough if we were wearin' butternut brown," Aaron Meachum said, spitting a stream of tobacco juice onto her porch. "The whole damn McKee family's secesh; everybody 'round here knows it."

"Is that true, ma'am?" the captain asked. "I see no men about. Are they with the rebels?"

"My husband is in Springfield trying to earn a few dollars. His eldest son is with Bedford Forrest up Tennessee way; his second boy's with the Union blockade at Charleston. The two youngest went off with Sterling Price after he whipped y'all at Wilson's Creek in '61."

"Rebels," Meachum spat.

"Three Confederates," Polly corrected, "and one Federal. At least they're *real* soldiers, Captain."

"As we are, ma'am."

"Real soldiers don't ride with trash. This fella, Aaron Meachum, is a jayhawker who was murdering and burning in Kansas long before the war. He runs easier with coyotes than with men."

"Mr. Meachum isn't actually a member of our unit, ma'am; he was retained as a guide."

"Well, he doubtless knows the trails through these hills. He's used most of them running from the law. If he's your guide, Captain, you're on the road to perdition."

"Armies are like families, ma'am; you can't choose your kin. We're seeking slaves and deserters, Miz McKee. I'm told you have slaves here."

"Who told you that? Meachum? Captain, this ain't no plantation. We raise saddle horses and draft animals, and we're only three days from the Illinois line. Even if we held with slavery, and we don't, it's tough enough to keep animals from runnin' off to say nothin' of men. Our stock's been stolen, our crops burned. We had no slaves before the war and we've surely no need of them now. There's only me and my boy here, you have my word."

"In that case a search won't take long," Gilliaume said. At his nod, the troopers and Meachum began to dismount.

"No!" Polly's voice cracked like a whip, freezing them as she snaked the scattergun from inside the open door, leveling it at Gilliaume, cocking back both hammers.

"Ma'am, be reasonable, you can't possibly prevail against us."

"It won't matter to you, Captain. Or to Meachum. Or to one or two near you. My boy is covering you from the barn with a ten-gauge goose gun loaded with double-ought buckshot. If I fire, so will he."

"You'll still die. As will your son."

"No matter. We've only a little flour and some corn meal. My boy's legs are bowing 'cause Rebs butchered our milk cow. Soldier boys have taken all but the gleanings of the fields. For God's sake, sir, your animals are better fed than most folks around here. We have nothing for you. Unless Old Sam Curtis is passing out medals for murdering women and boys."

Gilliaume stared coolly down at Polly, ignoring the shotgun muzzle, taking her measure. She knew that look. Death had pushed past him to kill his friends so often that he was weary of waiting, impatient for his turn.

But not today. "Gentlemen, the lady says she has no slaves and I believe her. And since there's obviously no forage for us here, we'll move on."

"You're lettin' her run us off?" Meachum said, outraged. "Our orders say deserters, slaves, and arms. She's armed, ain't she?"

"So she is," Gilliaume said wryly. "Personally, I interpret our orders to mean military arms, not rusty shotguns, but you have my permission to disarm her if you wish, Mr. Meachum. But kindly give me a moment to back my mount away. This is my best coat and bloodstains are damned bothersome to remove."

Clucking to his gelding, Gilliaume backed off a few paces, touched his hat brim to Polly, then turned away. The other riders followed. Leaving her to face Meachum alone. She shifted the shotgun, centering it on his chest.

"You got the edge today, Polly McKee." Meachum spat. "But this ain't over. I'll be back."

"But not by daylight I'll wager, you jayhawk son of a bitch. If you ever set foot on my land again, Aaron Meachum, I'll blow you out of your raggedy-ass boots. Now git! *Git!*" she roared into the face of his mount, spooking the beast. It shied away, kicking. Meachum sawed at the reins but the brute's manners were no better than its owner's. Bucking and snorting, it sprinted off to rejoin the others, with Meachum clinging to the saddle horn, cursing his animal and Polly all the way.

The laughter and catcalls that greeted him echoed off the hills. It wasn't much comfort, but it was something.

She waited on the porch, her old scattergun in the crook of her arm, watching the troop splash through the creek and vanish into the woods beyond. And then she waited a bit longer, until she was dead certain they were gone.

Stepping into the house, she carefully stood the shotgun in its customary place by the door. And then, in the sweet-scented silence of her parlor, she released a long, ragged breath. And hugged herself, fiercely, trying to control the trembling.

IT WAS A DAY for visitors. A little before noon, working in the barn, Polly heard the *tlot, tlot* of approaching hoofbeats. Meachum? Not likely, not openly. She peeked out through the crack of the door.

A single-seat Stanhope buggy was coming up the road from the west, a lone woman at the reins. Turning the rig in at the gate, she guided her animal down the long lane, slowing it to a walk as she approached the farmhouse.

Polly stepped out, shading her eyes, waiting. Her visitor was dressed warmly for travel, a fine, seal plush cape over a tailored woolen suit, the first new clothes Polly'd seen since . . . she couldn't remember how long.

"Afternoon, ma'am. Can I help you?"

"Pleasse, I'm becomp lost," the woman replied, her accent harsh. Hessian. Polly's eyes narrowed. "I left Corridon this mornink—"

"Just wheel that buggy around and head out the gate, miss. A mile farther on, the road splits. The north fork will take you to Centerville."

"I'm not going to Centerville."

"Look, ma'am, I haven't got all day—"

"Pleasse, I'm seeking the McKee place," the Hessian woman said desperately. "Is it far from here?"

Polly stepped closer to the buggy, frowning up at the woman. Younger than she thought, face as pale as buttermilk, nearly invisible eyelashes. A bruise and some swelling along her jaw. Still, all in all, a handsome girl, Hessian or not.

"What do you want with the McKees? Who are you?"

"My name is Birgit Randolph. My hussband is Tyler Randolph. He iss a cousin to Angus McKee. He—"

"I'm Polly McKee, Gus's wife. I've known Tyler since he was a sprout, but I still don't know who the hell you are. Tyler ain't married."

"We married earlier this year. We met when he was with the state militia in Saint Louis and became friends. He was very . . . dashing. After the riots he joined General Price. We wrote back and fort' when he was in Arkansas. This past April he came for me and we were married."

"What do you mean he came for you? Came where?"

"To Saint Louis. Tyler iss not a soldier anymore. He was wounded at Pea Ridge. He is discharged now."

"Wounded how? How bad?"

"His leg. Shot. It is mostly healed, but he limps. It causes him pain, I think. He never says. He's very . . . stubborn."

"That sounds like Tyler. Where have y'all been stayin'?"

"At his farm near Mountain Grove."

"I'll be damned," Polly said, shaking her head. It was too much; first, Meachum and his jayhawks, now a half-daft Hessian woman claiming to be kin. The damned war was making the world a madhouse.

"Well, you might as well step in out of the wind, miss—I mean—Mrs. Randolph. I'm afraid we're out of coffee—"

"I haff tea and some sugar," Birgit said, offering Polly a three-pound sack. "Tyler said the plundering hass been bad here."

"We get hit by both sides," Polly conceded grimly, leading the way. "Come into the kitchen, I'll make us some tea."

Birgit hesitated just inside the door. Though the walls hadn't seen paint in years, the small farmhouse was immaculate.

"You have a nice home. Very clean. Even it smells nice."

"What did you expect? A pig pen?"

"No, I—please. I know I don't always say things right but I don't mean to make you angry. I think I've come at a bad time."

"There aren't any good times nowadays. And exactly why have you come, ma'am? What do you want here?"

"Tyler—told me to come to you. He hoped you can drive me to Saint Louis, then bring the buggy back here. He will send for it later."

"Send for the buggy? But not for you? Why? Farm life too rough for your taste?"

"No. I grew up on farm in Bavaria. I'm not afraid of work."

"What then? Ah, the lame dirt farmer isn't a dashing rebel lieutenant anymore? So you go runnin' home to Mama. Sweet Jesus, serves Tyler right for marryin' a Hessian in the first place."

"I'm not Hessian."

"Don't lie to me, I know damned well what you are!"

"I'm not!" Birgit glared, flushing, not backing off an inch. "My family is German, but we are come from Freystadt in Bavaria! Hessians come from *Hesse*! I'm not Hessian! And I didn't leaf Tyler. He drove me out!"

"What are you talking about?"

"It's true! I tell him our child is growing in me, and he got terrible angry. He says I must go back to my family. And I say no, and he says I must obey him. Still I say no. And he . . . struck me!" Her hand strayed to her bruised mouth, her eyes brimming. "And now I am come here, and you are angry with me, too—I don't know why—but I don't anymore know what to do. I don't know what to do!"

Polly knew. Wordlessly, she wrapped the younger woman in her massive arms, holding her while she sobbed like a lost child. Which she was, in a way. Good lord, the girl couldn't be more than seventeen or eighteen. Polly was barely forty, but Birgit's age seemed like a fever dream, dimly remembered now. The low moan of the blue enameled teapot broke the spell.

"I'm sorry," Birgit said, pulling away. "This is my own trouble. I shouldn't burden you."

"Don't talk foolish," Polly said, lifting the kettle off the stove lid, filling two vitreous china mugs. "God help you, girl, we're family now. Sit yourself down at the kitchen table, we'll work something out."

"But how?" Birgit asked numbly, sipping the steaming brew. "Tyler doesn't want me. He doesn't want my child."

"That can't be true. He had to snake through half the damned Union army to marry you. Discharge papers or no, he could have been lynched or thrown in prison any step of the way. Tyler's a stubborn boy; all the Randolphs are, and the McKees, too. There's no quit in any of 'em. If he was willing to risk dyin' to marry you in April, he hasn't changed his mind. There must be more to this. How are things between you two? Has he hit you before?"

"No, never, never. It's been good with us. The best. But this last month, he's . . . dark. Far off. He stays up nights, watching. There are fires in the hills near the farm. Deserters, he says. Or jayhawkers. Then a few days ago, men took our plowhorse. Five of them. Came up on Tyler in the field and just took it. He doesn't speak to me since. I thought telling him of the baby would cheer him but . . ." She swallowed, shaking her head.

Polly sipped her tea, mulling it over. "He's afraid," she said simply.

"Afraid? Tyler?"

"Oh, not of dyin'. After all the warrin' that boy's seen, death's less troublesome than a drunken uncle. It's you he's afraid for. Afraid he can't protect you. Or your child. That's a terrible fear for a man to face, especially a soldier like Tyler. He's seen the killing, knows what can happen. And in his heart, he's afraid of failing you, though I doubt he realizes it."

"So he drives me away?"

"Looks like it."

"What do I do?"

"Depends. Maybe he's right. God knows there's trouble in the wind around here."

"You stay."

"This place is all we've got. You'll be safer in Saint Louis, Birgit. Maybe you should go home."

"No. Tyler is my home."

"You sure about that? You seem awful young to me."

"It's true, I am, maybe. But I know. When I met Tyler, Saint Louis is full of young soldiers. Thousands. And I am at a cotillion, and Tyler is laughing with friends when he sees me. And he walks over and we talk a minute. No more. And I already know."

"Know what?"

Birgit eyed Polly's wind-weathered face a moment, then shrugged. "Laugh if you want, but I look at Tyler and I see . . . our children. I see my life. With him. But maybe you're right, maybe I am just . . . Hessian."

"No. I was wrong about that. And about you. I'm sorry for that. And Tyler was dead wrong to treat you like he done, though I can't fault his reasons."

"I don't care about his reasons. He's wrong to push me away. And I was wrong to leaf. I want to go back."

"It's not that simple. These are dangerous times, he's got good cause to fear for you."

"I know. I am afraid, too. But I'm more afraid to lose him, to lose what we have together."

"Havin' a stout heart's all well and good, darlin', but it ain't hardly enough. There are men in these hills who'd kill you for your horse or a dollar. Or no reason at all. And the truth is, Tyler can't always be there to protect you. You'll have to protect one another. Do you know about guns?"

"A little. Tyler bought me a pocket pistol. He tried to teach me but I'm terrible with it."

"Just like a man," Polly said dryly. "Give the little lady a little gun. Know the trouble with pistols? Men won't believe women can shoot. You have to kill 'em to prove it. Or die tryin'. That there's a woman's gun," she said, indicating a coach shotgun beside the back door. "No skill required, only sand enough to touch it off. You still have to watch out for border trash, but they'd better watch out, too. I can teach all you need to know in twenty minutes. If you'd like."

"Yes, I would. Thank you."

"We'll finish our tea first, talk a little. These days I seldom see other women. I work like a man, dress like one. Sometimes I think I'm turning into one."

"I think you are very much woman, Mrs. McKee. And your home—now don't be mad with me—*is* very clean. It even smells clean. What is that scent?"

"*Eau de Lilac.* Lilac water. Before the war, with the boys home and their clothes and boots and such, sometimes it'd get to smellin' like a horse barn in here. Lilac water helps. I'm surprised you can smell it at all; I've watered it down somethin' fierce tryin' to make it last. The boys each promised to bring me a fresh bottle when they went off soldierin'. "

"You say *boys.* How many?"

"Angus had the four older boys by his first wife, Sarah. She died of the consumption, quite young. It wasn't like you and Tyler with us, me and Gus didn't meet at no dance. I was orphaned, livin' with kin, and Angus needed a mother for his boys. I was only fifteen when we married. We've got a boy of our own now, Jason, and I lost a girl at childbirth. It ain't always been easy, but we've built ourselves a life here. It was a good place before the war. We'll make it so again."

"But you . . . care for him? Your husband?"

"Oh, surely. But Gus is . . . a bit older, set in his ways. But we're a good match, mostly we pull together like a yoked team. But I can't say I've ever had a moment like you talked about, no . . . special feeling like that. We just make the best we can of whatever comes. To be honest, he's been gone so long I wonder sometimes if things will be the same with us . . . afterward."

"Gone to where?"

"The hills. I tell folks he's in Springfield, but he's not. After Price's troops got drove down to Arkansas, both sides were raidin' the border, runnin' off our stock. So Angus took the last of our horses up into the hills. Been movin' around with 'em since, hidin' 'em away so us and the boys can start over when the war ends. If it ever does. When he left we thought it'd be few months, a year at most. Seems like forever now."

"Maybe not much longer. Tyler says it will end soon."

"Darlin', I've been hearin' that ol' song since '61."

"No, it is true. Tyler saw a paper. The Federals have all the Shenandoah Valley. Price's men are scattered. Hood is retreating from Atlanta and the city is burning."

"Atlanta burning? But why?"

Birgit shrugged helplessly. Even in faultless English, no words could explain the madness on the land.

"Dear God," Polly said, slumping back in her chair. "This war may stop someday, but it won't be finished for a hundred years. No wonder the hills are fillin' with deserters and the jayhawkers are on the prowl. Both sides smell blood. You need to get home, girl, if that's what you mean to do. But first I'm gonna teach you a little about killin'. In a lady-like fashion, of course."

In half an hour, Polly instructed Birgit in the basics of the short-barreled coach gun. Pointed and fired at close range, the stunted scattergun would erase anything in its path from a poplar stump to three men standing abreast.

The girl took to the gun as a practical matter, learning to dispense death in defense of herself and her own with no more compunction than killing a coyote after chickens. Or a child.

Neither woman derived the pleasure men take from slaughter. It was a chore to be done, perhaps more dangerous than some, but also more necessary. At the lesson's end Birgit could manage the coach gun competently. And as she seated herself in the buggy to leave, Polly placed the stubby weapon on her lap.

"You take this with you, I've got another. And if there's trouble on the road, don't hesitate. These boys been killin' each other regular for a long time, they're damned quick at it. Surprise and that gun are all you have."

"I'll manage. If nothing else, I think Tyler will hear me out when I explain how things will be with us now."

"I expect he will at that," Polly grinned. "You can make Corridon before dusk. Stay the night there, move on in the morning. You'll be home before supper."

"And in spring, when my time comes for the baby, can I send for you?"

"Of course, darlin', surely. I'll come runnin' and we'll haul that child into this world together. I'll see you then, Mrs. Randolph, maybe sooner if this madness ends and our boys come home. Meantime, you take care, hear?"

Jason brought in a load of kindling he had gathered in the woods and after feeding him, Polly sent him down the valley to stay over with a cousin, as was customary during the nights of a new moon.

But instead of finishing her work in the barn, Polly spent the last of the afternoon cleaning the house, absurdly pleased that Birgit noted how well she kept it. Only women's opinions matter. Men wouldn't notice a slaughtered hog on the sofa unless they had to shift it to sit down.

With the house immaculate, Polly hauled the copper bathtub into the kitchen and put water on to boil. And for a moment, she glimpsed herself in the hall mirror. And couldn't help thinking how fresh and young Birgit looked. Her own face was growing leathery, weathered by the wind and the work. She wondered how Angus saw her now, and wondered if she'd ever truly feel like a woman again . . .

Gunshot. A single blast, echoing down the valley like distant thunder. Polly froze, listening for another. Nothing. Which might be good. Because she was sure she'd recognized the bark of a coach gun. And not many used them. Banking the fire in the kitchen stove, she took her own gun and eased out onto the shaded porch. To wait.

An hour crept by. Half of another. Dusk settled over the hills and still she waited, standing in the shadows. A sliver of silver moon was inching above the trees when she heard the distant drum of hoofbeats nearing, then the clatter of a wagon as the Stanhope buggy burst over the crest of a hill, hurtling madly down the moonlit road toward the farm.

Polly was up and running as the buggy skidded through the gate into the yard. Birgit sawed on the reins, yanking her lathered, gasping animal to a halt. Her face and clothing were mud-smeared and filthy, hair awry, eyes wild.

"What happened?"

"A man came out of the woods, grabbed the horse. I warned him off but he won't let go. I struck him with the buggy whip and he rushed at me, grabbed me, tried to drag me down and"—she swallowed—"and I shot him!

"He pulled me from the buggy as he fell and I ran into the woods. Lost. Couldn't find my way. After a while I came out on the road. And I see the buggy. He's laying by it."

"Dead?"

"I—think so," Birgit said, gulping down a sob. "I'm pretty sure. His head—oh, God. Yes, he's dead. He must be."

"It's all right, girl. You did right. But we're not out of this. Is the body in the road?"

"By the side, yes."

"And the gun? Where is it?"

"I—lost it when I fell. I don't know what happened to it."

"All right, now listen here to me," Polly said, seizing the girl's shoulders. "We have to go back. Now."

"I can't!"

"We *have* to! Don't matter if he was Federal or Reb, if his friends find him kilt they'll come after us, 'specially if that gun's nearby. Too many people know it. I'd go alone, but I might go past him in the dark. Can you find that place again?"

Birgit nodded mutely.

"Good. Wait here. I'll get a shovel."

THEY NEARLY MISSED HIM. Moonlit, dappled with shadows, the road was a slender ribbon threading through the darkness of the hills. Birgit wasn't sure how far she'd traveled or how long she'd been lost. But she recognized the spot. And the crumpled form beside the road.

"Wait here," Polly hissed, stepping down from the buggy, her shotgun leveled. No need. The blast had shredded his upper body. She could smell the reek of death from ten feet away. Not just the stench of blood and voided bowels, but the sickly sweet odor of gangrene as well. Couldn't tell if he was Reb or Federal. Linsey-woolsey shirt drenched with blood, canvas pants, broken-down boots. The strays of both sides had been living off the land so long they much resembled each other. Especially in death.

"Is he . . . ?" Birgit whispered.

"Oh, yes. Dead as a stone. He was dyin' anyway. Got a bandaged wound on his thigh and it was mortifyin'. Gangrene. You probably did the poor bastard a favor, girl. Let's get him underground."

Straining, stumbling, the two women tried to drag the reeking corpse into the trees, but he kept snagging on the underbrush. In the end, Polly lifted him by the shoulders while Birgit took his legs, and they carried him bodily into the forest.

Spotting a natural trench at the base of a fallen sycamore, Polly widened it with her shovel, then they rolled the corpse in and covered it over with dirt and forest debris.

"Leaves are already fallin'," Polly panted, straightening. "A day or two, it'll be like we was never here."

"We should say words for him," Birgit said.

"Pray? For a damn road agent?"

"We can't just leave him like this. It's wrong." Her voice was shaking.

"All right, girl, all right. Do you know what to say?"

"Not—in English."

"Then say it in Hessian. Or whatever that place is you're from."

"Bavaria. But the language is the same."

"Well, I expect the good lord understands 'em all, and this poor devil's beyond carin'. Go ahead."

Kneeling silently in the moist forest mold beside Birgit while she prayed, Polly didn't understand a word of it. Yet somehow she felt better as they made their way back to the road. The girl was right. A proper buryin' was the decent thing to do, even for no-account border trash.

They found the gun in the brush beside the road where Birgit had dropped it. After reloading, Polly handed it up to the girl in the buggy.

"You drive on now. Corridon's less than an hour away and you'll be safer travelin' this time of night than in daylight. You shouldn't have no more trouble, but if you do, well, God help 'em."

"But what will you do?"

"Walk home. I been in these hills my whole life; moonlight's as bright as a lantern for me. Don't worry. You just take care of yourself and that baby. I'll see you come spring, girl. I promise."

Polly watched until the buggy disappeared, then set off for home, a long, weary march. It was well after midnight when she finally trudged up the lane to her home.

She'd thought Angus might be waiting. He usually came down from the hills for provisions on the first night of the new moon. But he wasn't there, at least not yet.

Exhausted, she relit the kitchen woodstove to warm the water, then stumbled into her bedroom. By the light of a lone candle, she filled the basin from the pitcher on the washstand, then stripped off her shirt, hanging it carefully on the doorknob to avoid getting bloodstains on the bedspread.

But as she plunged her arms in the basin to rinse off the gore, the scent of it came roiling up, suffusing the air, a powerful sweet-sour blend of gangrene and . . .

Lilacs. Stunned, Polly stared down at the basin, already reddening with blood. Leaning down, her face just above the water, she drew a long, ragged breath. Dear God. It was *Eau de Lilac.* Full strength, undiluted.

Her throat closed so tightly she could hardly breathe. Still, she forced herself to take her shirt from the doorknob to sniff a bloodstained sleeve. It was drenched with lilac water. No doubt about it.

The—person—Birgit killed must have been carrying the bottle in his shirt pocket. The shotgun blast splattered it all over his chest.

With a low moan, Polly sank to the bed, burying her face in her hands, rocking. No tears, her agony was soundless and soul deep, a pain so savage she thought she might die. And wished she could.

Which boy had they buried? She'd never looked into his face, hadn't wanted to. He was just another lost scarecrow of war, another starving, walking corpse, looking for a place to die.

Or to kill. Why had he attacked Birgit on the road? Too sick to walk any farther? Or had the war bled the pity from him, made him into another Meachum? Taken his soul?

Wasn't sure how long she sat there. Must have fallen asleep. Because she woke with a start. Someone was moving in the kitchen. And for a wild moment she thought she'd been mistaken, the boy hadn't been dead, somehow he'd clawed his way out of the earth . . . but no.

In the kitchen Angus was fumbling with a lantern.

"Don't light that," Polly said, carrying her candle to the table. "Cavalry was here today. They might be watching the house."

"Whose cavalry?"

"Federals, out of Jefferson City."

"Oh." In the flickering shadows, her husband's seamed face was hewn from granite, his beard unkempt, his graying hair wild. She wanted to hold him, to feel his strength. But it wasn't their custom. And she wanted no questions.

"You're late," she said, her voice quiet, controlled. "It's nearly three."

"I walked in. Took longer than I figured."

"You walked? Why?"

He avoided her eyes, almost sheepishly. "I loaned out my horse."

"The mare? Loaned it to who?"

"Some boy. Union deserter from Curtis's outfit. Came stumblin' into my camp yesterday. Nice boy. Family's got a farm up near Cairo, Illinois. He needed to get home. So I put him on my horse and set him on an old jayhawk trail. Figured I'd be better off with him gone than hangin' around the hills tellin' his pals about the crazy old man hidin' in the pineywoods with his raggedy-ass horses. Told him I'd send one of the boys for the animal after the war."

"Might not be too much longer. Had a visitor today, Tyler Randolph's new wife. She said the Federals burned Atlanta. Hood's retreating."

"Might be," he nodded. "I've been seein' a lot of strays in the hills, mostly Rebs but some Union. Federals are shootin' deserters now. Huntin' 'em down like coyotes. Is that why the cavalry came?"

"That, and to steal anything that wasn't nailed down. Aaron Meachum was with them. Gave me some mouth, nothing I couldn't handle."

"Meachum," Angus rasped, his eyes narrowing. "That bloodsuckin' scum's ridin' high now, got the Hessians around him, thinks he's safe. But when this is over and the boys are home, we'll be payin' a visit to that jayhawker sonofabitch—"

Polly slapped him, hard! Snapping his head around! He stared at her in stunned disbelief.

"No! By God, Angus, when this is over, it's truly gonna be over for us. We've given enough, bled enough. Let the dead bury the dead. No more killing, no more burning, not for revenge nor anything else!"

"What the hell's got into you, Pol?"

"I met Tyler Randolph's wife! And she's Hessian, except she's not—she's from some other place in Germany. But she's a fine girl! And God willing, she and Tyler will have children. I can midwife for her, and they can come visit on a Sunday, stay at Christmas, maybe. But so help me God, Angus, if you ever say any more about killin' or use that word *Hessian* to me again, I'll leave you! I'll take our boy and go! Do you understand?"

Tears were streaming now, she couldn't stop them and didn't care. Angus eyed her like a stranger, utterly baffled. He touched his lip and his fingertip came away bloody.

"No," he said slowly, "I don't understand. But I think it's a damn sight more than we can talk through tonight. I better go. Need to be in the hills before sunup anyhow."

"No! Not yet. You came in for warm food and a bath, and you're damned well gonna have 'em!"

"I came in for a kind word, too. But I guess I'll settle for a bath."

"Good!" Polly carried the steaming buckets from the woodstove to the tub, filling it with practiced ease as Angus warily unbuttoned his shirt, watching her all the while.

When the tub was full, he turned his back and so did she, giving him privacy, as was their habit.

But not tonight. Instead, she turned and watched him strip off his frayed shirt and the tattered union suit beneath. Saw his pale, scrawny frame, the lump on his shoulder where a horse had broken his collarbone years ago, his flat butt, the hipbones showing through.

My God. He'd been up in those hills for nearly three years, living with their animals, living *like* an animal. Freezing and going hungry. For her. For their boys. With no complaints.

As he turned to climb in the bath, he saw her watching and colored with embarrassment. But he said nothing. Just eased his aching bones down in the steaming water with a groan.

But in that briefest of moments, when their eyes met, she'd seen her life. With him. And nothing else mattered. Nothing. Not the hunger, not the war, not even the boy lost in the forest. Somehow they'd get through this. They would.

Ordinarily she left him alone to bathe. Instead she knelt behind the tub and wrapped her arms around his narrow shoulders, holding him. "I'm sorry," she said, after a time.

"No need. Up in them hills I forget how hard it must be for you holdin' on here alone. Comin' home feels so good to me that . . . well, I forget, that's all. Are you all right?"

"I will be. When all this is over."

"Soon, maybe. And you're right. When it's finished we'll get back to some kind of life. Make up for these sorry times. All of us. I miss you, Polly, miss our boys, our home. Even miss the way it smells, like now. What's that stuff again?"

"*Eau de Lilac,*" she said. "Lilac water."

# The Price of Coal

### *Edward D. Hoch*

I n September of 1864, at the age of nineteen, I left home in Liverpool and signed on as an ordinary seaman aboard the newly launched schooner *Night Owl*, bound for Halifax. It was not until I was on board and sailing into the open sea that I learned the true nature of the ship.

"She's a blockade runner," my new friend Robinson told me, gazing out at the wake we were leaving in the Irish Sea. "We'll be lucky if we aren't blown out of the water by a Union gunboat."

"Go on! You're trying to scare me! The captain's as English as we are."

Robinson was a jovial lad, not much older than me, who was always kidding about something. We bunked together belowdecks and the hot, crowded conditions made us companions at once. "The captain's only a front until we reach Confederate waters. That's so the ship won't lose her mercantile register. But the other officers are all Confederates. Couldn't you tell by their Southern accents?"

He went on to explain that several small, fast ships had been built for the Confederacy in England and Scotland, with more on the way. The *Night Owl* was a two-funneled side-wheeler, long and low with a molded steel hull, perfect for the tasks it would be called upon to perform. I felt rather foolish listening to him instruct me in such things that I should have known. "What cargo are we carrying?" I asked finally.

"Tea, on this run. But we'll be picking up the real cargo somewhere below the Mason-Dixon Line."

"I thought we were bound for Halifax."

"That's just the first stop, to make it look good. Block-ade-running was quite successful in the war's early days, but each year it grows more dangerous as the Union builds up its navy. Some say the South should be building more cruis-ers to break the blockade."

The journey across the North Atlantic seemed placid enough to me, though it was my first taste of the ocean and every day brought new discoveries. I marveled at the way gulls followed the ship, waiting for each day's garbage to be thrown off the stern. It was my first voyage on a side-wheeler, and the ship moved with remarkable speed. She was painted white, which had surprised me from the moment I first saw her, but Robinson explained that was to make her elusive when pursued by Union vessels in the North Atlantic Blockading Squadron.

In less than a week's time we were sailing into Halifax Harbor. Two days later, on the first of October, we entered the harbor at Wilmington, North Carolina, without incident, under the watchful guns of Fort Fisher. I was anxious to get ashore in this new country, but our superior, a boatswain's mate named Roger Frye, ordered us to stay on board. "We'll be loading a new cargo and leaving port within forty-eight hours," he told us. "Captain Morguane will be speaking to you directly."

Once we'd left Halifax and sailed down the Atlantic coast into Confederate waters, I'd become aware that our British captain was no longer in charge. An American, one of the Confederate officers on board, had assumed com-mand of the ship and was taking her into port. Morguane was a Southern gentleman with coal-black hair and mustache, and when he spoke to us he came right to the point.

"Gentlemen, this ship is now under the command of the Confederate States of America. We will be transporting cargo to and from the islands of Bermuda, Cuba, the Bahamas, and elsewhere. At times we may be in some peril, but my job will be to bring both crew and cargo home safely. I promise you I will do that. If any of the English seamen who joined us in Liverpool wish to leave the ship now, they may do so and we will attempt to arrange safe passage back home. For those of you who stay, there will be a bonus paid after the successful completion of our first voyage."

The other crewmen and I exchanged glances. Most of them had known what they were getting into, and there was no quitting now. The promised bonus, like a pot of gold at the end of some illusionary rainbow, was enough to hold us in thrall.

"Good!" Captain Morguane exclaimed. "A united crew is a happy crew. Now a word about our ship. The *Night Owl* and its sister ship the *Night Hawk* were built to specific dimensions. The cargo hold has a capacity of 850 bales of cotton, and that is what we will leave with in two days' time. The cotton is the currency with which the Confederacy purchases what it needs from other countries. Over the past year I have made thirty-three successful runs on various ships, bringing in meat, lead, saltpeter for explosives, shoes, blankets, coffee, rifles, cannon, and medicines. Occasionally, there are passengers who must reach the Confederate States on important business. When we leave here with our cargo we will sail due east to Bermuda, where we will trade the cotton for shoe machinery and two hundred tons of coal."

Later, when we were in our bunks, I wondered aloud about our chances of trouble. "Are the Northern ships heavily armed, Robinson?"

"That they are, but we are faster with our light arms. Even with a heavy cargo we should outrun them easily."

On the morning of our arrival at Bermuda, Roger Frye had us scrubbing down three of the ship's passenger cabins in preparation for two women and a man who would be joining us on the return trip.

"What a waste of time," I grumbled to Robinson, scrubbing the floor on my hands and knees. "No one has used these cabins since the ship was launched. How could they be dirty?"

"The salt air gets into everything," he said. "You'll learn that soon enough, lad."

I resented being called a lad by someone only a couple of years older than I was, but I let it pass. "Two women and a man. Are they traveling together?"

"Don't know. Probably not, if they need three cabins."

As with our other stops so far, the crew was not allowed ashore at Bermuda. The bales of cotton were quickly unloaded, but it was already growing dark, and the captain decided to wait until morning for the new cargo. In the fading light I could see that the mid-Atlantic harbor was a port for other ships as well as ours. Some were low-slung blockade runners, easy to identify now that I recognized their sleek lines and iron-hulled sides. Most were side-wheelers like the *Night Owl.*

"See that one?" Frye asked, coming up from the hold to join me at the railing. "It's our sister ship, the *Night Hawk.* She's just pulling out. I served on her for a couple of runs. That's why they put me on this one."

"Where's she headed?" I asked.

"Who knows? Maybe the same place we are."

"How does all this cargo arrive in Bermuda?"

"It comes from countries like England that are sympathetic to the Confederate cause."

"Why England? Slavery was abolished in the entire British Empire more than thirty years ago." At least I'd learned that much during my school days.

Roger Frye laughed. "Maybe I should have said countries like England that are unsympathetic to the Union cause. Anyway, their ships can't sail into the blockaded area, so they leave their cargoes here, or in Havana or Nassau, for the blockade runners to pick up in exchange for cotton."

It was a world I'd never known in all of my nineteen years, but I was learning about it quickly.

IN THE MORNING I was awakened by the first glimmers of the rising sun through our porthole. "Time to go to work," Robinson muttered, turning over in his narrow bunk.

What passed for breakfast was served in the ship's galley, and when we finished we went out on deck. A line of horse-drawn wagons had come onto the dock, filled with loads of coal. I recognized Captain Morguane on the bridge of the *Night Owl*, observing the entire operation with a stout red-faced man by his side. Even at that distance I could see that both men were counting the loads as they were hoisted on board. "Who would that be?" I asked Robinson.

"Beats me."

Before long, a carriage arrived carrying a stout woman who appeared to be about my mother's age. She had her belongings in two carpetbags, and Frye immediately ordered us down to carry them on board for her. "You've booked passage with us?" Robinson asked her, though there was no other reason for her presence on the dock at this hour of the morning.

"I have," she told him. "Please inform your captain that Selma Quiggin has arrived."

"The captain is checking the cargo right now," Robinson told her politely. "Let us escort you to your cabin, and I will see that Captain Morguane is informed of your arrival, ma'am." It always amazed me that he could speak like a gentleman when the occasion called for it. He picked up her bags and led the way up the gangplank.

Because two other passengers were expected, I asked Frye if I should remain on the dock to assist them. "They've already arrived," he told me, gesturing up toward the ship's bridge. "That's Simon Kostner, and his niece is traveling with him. He's the agent handling the coal sale, and they're counting the loads to make sure he delivers the full shipment."

I didn't see Kostner's niece until I passed her with her uncle, making their way to an early dinner in the officers' mess. She was an attractive young lady, about my age or a bit older, with ringlets of brown hair framing a soft and attractive face. Her long white gown might have been more suitable for a ballroom than an officers' mess. I heard her uncle address her as Mignon. Robinson and I ate early, too, because the *Night Owl* was sailing with the tide, and we had to be at our stations to cast off.

As we moved out of Bermuda Harbor into the open sea, I returned to the deck near the officer's mess, hoping to catch another glimpse of the young lady. She appeared within ten minutes, accompanied not by her uncle but by the older woman, Selma Quiggin. "Have you never been to America, dear?" the woman was asking.

"Yes, but not to the Confederate States," Mignon responded. They passed without seeming to notice me at the rail.

A few minutes later I'd taken out my tobacco pouch and was rolling a cigarette when Mignon returned alone, walking directly up to me. "What is your name, boy?" she inquired.

I was momentarily at a loss for words. When she repeated the question, I managed to stammer out, "Phillips, miss."

"Are you allowed to smoke cigarettes on deck, Phillips?"

"We're not carrying any combustible cargo, miss."

She stared into my eyes, not quite smiling. "Isn't coal a combustible cargo?"

"I—" I felt she was trying to trick me or mock me, but at that moment I couldn't come up with a good answer.

"I've seen you watching me, Phillips. You have been watching me, haven't you?"

"I may have noticed you on the way to dinner."

"Do you find me attractive? Am I as pretty as your English girls?"

"Oh yes, ma'am."

"Perhaps we should inspect the ship's hold together, to make certain the coal has not caught on fire."

"I don't think I should—"

She cut off my words with a wave of her hand. "Or should I tell my uncle you were rude to me?"

She opened a hatch door and disappeared quickly down a flight of steps. I had no choice but to follow her. "You shouldn't be here," I told her.

"Why not? It's my uncle's coal."

"Not anymore. He traded it for that cotton we unloaded."

She reached the deck of the cargo hold and waited for me. "You're not so smart. The cotton paid for the shoe machinery. The coal was paid for in gold by your captain."

"Gold?"

"Gold coins from the San Francisco mint. No one is foolish enough to accept Confederate money in payment. Uncle Simon has a bag of them in his cabin that must weigh thirty pounds."

We'd reached the forward hold, and she opened the bulkhead door without trouble. The choking odor of coal dust assaulted my nostrils. "We can't go in there," I told her.

"Have you ever made love on a pile of coal, Phillips?"

I grabbed her arm and yanked her out of there. "No, and I'm not going to start now! That dress is much too pretty to be smeared with coal dust." I closed the bulkhead door and pulled her up the steps behind me. "It's no wonder they say women are bad luck aboard ship."

"What about Selma Quiggin? Is she bad luck, or just the pretty ones?"

"You're impossible! I don't even know what either of you are doing on this ship."

"Running the blockade, like everyone else. Selma Quiggin is carrying vital dispatches for President Jefferson Davis. My uncle is returning home with his profits from the sale of the coal."

We reached the open air of the deck, and I was relieved to breathe fresh air again. "And why are you traveling with him?" I asked.

At first she didn't answer, and I expected another of her attempts to shock me. But after a moment she said, "My father was killed in the war last year. Uncle Simon thought the trip with him might help take my mind off it."

"I understand many good men have died fighting for the Confederate cause."

She averted her face and shook her head. "He fought on the Union side. He was a captain, killed at Gettysburg."

"And his brother sells coal to the South?"

"There are many brothers on opposite sides in this war. It has torn families apart. But Uncle Simon is in it more for the money than anything else."

Before she could say more, we were interrupted by Selma Quiggin, strolling the deck in the moonlight. She had a colorful shawl wrapped around her dress, though the evening was mild. "Lovely night, Mignon," the stout woman said. "Perhaps too lovely, if we wish to slip safely through the blockade."

"I have confidence in Captain Morguane," the young woman answered. "Miss Quiggin, this is Mr. Phillips, one of the *Night Owl*'s able seamen."

I blushed a bit as I bowed to the woman. "Only an ordinary seaman so far, Miss Quiggin. It's a pleasure to meet you."

"If you'll excuse me," Mignon said, "I think I'll retire to my cabin."

"Are you on duty, Mr. Phillips?" the woman asked when we were alone.

"We're always on duty, ma'am. Would you like me to escort you to your room?"

"That would be kind of you. I don't quite have my sea legs yet."

I offered my arm and guided her down to the cabin deck. Her room was just across the passage from those of Kostner and his niece, and adjoined Captain Morguane's quarters. As I remembered from scrubbing their floors, none of these cabins were very large. The *Night Owl* had not been built for pleasure cruising.

Selma Quiggin handed me the key to her cabin, and I was about to unlock the door for her when Mignon suddenly burst forth from the cabin across the way, her face white as chalk. "My God, someone has killed my uncle!"

I ran to the door, fearing she would swoon at any moment. Selma followed, and she helped Mignon across the passage to her cabin while I ventured inside. Simon Kostner's cabin was dark, and I had to relight the oil lamp before I could make out the terrible sight that had greeted Mignon. Kostner was propped up on the bed, holding his bloody stomach with both hands. His eyes were open but there was no doubt that he was dead.

I HURRIED ACROSS TO the captain's cabin and knocked on the door. There was no answer and I was wondering what to do next when Roger Frye happened along the passage. "Is that you, Phillips? What are you doing at Captain Morguane's door?"

"There's been a terrible accident! Simon Kostner is dead."

Frye quickly followed me into Kostner's cabin and closed the door. "This is terrible," he said after a quick examination of the body. "He's been stabbed several times. Do you see a knife around anywhere?"

"No, but the porthole is open. It could have been thrown into the sea."

"Captain Morguane is on the bridge. Go summon him while I stay with the body," Frye instructed me. "Say nothing to anyone else."

As I started down the passageway, Selma came out of her cabin. "Mignon is still unconscious, but I think she'll be all right. It's just the shock of the thing. I want to see if they have any smelling salts on board."

"Come along," I told her. "I'm on my way to inform the captain now."

"She had his blood on the front of her dress," she told me, trying to wipe a spot away with her handkerchief. "This is a terrible thing. Why would anyone want to kill him?"

"I understand he received payment in gold coins for the coal. Someone might have wanted them."

I led the way up the stairs to the bridge, with Selma puffing behind me. Captain Morguane was startled at our sudden intrusion into his private realm "What is the meaning of this?" he demanded.

"There's been a killing," I managed.

Selma chimed in with the details. "Someone has stabbed Simon Kostner!"

Morguane's head jerked at the news. "Kostner? Dead?"

"In his cabin," I hurried on. "Mr. Frye sent me to summon you."

"And do you have any smelling salts on board?" Selma added. "Finding the body was quite a shock for Kostner's niece."

The captain surrendered the wheel to his first mate and opened a small medicine cabinet. "Here's your smelling salts. Now let's get down there."

Selma returned to her cabin to minister to Mignon, while I entered Kostner's cabin where Frye stood guard. Captain Morguane took one look at the dead man on the bed and averted his eyes. "Are we to believe that some member of our crew killed him?" he asked Frye.

"It appears so, sir, unless it was one of the ladies."

"They were both in my company on deck shortly before the body was discovered," I said, but from the look the captain gave me, I realized immediately that I should not have admitted to conversation with the passengers.

"Know your place, lad, if you wish to get ahead in this man's navy."

I was about to apologize when Selma Quiggin appeared at the door supporting Mignon. "I must see him again," the poor girl managed between her tears. "I could not believe my eyes when I entered the cabin earlier."

Morguane moved quickly to block her view of the body. "Stay back, miss. It is not a pleasant sight."

"I tried to keep her away," Selma assured the captain.

He stepped over to Mignon and said in a kindly voice, "I know this has been a terrible experience for you, Miss Kostner. If you could tell me exactly what happened . . . "

She took a deep breath and began to speak. "I was returning to my cabin when I noticed that my uncle's door was slightly ajar. I knocked and pushed the door open. When I went in, I saw all this blood and I panicked."

"You saw this in the dark?" I asked, remembering how I'd found the cabin.

She shook her head. "The lamp was on. I must have blown it out in my confusion. I wanted to blot out what I'd seen."

"Take her out, please," Captain Morguane requested. "We have work to do here."

Mignon wished to rest in her own cabin, and I accompanied them there. While Selma turned up the lamp, I sat on the edge of the bunk and tried to comfort the dead man's niece. "I'll be all right," she assured me. "It was just the shock of seeing him. I fainted right away."

Selma left us the smelling salts and returned to her cabin. Frye stuck his head in the door to say, "I'll need you in five minutes, in Kostner's cabin. The captain has sent me to find Robinson, too."

When they were alone Mignon took my hand. "Forgive me for how I acted earlier, belowdecks. I was only playing with you. I'm not that sort of girl." The color was beginning to return to her face.

"I'm glad. I want you as unspotted as your gown. That coal would have ruined it."

She smiled. "You're nice. Perhaps I can make an able seaman of you yet."

"Tell me about your uncle. Who could have killed him?"

"Anyone after that gold, I suppose. It's a great deal of money in these desperate times."

I remembered Frye's summons. "I must return to work. I'll try to see you later."

When I reached the dead man's cabin I found Frye and Robinson already at work. The body had been placed in a canvas bag. "Will he be buried at sea?" I inquired.

Frye shook his head. "We must take him back to establish the cause of death, in the event there is an arrest and a trial. Help us carry him below, Phillips, and then we'll return here."

We placed the body in a large locker and came back up to the cabin deck. "What happened?" Robinson asked me, and I quickly filled him in, omitting my aborted escapade with Mignon.

Back in the cabin Frye said, "We're to search everywhere for the gold coins Captain Morguane paid Kostner for the coal. The captain is convinced they were the motive for the crime. If we don't find them here, we're to search the women passengers' cabins and then the crew quarters."

"Surely he doesn't think Mignon would have killed her own uncle," I protested.

Frye looked at me and muttered, "You've a lot to learn, lad."

"What does that mean?"

He didn't answer but Robinson told me later, while we searched. "Middle-aged uncles sometimes travel with young nieces who are not really their nieces."

"What? What are you saying?"

"It's the way of the world, lad."

"I don't believe it. You can't say that about a girl like Mignon."

We searched her cabin along with Selma's but found nothing. Then we moved on to the crew's quarters, and storage facilities belowdecks. We found nothing. Finally, toward daybreak, Frye reported our failure to the captain. "Did you search my cabin?" he asked the boatswain's mate.

"No sir."

He handed Frye the key. "Do so, now!"

But there was nothing. Robinson and I were finally allowed to sleep as the sun rose in the eastern sky.

THE WINDS WERE WITH us as we made our way due west through the breaking waves toward Cape Fear. The captain said we should make port in two days' time. Simon Kostner's death had been announced to all, but the manner of his dying was spread only in whispers. Robinson and I spent our working hours in more unsuccessful searching for the missing gold, and I saw nothing of Mignon.

"You know what I think?" Robinson asked me on our last day at sea. "I think the killer dropped the gold out that porthole to a waiting boat."

"That would be risky at night. What if he missed?"

"Maybe he dropped it into the water with a rope attached, so he could haul it up later."

That made more sense to me, but a tour of the railings around the decks revealed no mysterious ropes hanging into the water.

The captain had estimated we would be within sight of Cape Fear by dark, and everyone knew that was the most dangerous time. If we were sighted by the North Atlantic

Blockading Squadron, they would surely try to board us or even sink us.

"Will we be able to make it into port in the dark?" I asked Frye.

"There are treacherous waters, but the lighthouse will guide us."

Wind-driven clouds had been building up all afternoon, and as we came in sight of land a heavy fog began to settle in. It was just then that the ship's whistle sounded, alerting the crew that an enemy ship had been sighted. Robinson grabbed up a spyglass and scanned the horizon. "There she is," he announced grimly, passing the glass to me.

The ship's guns seemed monstrous to me, even at that distance, easily capable of blowing us out of the water. They were signaling us to heave to for boarding, but the captain ignored them and stayed on course for Cape Fear. Suddenly, as the Union ironclad closed the gap between us, I saw a puff of smoke and heard the cough of a cannon. Almost at once we were hit on our upper deck near the bridge, and we heard a scream of agony.

As the ironclad moved into position to fire again, Captain Morguane changed course. "He's trying to reach that fog bank," Robinson shouted. "It's our only hope!"

Frye joined us from the upper deck, his face ashen. "That was a thirty-pounder. It took off Match Madick's leg. He's probably a goner. They were aiming at our front stack."

The Union warship fired again, but this time the ball passed across our bow. Then we slipped into the fog bank and were safe for the moment. "Will they find us?" Robinson asked.

"Not in here, but we have to emerge sooner or later. And then we have to make it into port somehow."

Our two women passengers, terrified by the cannon fire, had appeared on deck. "Are we going to sink?" Mignon asked.

"No fear of that," Frye reassured her. "Captain Morguane will get us out of this, with a little help from the fog."

Selma Quiggin, holding her sizable waist, had gone to the railing to peer through the fog. At that moment the cannon's roar reached us again, but the ball came nowhere near. "Will they keep on until they hit us?" she asked.

Robinson shook his head. "Not likely. They'll save their ammunition until they have a visible target."

Mignon suddenly gasped, and I saw that the front of her frock had a spot of blood on it. I hurried to pull her out of the way as blood continued dripping from the upper deck where the crewman named Madick lay dying. "Stay away from there," I cautioned, but I could not take my eyes from the blood on her dress.

"Is everyone here safe?" Captain Morguane asked, climbing down from the bridge. "We've suffered one serious casualty, but the ship seems secure. If we can sail out of this fog bank, I think we can make it into Wilmington."

"Captain—," I managed to say, catching his attention.

"What is it, lad?"

"I think I know what happened to Mr. Kostner."

"There'll be time for that later. I have to get back to the bridge now."

Robinson was staring at me. "What do you mean, Phillips?"

"The blood on Mignon's dress."

All eyes were on her then, as she tried to wipe it away. "It reminded you of her uncle's blood?" Frye asked.

I shook my head. "It reminded me that there was no blood on her dress after Kostner's body was found. I even remarked to her how unspotted it was. And yet Selma here explained away the blood on her own dress by saying it had come off Mignon's when she helped the girl. That couldn't be true."

Selma Quiggin laughed harshly. "Are you saying I killed that man?"

"Yes, and hid the blood with that colorful shawl you wrapped around yourself, even in this mild air."

The ship was free of the fog bank now, with the Cape Fear lighthouse within sight. The captain was distracted from the conversation by something he saw in the channel. "Hand me that spyglass," he told Frye.

"You did kill him," I told the woman. "How else could you know he'd been stabbed when the cabin was in darkness and you only stood at the door for an instant."

"I never said—"

"Yes, you did. When we went up on the bridge you told the captain he'd been stabbed."

Frye was at the captain's side. "What are you seeing, sir?"

"It's our sister ship, the *Night Hawk*. The Union raiders have sunk her in the channel. I don't know if we can get around her. The sea is quite rough."

The next hour was a nightmare, with Selma Quiggin and Kostner's murder forgotten for the moment. Captain Morguane took control of the wheel and tried to guide us into the channel past Fort Fisher. But darkness was falling fast, and the smoldering wreckage of the *Night Hawk* left us too little room to maneuver. Just after sunset we ran aground on a sandbar. The captain gave the order for the passengers and most of the crew to abandon ship, which meant wading through the rough surf to the shore. With less weight Morguane hoped to free his grounded ship.

We went down the gangway to the water, and I held tight to Mignon all the way in. No one noticed what happened to Selma Quiggin and perhaps no one cared. At daybreak, with the *Night Owl* still stuck fast to the sandbar, we found her body washed up on shore. Simon Kostner's stolen gold coins, the sale price of the coal, were found in a money belt around her ample waist. It was one place we hadn't searched, and the weight of them had pulled her down beneath the foaming surf.

WHEN MORGUANE WAS UNABLE to free his ship from the sandbar after a week of trying, Robinson and I were given passage back to Bermuda aboard another blockade runner. From there we would return to England. I wanted no more of the war at sea.

I told Mignon I would write to her, and I did, but so far our paths have not crossed. It's a big world, and a big ocean between us.

# Last Hours in Richmond

## Brendan DuBois

In the fourth year of the War of Secession, Mary Stuart-son of Richmond, Virginia, was in the rear of Colling-wood's Grocers, thinking sourly of a time not so long ago when she and her husband could have purchased this entire store and its belongings with as much effort as it took to prepare a bank draft. Now, in this cold winter, when each day seemed to last forever, along with the cold and mud, with her family shattered and her family fortune nearly gone, she found herself dickering over the price of a shrunken ham.

"Come now, Mister Collingwood," she protested. "Tell me again what price you're asking for this sorry piece of meat?"

Collingwood smirked, wiping both hands on his dull gray store apron. In this part of the store, the windows were smeared and dark, not allowing hardly any light inside. The shelves themselves were empty, having been empty for

months. Like most shopkeepers in this embattled Confederate capital, what few goods that existed were kept securely in
rear rooms.

The shopkeeper said, "Madam, truly I'm grieved by
what you say. The fact that I am offering this ham to you at
this price shows the high esteem in which I hold you as a customer. The price is fair. You cannot do better at any other
establishment, if even they have any hams left."

"But three hundred dollars!" she said, hardly even
believing the words as they left her mouth. "Three hundred
dollars for a ham!"

Collingwood shrugged. "If you don't take it at that
price, madam, then some other lady shall come in and pur-
chase it for four hundred. Supply and demand, Missus Stuartson. Supply and demand. With you at your boarding
house, you should know better than anyone."

She looked at the smug face and freshly washed beard,
the plump cheeks. She wished she could shoot the man,
shoot him right here in his store, but the damnable
scoundrel was right. Supply and demand, and with Richmond being strangled each day by the damn Federals, everything was in short supply. Save for cold, hunger, and despair.

Mary went through her cloth bag, pulled out a rolled-
up piece of cloth. "I don't have that kind of money with me,
Mister Collingwood. But what I do have is this."

She unrolled the piece of cloth on the wooden counter,
revealing a heavy gold watch and chain, and a man's gold
ring. She saw the look in the shopkeeper's eyes as he picked
them up and examined them. He looked over at her and
said, "Deal, Missus Stuartson."

She shook her head. "Not so fast. I want some coffee, as
well. Mister Stuartson so enjoys a cup of coffee."

"Coffee!" he exclaimed. "Why, I don't think—"

She made to take back the jewelry. "I know for a fact
you have coffee, Mister Collingwood. You sold some here
yesterday. That's the arrangement I desire. Ham and coffee
for this jewelry. Or I go elsewhere."

The grocer finally nodded and went back into a rear storage area, and when he returned, he wrapped up both the ham and a small bag of coffee in an old copy of the *Richmond Examiner*. Mary didn't bother reading the headlines as the old newspaper was used as wrapping paper. All of the headlines these past months had been filled with bad news. It was horrible enough to read them once. She need not read them again.

As he passed over the small bundle, the well-fed grocer seemed almost apologetic. "It's the terrible times we live through, Missus Stuartson. These terrible times make all of us do what we can to survive."

"Yes, you're right, Mister Collingwood," she said, putting the package into her cloth purse. "We do what we can to survive."

OUTSIDE, THE COLD FEBRUARY wind seemed to cut through her as she navigated along the muddy streets, holding up her skirts with one hand. With her other hand, she kept it inside her bag, holding on to the revolver that belonged to her husband. In the four short years since this city had become the capital of a new nation, the population had almost tripled and what little police were here could not handle the increase in forgers, robbers, and deserters that crowded these muddy avenues. It seemed each week that besides the war news, the newspapers had breathless stories of murders most foul, and men and women gone missing in the dark alleys and streets of Richmond after dark.

Wagons went by, horses with their ribs showing through, carrying whatever goods still dribbled into Richmond. They were followed by a line of colored men, walking slowly, most of them barefoot, carrying shovels and picks over their shoulders, heading out to strengthen the city's defenses. She kept her eyes about her, knowing that some desperate men—and even desperate women!—were not above robbing women as they left shops, trying to steal what little they had. She remembered a time earlier, when Mister Collingwood had been more cheerful and open with his store, and how he always had a sweet for her son, Tom, and her daughter, Lucinda. Now Tom and Lucinda were dead, he on a battlefield in Pennsylvania, and she in a common grave here in Richmond after a long illness, and no sweets were to be had, ever again.

As she turned a corner, only a few blocks away from her home, she heard the distant rumble of cannon fire, as the damn Federals kept pressing on. *What this war has done to us,* she thought, *all of us.* There had been a time when she wouldn't have gone out even for such a short distance without a matched pair and carriage, and her clothes would have been clean and crisp. Now, like most of the women passing her by, she wore black, in perpetual mourning for her family and her nation, and the horses had been taken into service for the army. And these poor women in this city, nearly two years ago exactly, they had finally had enough and a food riot had erupted. Stores had been robbed and burnt, and they had stopped only when President Jefferson Davis himself, the mighty Sphinx, had arrived to plead the women to disperse, before the militia would fire upon them. Oh, the horror, of seeing good men of Virginia preparing to fire upon their own mothers, wives, sisters, and daughters.

Mary paused at the small gate to her house, tears suddenly filling her eyes at what she saw. Once her house had been the envy of the neighborhood, as her husband's business thrived with all of the shipping traffic coming and going on the James River. But now the house looked old and tired, with broken panes of glass being filled in by newspaper. The white picket fence around the house had long been broken up and burnt for fuel, leaving only the granite posts for the main gate. And her husband's business had collapsed—as so many others had—when the Union Navy's blockade had put its foot upon the throat of so many Southern ports.

She gathered herself up and went up to the house, forcing the tears to stop. Their house had been taking in guests now for nearly two years, ever since her husband had returned wounded from Pennsylvania, at a place called Gettysburg. Henry had not said much for months, grieving for their lost victory and their lost son, Tom. But as she had said to the grocer, they did what they had to do to survive, and turning their comfortable home into a boarding house for strangers had been that first, dramatic, and dark step into their new lives.

INSIDE THE HOUSE IT was damp and cold, and she went past the parlor and to the kitchen, where the cabinets were firmly locked. She took a ring of keys and unlocked the cabinets, tried to come up with a decent dinner for her three guests. They paid in many ways—from notes from other Southern cities to foreign money to even Union greenbacks—but even then, coming up with a meal was always a struggle. She looked through her meager possessions, trying to think of what she had down below, in the root cellar, also firmly locked and chained. Before the war, house breaking was almost unheard of in these neighborhoods of Richmond, but with each passing month of the war, more and more houses were entered by the hungry and the cold.

There was a noise and she turned. The door leading to the cellar opened and Henry came up, wearing heavy cotton pants and a well-patched shirt. His face was lined and his beard had turned white, ever since coming back from Gettysburg, and his eyes always had the look of being so very tired. She ached at seeing him there, the once-strong and confident man who had wooed her heart and soul. Now he was strong no more, and the firm arms which had held her tight over the years had been shattered as much as their family. His right arm was withered and his left arm—struck by a Union ball—had been amputated just below the elbow.

He bowed slightly. "Good day, wife."

She came up to him, kissed him on the cheek. "And good day to you, husband. Is there any news?"

He shook his head, reached into the doorway of the stairway and pulled out a dirt-encrusted shovel. "We have another guest. A Major Tomlison. A dandy officer, he is, with nice long sword and bright shiny boots. Officers." He spat the word out like an epithet. "The kind who knows everything about men and war from some damn Prussian drill manual. Officers. He looks as stupid as the officers who sent us up to that ridge in Gettysburg, right into the face of all that cannon . . ."

"Henry," she said simply, seeing how his expression had changed, how he was reliving those horrid moments. "Henry, it will be fine. Will you fetch me wood for dinner?"

He looked up, gave her a weak smile. "It will be my honor."

*Honor*, she thought, looking up again to the cabinets. One of the words that was on the lips of many a noble Southerner who fought his way to battle. But would honor help her now feed an unexpected fourth guest?

THE EVENING MEAL WAS simple, fried mush and day-old bread, smeared with molasses, and boiled turnip greens that she had canned last fall. As she served her guests—all men—she looked at all of them in turn. There was a Mister Cloutier from Louisiana, a representative to the Congress who no longer represented his voters, since they were all now under Union occupation. A Mister Puddleton, a quiet man who wrote for the Richmond Examiner and who sat next to Mister Gray, who worked in one of the struggling banks. These three had been here for months, and while they all had their foibles and difficulties, she had gotten used to them. In a way, they had almost become family to her.

But now this evening, there was the new guest, Major Tomlison, and she recognized what Henry had said: the man was certainly a dandy. The other three men's clothes were worn and ill-repaired, but the Major's uniform was shiny and freshly cleaned. He had a thick mustache and his eyes seemed merry, and he wore heavy gold rings on both index fingers.

As she served the simple meal, she listened to the bits of conversation from the men, wondering how long this could last, how long all of them could last in this besieged city.

". . . Grant's getting more troops, that's what we've heard . . ."

". . . more prisoners tried to escape from the warehouses last night, but all of those poor wretches were recaptured . . ."

". . . another murder was reported down by Rockett's Landing, a man with his throat slit and tossed into the river . . ."

". . . colored troops, fighting for Virginia. Can you imagine that, colored men with guns? We should just surrender to Lincoln if that ever happens . . ."

Then, a strong voice, booming over the others: "I hear the war will be over within a month, and on terms favorable to the Confederacy."

She stopped serving, looked at the confident officer who had just uttered those remarks. Major Tomlison looked about, nodded again. Mister Puddleton, the newspaper man, quietly spoke up. "And what brings that opinion to the fore, Major?"

The major spooned up some of the fried mush. "No matter how many troops and cannon and ships the Yankees have, we have something they don't. General Lee. You mark my words. The Yankees are tired after so many years of war. A couple of more sharp victories against the Yanks, and then they'll sue for peace, and Britain will finally come around to help us. Just you wait and see."

Her husband, sitting at the end of the table, kept quiet, but his face glowered and his lips were pursed. Mister

Cloutier coughed into a handkerchief and said, "Begging the Major's pardon, but after our setbacks at Vicksburg and New Orleans and Atlanta . . ."

The major turned on him. "Are you a defeatist? Sir? Is that what you're saying?"

Mister Gray, the bank man, took off his spectacles and rubbed at the glass with his napkin. "My brother is a captain, serving in the lines near Petersburg. His men are nearly starving. They have no shoes, no coats, and damn little powder or shot. They may have General Lee and other fine generals, sir, but the Federals are well-fed and well-armed and well-rested."

Major Tomlison swallowed another spoonful of mush. "The odds have been against us, right from the start. Just you see. General Lee is the best general this continent has ever seen. And he'll achieve another series of noble victories, just you see. Then old Abe will have to give us what we want and leave us alone."

Her husband spoke up. "Like Gettysburg, do you mean? Another noble victory like Gettysburg?"

Mary stepped in, raising her voice. "Now, now, gentlemen. Let us have no more talk of war at this table. We talk so much about it, day in and out. Let us have at least a few minutes of peace."

The major's face was reddened and she saw how her husband stared at him, hatred in his eyes. She sat down and began eating, the food nearly tasteless.

AFTER THE WASHING AND the cleaning, the men retired to the parlor, where Mister Cloutier, the congressman, passed around a pouch of tobacco, and soon all four of her guests were sitting on her fine chairs, smoking pipes and talking in low voices. She lit a small fire in the fireplace, which was enough for a little heat and hardly any light. She trusted these men not to go through her meager supply of firewood, and as she finished cleaning in the kitchen, her husband Henry came in.

"Did you hear that arrogant officer, that stupid young pup?" Henry demanded. "A few more victories and all will be won. Bah! Such stupidity! Did you hear what he said?"

"Yes, yes, I did," she said, putting away her dishes, suddenly tired of it all. She missed everything so much, from the voices and touches of her son and daughter, from a time when the house was snug and warm and oil lamps kept everything well lit, to feasts and meals that went on for hours. And laughter. She could not remember the last time she had laughed long and loud.

Henry stepped closer. "I'm sorry, Mary," he said, his voice low. "I'm sorry I raised my voice back there, at dinner. Just seeing that officer, full of himself and nonsense . . ."

She wiped her cold hands. "It's all right, Mister Stuartson. It is quite all right."

He shook his head, and his eyes glistened in the dim light. "No, it's not all right. I should have never let Tom out of my sight. Not once. But the smoke and the cannon fire . . . That's when I missed him, Mary. Just for a moment. And when the smoke cleared away, I managed to find him, Mary. Our only son. Dead in a field. I tried to drag him back to our lines but by then, I was wounded. I tried, oh Lord, I tried . . ."

She reached over and stroked his lined cheek. "I know you tried, dear sir. I know you did. You did what you could."

Her husband only nodded. She went on. "I am about to retire. And you, dear husband?"

"I . . . I have a little work to do. Then I shall join you."

"Very well."

LATER THAT EVENING SHE was in their bedroom, and at a small writing desk, lit by a single candle, she wrote a letter to her sister Carol, who lived in Charleston, South Carolina. She had not heard from her sister in over a month, which was not unusual, considering the state of the mail service. Yet she refused to give up, and she wrote Carol once a week. She tried to keep her letter as bright and as cheerful as possible, knowing that Charleston was under a worse siege than Richmond, with Union navy forces shelling almost every day. Poor Carol had no need to know of her own sister's difficulties.

As she wrote, she often looked up to the wall, where a framed sampler hung, outlining the alphabet and the first nine numerals. Her daughter, Lucinda, had done this sampler almost seven years ago, and she remembered with pride how nimble and quick those fingers had been, bringing everything together. *My poor dear,* she thought. *Never again to sit at my side in the parlor, to laugh and gossip and to sew, never again.* Two winters ago she had caught ill, and what few doctors remained in Richmond had been no help. She had done what she could as her daughter burned with fever, and her husband had stood there as well, still gaunt and pained from his wounds.

In the end, she had simply expired in her sleep, her poor little girl's heart finally giving out. Oh, how did she survive those dark days, knowing she and Henry were now childless, their son and daughter taken away in this damnable war . . .

She looked down at her desk, finished the letter, and then folded it over. It was late. Where could Henry be?

IT WAS DARK. SHE awoke at the sound of her husband, entering the room, carrying a small oil lamp. She sat up. "Husband, are you all right?"

He put the lamp down on a nearby table. "Yes, I am . . . I am just so tired, that's all."

"Then come to bed."

He cupped the lamp with his sole hand and blew out the wick. She noted how stained and dirty his fingers were, dirt encrusted under his fingernails. She remembered a time when he would have never even allowed himself to be seen in such a condition, never mind retiring to bed with dirty fingers. *But we've all changed,* she thought. *This war is much more than a war of brother against brother. It's a war against our entire way of life, the way we think and eat and act, and we're losing so desperately.*

The bed shifted as he slowly climbed under the covers. She moved over and rested her head against his shoulder. She could feel his heart beating wildly, and she wondered how he was feeling.

"Henry, is everything all right?"

"Yes, yes, Mary. Everything is fine. Nothing to worry about. It's just that I'm . . . I'm so very tired. I feel like I could sleep for a month, my dear. I really do."

She reached up in the dark and gently stroked his face. "One of these days, husband, one of these days it will be warm and sunny and the war will be over, and we will have enough to eat and we will be warm. Never again to be cold and hungry. One of these days."

He breathed out. "Yes, one of these days."

She cuddled closer to him, the only man she had ever loved. "I have lost my son and my daughter. All I have now is you. And I will do everything in my power to keep you, husband, forever."

She rested on his shoulder for long minutes, until he finally drifted off to sleep.

In the morning she prepared breakfast, some of the ham she had purchased the day before from Mister Collingwood, served with a single fried egg and a thin slice of toasted bread. It was served with coffee made from chicory; the real coffee she had purchased yesterday would be saved only for her husband.

When she had set the table, she looked and noted an empty chair. "Has anyone seen the good major?" she asked, after placing down the food platter. Mister Cloutier said, "I recall hearing his door open up during the night. But if he ever came back, I was asleep."

Henry said, "Perhaps the young officer is sleeping off after a night of carousing down by the docks."

Mister Gray said, "If that's the case, then he'll be lucky to be alive. There are rough gangs down there, gangs who will even take on well-dressed officers."

Henry made to leave the table. "I'll go upstairs and see if I can't wake him."

Mary shook her head and left the dining room. "No, you men eat before it gets cold. I'll see if he's awake or not."

She gathered up her skirt as she went up the stairs, to the first room on the left. It had been a room for her sewing and needlepoint, and it was rather small, but with a bed and wash-stand, it was much better than some of the other rooms being rented out in this crowded city. Mary rapped twice on the door. "Major Tomlison? Are you awake? Major Tomlison?"

There was no answer. Well, that was that, then. She tried one more time and then went back to the dining room. Henry said, "What, then? Will he be joining us?"

She sat down, placed a napkin in her lap. "I knocked on the door three times, and raised my voice as well. There was no answer, and I shan't delay breakfast any more."

As she picked up her knife and fork, she noted the looks of the men around her, staring self-consciously at the empty chair and the plate in front of it. Mary noted the looks and then reached over and retrieved the plate. "And if he can't bestir himself to join us for a meal, then I won't waste the food."

Carefully, she cut the fried egg and ham slice and bread into five pieces, and then passed the plate towards Mister Cloutier, who smiled as he placed the extra food onto his plate. Then he passed the plate towards Mister Gray.

"If we're fortunate tonight, then perhaps the good major will sleep through the evening meal as well," Mister Cloutier said, and the other men laughed.

But not Henry. He bent down to his plate and resumed eating.

LATER IN THE MORNING, as she was preparing the daily wash of the sheets and linens, there came a knock at the front door. She went to the foyer, wiping her reddened hands on a towel. When she opened the door to the cold February air, two officers were standing there, hats in hand, bowing in her direction.

"I'm sorry, gentlemen," she said. "I've no more rooms to rent. Perhaps you could try Missus Green, four houses down."

Both officers looked alike, tired eyes and chest-length beards. The one on the left spoke up. "Begging your pardon, madam, but we're not here to rent rooms. We are making an inquiry concerning one of your guests. A Major Tomlison."

"And how can I assist you?" she asked, holding herself tight against the February wind.

The officer on the right said, "I am Captain Slater, and this is Captain Abrams. We are on the staff at the War Department. Major Tomlison was supposed to meet with us there at nine this morning. As you can note, it is nearly eleven."

"I'm afraid I've not seen the major since last evening's meal," Mary said, looking into the tired eyes of both officers.

"So he is staying here?" Captain Abrams asked, hat still in his hand.

She shrugged. "He paid up for two nights. Where he goes is his business."

Captain Slater asked, "Did he join you for breakfast?"

"No, he did not."

A team of horses went by, spraying mud up from their hooves, hauling a gun carriage. The men riding the horses looked so tired that they could fall asleep on the backs of the animals. For some reason Mary watched them until they turned the corner.

Captain Abrams cleared his throat. "If we may, madam . . . I mean, with your permission. Could we see his room? Please?"

She hesitated, looking at them, wondering why they were here. This dandy of a major, her husband had noted. What possible use could he be to the War Department? Or to the Confederacy? She sighed, opened the door wider.

"Do come in, gentlemen, but mind your boots. I've swept and cleaned this doorway this morning. I have no urge to do it again."

She went up the stairs and the two officers followed her, keeping quiet. She could sense their embarrassment and difficulty, but she had no sympathy for either of them. At the War Department, they were out of the way of Union cannon or Union riflemen, and she was sure they both ate better than the men in the lines.

At the bedroom door she knocked, twice. "Major Tomlison? Sir, are you ill? There are men here to see you."

There was no answer.

Mary turned to the two officers. "That's the response I received earlier this morning, gentlemen."

"And you did not enter?" Captain Slater asked suspiciously. "To see if anything was amiss?"

"Sir," she said, trying to sound shocked. "If the major did not want to come down for breakfast, what business is that of mine?"

Captain Abrams moved closer. "Madam, if you will . . . could you please open the door for us?"

She looked at them both again, these well-fed and well-bred officers who thought they were fighting for honor and nobility and everything that was grand about the Confederacy. Mary felt cold again and lonely and wished for nothing more right then than for enough fuel to fill the fireplace, to empty this house of its cold and dampness.

"Of course, Captain," she said. "At your request."

Mary unlocked the door and opened it up. A small window on the far wall gave enough light to show a small bed, nightstand with white jug and basin, and a wooden chair. The wallpaper was beginning to peel away. The two captains entered the room, followed by Mary. The officers looked at each other. The bed was made and did not appear slept in, which made sense, for Major Tomlison was not there.

Captain Abrams spoke up. "His luggage. Did he leave it here in this room, or someplace else in the house?"

Mary said, "All guests here are responsible for their own belongings. I know not where they may be."

Captain Slater looked about the room and out the window. He turned and said, "Madam, earlier you mentioned something about a guest hearing something. Again, what was said?"

"One of the guests, a Mister Cloutier," she said. "A representative to the Congress. He said the door opened during the night, and that Major Tomlison left. But he also said he fell asleep before noticing whether the major had returned."

Captain Slater did not look happy. "Is it possible somebody entered the house at night, to spirit away the major?"

"For what reason?" Mary asked.

"I do not know, madam," Captain Slater said, again looking out the window. "This city is full with Union sympathizers and spies. Major Tomlison had a sensitive position at the War Department. If he had been captured and made to talk . . ."

Mary shook her head. "My husband promptly locks the door at eleven. We have a rule for our guests, that they must be back in our home by then. And I assure you, Captain Slater, that our door was not broken into last night."

The two captains looked at each other, and then Captain Abrams said, "Madam, you have been of service. If Major Tomlison returns, or if you hear any news of where he might have gone, please let either of us know. We can be contacted at the War Department."

"Certainly," she said, leaving the room, and the two captains followed her. As she led them out to the entrance way, Captain Slater turned and said, "This is quite a lovely house, madam."

She smiled. "You do me a service, sir. At one time this house was grand, quite grand. Until . . . well, until circumstances forced my husband and me to open our home to boarders. My husband is an invalid veteran, gentlemen, and we had to do what we could to survive."

Captain Abrams nodded and Captain Slater, the one with the suspicious look about him, touched the brim of his hat in a salute. "Madam, so many of us now do that. In order to survive. Good day, madam."

"And good day to you both," she said.

WHEN THE DOOR CLOSED, she looked out the small door window, until she saw that they had made their way out of sight. Then she went back to the kitchen, splashed some cold water on her face, and then stood before the cold stove, shivering. She looked out the rear window, to the tiny garden where she raised potatoes and turnips these past three summers. Henry was nowhere to be seen. She shivered again, took a lamp down from a shelf, and lit it with a sulfur match.

Mary went over to the cellar door and opened it up. There were noises down there, and she made out the flickering light of a lantern. She called down, "Henry?"

There was silence for a bit, until she called down again. "Henry? It is I, your wife, Mary."

A weak voice. "What do you want, wife?"

She kept her voice steady. "I'm coming down. I must talk with you."

"Mary," came the voice. "Please don't come down. I insist."

"I am sorry," she said. "I have no choice."

She gathered up her skirt and went down the narrow wooden steps, holding the lamp out before her. The air was cold and dank, and when she reached the bottom of the stairs, she turned left. The cellar was made up of arched brickways, with a dirt floor, and in the distance, she saw her husband, head down, staring at his feet.

Mary went closer to him, lamp still held high, and then everything was illuminated as she got closer. Henry was standing there, shovel held in the crook of his half-arm, as he looked down upon the partially filled long hole at his feet. Mary came closer, feeling so cold she could shiver, and she lifted up the lamp and looked down at the hole. She felt like she couldn't breathe. Looking up at her from the bottom of the squared-off hole were the unseeing eyes of one Major Tomlison of the Confederate Army.

"Henry . . ." she said, her voice filled with sadness. "What is the meaning of this?"

"I'm . . . I'm sorry, Mary," he said. "It won't happen again."

She looked up at him, her voice now filled with anger. "You fool! I just had two officers from the War Department upstairs, trooping around this man's room, asking me questions. What would have happened if they had pressed me further, had asked me to come into the cellar?"

He said nothing, staring down at the shovel, his withered arm quivering, and tears came to his eyes. She reached over and hugged him. "I'm sorry, Mister Stuartson. So sorry to raise my voice."

"It's just hard, that's all," he said. "Trying to shovel such a hole with less than two arms. I didn't expect it to take so long."

"No, of course not," she said, looking around the cellar. "And we must be running out of room by now. This is the sixth one, is it not?"

"Yes, it is," he said, his voice filled with pride. "And we did well. Two rings, a watch, the sword and good leather boots. We did well."

She nodded in satisfaction, remembering the first time this had occurred. It had been an accident, that's all. An officer—whose name she could not remember—had gotten drunk at one of the port bars and had come back, and had assaulted her in her own room. Henry had been outdoors in the privy and when he had come back, his voice roaring with rage, he had split the officer's head in with a shovel.

There had never been talk of reporting the matter. Her honor was at stake . . . how could she face anyone in the society circles of Richmond, knowing what had almost happened? And there had been no witnesses, none at all, and so the man had been buried in the cellar. But not before being stripped of his money and valuables, and that one drunk officer had helped pay for food that late fall.

Now, five more men—all of them rich, arrogant officers—had followed the first one, and Mary had been surprised at how easy it had all been. Other officers had come to stay with them at their house, and so many had been fine, courteous men. But those who had been rich, who had been arrogant, who had the type of manner who would order a young boy like her son Tom into lines of Union cannon . . . well, that had been easy enough. Henry would bring them down into the cellar on some promise or another—usually the offer of a strong drink—and they would not suspect a thing. Why would they, with a man before them with only one arm?

Then, there was room in the cellar, and it being so cool, nothing untoward would ever happen. Henry took care of the digging and the disposal, and Mary would quietly exchange whatever goods they secured from the dead officers for food, for clothes, for fuel. And it being wartime, with so many troops moving in and out of Richmond, with desertions rising each month, no one had been missed.

Until this morning, with that stupid officer who had to be connected with the War Department. That had been a narrow escape. But now Mary looked around the cellar, knowing they were running out of room, running out of time.

"Henry," she said simply.

"Madam?" he said, resting wearily on the shovel.

"We must talk, of what is to happen next."

He looked puzzled. "What do you mean?"

Her chest felt heavy at what she was about to say. "The war is lost. You know that. We all know it. In a matter of weeks or months, the Federals will press through and Richmond will be occupied. When that happens, we cannot stay."

"Mary . . . This is our home . . ."

Her eyes filled with tears. "No, it is not. These are our last hours in Richmond. Your business is gone. Our children are gone. Many of our friends and relatives are no longer alive. There is no point in staying here. All I know now is how to run a boarding house, and with the war over, I will not stay in this city and continue to do such work. In wartime, yes. But not here, not in peacetime. And you and I know that the only way we have lived here these years has been because of them."

With that, she moved her hand with the oil lamp, motioning to the mounds of dirt that marked the guests who had come here and who had never left. Mary said, "When the Federals take control of Richmond, the chaos and disorder will eventually disappear. There will be martial law of a sort. And missing guests from a boarding house will be noticed, with the Union Army in charge. No, my dear husband, we must move from Richmond, as quickly as possible, when the time comes."

"To where?" he said, his voice weak. "Where could we possibly go?"

"North. To a large city. Perhaps Baltimore. Perhaps New York."

"New York!" Henry exclaimed. "Among those Yankees and bankers? New York?"

She gently touched his face. "You've told me several times, about how sometimes you have guilt about what you have done. In striking down officers of the Confederate Army. Even if they are sour men who deserve their fate, you've told me that it has troubled you. Am I correct, sir?"

"Yes . . ."

She moved closer, kissed his lined cheek. "Then think of what we can do in New York City," she whispered. "All of those rich Yankees. All of those smug, arrogant Yankees who supported the troops and raised the money to pay for their cannon and uniforms, and who voted for Lincoln twice, all so that you would be wounded and Tom killed and Lucinda made ill and me brought to the class of a boarding house owner. Won't that make you feel better? To strike against them, at their den in New York? Won't it, Henry?"

Finally he smiled, and then bent over to kiss her. "Yes, that is true. That would make me happy indeed. To set our efforts against Yankees, even if there is a peace. Now, if you will excuse me, madam, I must finish."

And then she was going to kiss him again, when the voice came down from upstairs: "Missus Stuartson? Missus Stuartson?"

Henry froze, his eyes wide, but Mary moved away and went to the bottom of the stairs. Up in the kitchen, Mister Gray was looking down at her. "Yes, what is it?" she asked.

"There's an officer here to see you," he said. "He says it is urgent. His name is Captain Slater, and he says it concerns Major Tomlison. The missing officer."

From behind her, she thought she heard Henry make a noise, but she moved forward, going up the stairs.

"Tell him I shall see him momentarily."

IN THE KITCHEN HER hands were shaking, and she washed her face again. To be brought to this . . . to face arrest and ruin and no doubt death . . . both she and Henry, hung by their neck or shot by a firing squad. She took a deep breath, went into the parlor, where Captain Slater, the suspicious-looking officer, was standing by himself by the cold fireplace. She remembered all of the fine parties and receptions that had been held in this very room . . . this room, which was now cold and whose curtains had been torn down and made into sheets for the guests' beds.

Captain Slater turned as she entered the parlor. He bowed to her and removed his hat. "Madam, if I may . . . please excuse this intrusion, but I must speak to you. Alone. Which is why Captain Abrams is not with me."

She stood still in the parlor, looking at him, glad that her skirts were hiding her quivering knees. "Go on, sir."

"It involves Major Tomlison. I believe you know why I am here."

By now her hands were shaking and she brought them behind her, holding them tight. She would not let this officer see her afraid. She would not let this young man think he had gotten the best of her. "Perhaps I do. But perhaps you will tell me."

His face took on a frown. "This is rather delicate, and I apologize in advance for any discomfort I may bring to you. But my station and my responsibilities force me to ask you the question."

*Oh, husband, how I wish you were here with me right now.* She cleared her throat and tried to keep her voice strong. "Then ask me the question, Captain. Do not be shy."

*Here it comes,* she thought. *Here it comes. The accusation, the questions, the demand of having her home searched . . . what would she do, oh, what would she say to him when the questions started.*

Captain Slater coughed and said, "Major Tomlison. His room."

"Yes? Would you care to search it again?"

"No, madam, I do not care to search it again. I was going to ask you . . . is his room available? To rent?"

It felt like the foundations of her home had turned to mud and that the house was swaying underneath her, for she felt seconds away from fainting dead away. "To rent?" she asked weakly. "You would care to rent his room?"

The officer nodded. "I am currently living in a loft over a horse barn, near the warehouse district. There are no amenities, no fireplace, and the meals are intolerable. Which is why I came back here by myself, and so quickly. This appears to be a very respectable house, in a very respectable neighborhood. So I ask you again, madam, may I rent that room?"

She then looked at him, at the polished boots and fine sword, and the heavy gold ring on his left hand, and the watch chain about his waist. An officer, true, but an officer assigned to the War Department, one who makes the plans and issues the orders and sends the troops into battle, especially one's husband and one's son . . .

"Of course," she said, bowing to him slightly. "We would be honored."

For the first time she saw him smile. "Madam, I am at your service."

And she smiled in return. "I am sure you will be, Captain. I am sure you will."

# Veterans

*John Lutz*

It began because Confederate Major General Henry Heth's troops needed boots.

In search of a new supply in a town called Gettysburg, Heth's men marched unknowingly toward death and history. They were noticed by Union soldiers serving under Brigadier General John Buford, who were bivouacked on a nearby hill. Buford sent for Union reinforcements. The ensuing Union troop movements were observed by Heth, who attacked. The newly arrived First Corps, led by Major General John Reynolds, took the brunt of the assault on McPherson's Ridge. Casualties were high, the Union's crack Iron Brigade lost more than half its men, and Reynolds was killed.

Corporal Will Faver, born in Oak River, Missouri, and a Union volunteer, survived. Grape shot had grazed his head, leaving a nasty gash, and a minie ball had taken a bite out of his left arm, but he was alive and still full of fight. Bandaged and determined, he rejoined Union forces on Cemetery Ridge, where they'd been driven backward to hold after fierce fighting.

The Rebs decided not to press the attack in the evening's waning light, so during that night the Yanks regrouped and waited. Reb troops were moving in from the north and west. Pickets were needed to take up position in those directions, well away from the main body of troops, to act as isolated look-outs and give warning of approaching Confederate forces. Dangerous assignments. Which was why Will Faver, wounded but not seriously, and mostly unknown by the men around him, was given picket duty. With a youth named Elliott Nance, a lean and sad-faced Pennsylvanian, Will was sent about half a mile north to take up position in a peach orchard.

There was a moon that night, and the two men were spotted near the orchard and had to break into a run when Confederate light artillery opened fire on them.

Will, who'd won many a picnic foot race in Oak River, simply put his head down and sprinted for the trees. Nance decided to weave to avoid the Rebel fire. Entering the cover of the orchard, Will heard the young trooper's shrill scream.

Will found himself alone in the orchard.

He moved farther into the shelter of the trees. It was June and they'd borne early fruit. The sweet scent of peaches rotting on the ground spooked him, reminding him of decay and death. His lost comrades in the First Corps . . . young Nance. Morose and afraid, he stumbled through the darkness beneath the tree cover, waiting for the artillery to be trained on the orchard. Will had seen wooded areas assaulted by artillery, leafless, blackened skeletal ruins where no life could survive. He hadn't much hope.

The ground dropped out from beneath him, and with a gasp of surprise he slid on his back into a dry creek bed. It would provide him some cover if the artillery decided to open up on the entire orchard. He scooted around to sit with his back braced against the slope of the hard dirt bank. And there he sat listening to his harsh, ragged breathing, living his fear, knowing his duty.

As he had so many times in danger, he slid his hand beneath his shirt and caressed the silver locket with

Sharleen's curl of blonde hair tucked beneath its oval lid. The metal warmed to his touch and calmed him. His faith returned. He would survive this night, this war, and get back to Oak River and live out his life with his wife and the children they planned on having. He knew at that moment that Will and Sharleen Faver would grow old together.

Then his brother said, "Move a muscle, Yank, and I shoot you dead as a stump."

Terror froze Will so he couldn't have moved if he tried. Then through his cold panic seeped warm realization. *The Reb's voice! He couldn't mistake that voice!*

"Luther?"

Luther Faver, Will's older brother, had taken sides in the war first, and joined the Tennessee Volunteers. He'd been in the tobacco business with partners in Memphis, and that was where his loyalties lay. Will was the brother who took over the family farm rather than let it lie fallow, married Sharleen, and sank his own roots deep and forever in Oak River.

"Luther? That you, Luther?"

The dark form of the Reb aiming his musket down at Will didn't move. Then slowly the long barrel of the gun dropped low and to the side.

"My God, it *is* you," Luther said, and scampered down into the gouge of the creek bed with Will. "How in the hell you been, boy?"

"Stayin' alive, I guess."

"Good thing we had orders to bring back prisoners if we could find 'em, or I'da surely opened fire on you when I saw you here." Luther, a tall man with a lean face and darker hair than his brother's, wiped the back of a hand across his forehead and took a swig from a canteen. He recapped the canteen and tossed it over to Will. "Seen Ma lately?"

And Will remembered that Luther wouldn't know their mother had died six months ago. Will had managed to return briefly to Oak River for her funeral. "Gone . . . ," he said, and took a long pull of water from the canteen.

Luther didn't say anything, just stared up at the night sky beyond the peach tree branches. "How 'bout Sharleen?" he asked at last.

"Good. Seen her last six months ago. Me an' her been workin' the farm. She's keepin' it goin' till I come back for good."

"Why'd you ever leave her, Will. You didn't have to fight in this war."

"Neither did you," Will said.

Luther looked surprised. "Me? Why, I had financial considerations."

Will nodded, understanding. "I plumb forgot you were a businessman." He capped the canteen and tossed it back to his brother. "Thing is, Luther, what are we gonna do now."

"Now?"

"I mean, about this here situation."

"I still don't understand why you ever left Sharleen," Luther said.

Will was trying to think of a good answer when Luther shot him between the eyes.

LUTHER SURVIVED THE REST of the war, sustaining only a slight gunshot wound in the Battle of Kennesaw Mountain the following year.

He returned to Oak River a hero. The Mason-Dixon Line ran close to the town, and veterans of both armies were welcomed home. People were eager for healing.

The second day home, Luther rode the aging horse he'd been allowed to keep the three miles out of town to the farm. It was where he'd grown up none too happily. He'd always been jealous of Will, who was the favorite and had gotten everything, from their parents' attention to . . . Sharleen.

Sharleen must have seen him from a window. She came out onto the porch as he approached the log house. The house itself didn't look bad, though it could use a little upkeep, some chinking between the logs and some paint on the shutters. And the porch roof sagged some.

Sharleen had aged better than the house. Though she looked older, she was still trim and beautiful, with her calm blue eyes, and her wonderful blonde hair pulled back now and tied in a swirl atop her head. She was wearing a faded flower-print skirt and a white blouse molded to her by the prairie breeze.

Luther reined in the horse a few feet in front of the porch and gave her back her smile. Then he stopped smiling. "I sure am sorry about Will."

Her smile left her face as if caught by the breeze. "So'm I, Luther. More'n you can know."

He dismounted and walked to stand at the base of the three wooden steps to the plank porch. "Place looks good, except for the fields for this time of summer."

"Frank Ames helps out some. Did some mending and painting last month."

Luther looked at her, fingering the brim of his hat held in front of him. "Ames survived the war?"

"He come back to Oak River six months ago. Lost him a leg at Gettysburg."

"Then he's lucky to be alive."

"He 'peers to think so," Sharleen said. She seemed to shake off her sadness and managed a bright smile that brought back memories to Luther. The smile had been there the night Sharleen had taken the walk with him among the cottonwoods in the moonlight, the times at the local dances when she whirled gaily to the music. The smile that was so uniquely hers was there when she'd won the turkey shoot one cold Thanksgiving, and when she filled in teaching at the schoolhouse, and when she and Will surprised everyone by saying they were getting married. The smile had been there on her wedding day. And no doubt on her wedding night . . .

". . . my manners."

Luther realized she was speaking.

"Do come on into the house," she was saying. "Luther?"

"Sorry," he told her. "My mind was wandering."

"It's no wonder," she said solemnly, "after what all you been through." Over her shoulder, as she led him into the house, she said, "Least it was over and final for Will after Gettysburg. Some small comfort in that."

The inside of the house was neat and clean if sparsely furnished. Will sat in a wooden chair at a square oak table in the kitchen. Sharleen had been cooking. The scent of baked bread was in the air, along with that of brewed coffee.

He watched the sway of her hips beneath her skirt as she moved to the wood stove and poured coffee into a tin cup. She set the cup in front of him, then sat down across from him at the table.

"Gotta be a rough life here for a woman alone," Luther remarked.

"Oh, I'm not alone." Her glance slid to an open doorway.

Luther didn't understand at first. Then he stood up, walked over, and peered into the room. A small child was sleeping in a wooden crib.

"That's Samuel," Sharleen said, when Luther had sat down again at the table.

"Will's son," he said with a forced smile.

"The precious thing he left me," Sharleen said. "I got Samuel. And I got Frank Ames."

Luther took a deep breath. "Sharleen, is Ames . . . ? I mean, are you and him . . . ?"

She appeared surprised, touching the side of her neck lightly in a way he remembered she'd done long ago when she was embarrassed. "Oh, no! It's nothing like that, Luther."

"Maybe not to you, but what about to him?"

She seemed to think on the question. "I don't believe so, and a woman oughta know. I think it's just he's a kind man and he runs the bank and's in a position to help out now and again. I know I'm not the only one he's helped."

Luther raised his eyebrows. "Runs the bank, does he?"

"Surely does. You remember he worked there before leaving to fight. Well, old man Scopes retired and sold his interest to Frank. There's partners and a board, but Frank's president and makes the decisions."

"I'll talk to him," Luther said, and took a sip of coffee.

" 'bout what?"

"Getting a loan to run some irrigation to the fields, turn the soil, and put in some good seed for spring planting. That horse I got out there ain't worth much, but he surely can pull a plow."

He couldn't read the expression on Sharleen's face.

"Luther . . ."

"Remember," he said, "I was raised here on this land. It ain't that I see it as mine, but you and Samuel are family, and nothing can change that." He gave her a reassuring smile. "With what happened to Will and all . . . I mean, I feel duty bound to help."

She studied his face, then nodded, stood up, and poured him some more hot coffee. "It ain't as if we don't need it," she said.

"You done all right," Luther said.

"The Lord knows I tried." She lowered her head, almost as if she were going to pray, but she began to cry quietly.

Luther got up, strode around the table, and hugged her to him until her back stopped heaving and she wiped her nose and was calm.

He caressed her cheek with the backs of his knuckles and she turned her face away. He walked back to his chair and sat down.

"Coffee was something we could never get enough of during the war," he told her. "Towards the end, we'd make it outta most anything we could grind between two stones." He shook his head glumly. "There was lots of things we couldn't get enough of."

"I just bet there was," Sharleen said.

Luther went to see Frank Ames the next morning at the Oak River Bank. Ames was a small man with a jutting chin and bushy dark mustache. He looked startled to see Luther, then stood up behind his desk and shook hands with him. That he'd stood up surprised Luther, as Sharleen had said Ames lost a leg to the Yanks.

"I'm real glad to see you made it back here safe and sound," Luther said.

Ames smiled. Though his angular face hadn't changed much, his gray eyes were a lot older than when he and Luther had competed in the county games five years ago. "Safe, maybe. But I'm not exactly sound, Luther. Lost a leg."

"Wouldn't guess it."

"Got a wood one, foot and all," Ames said, and limped out from behind the desk. "Don't have to work my boot off and on it, anyway. Silver lining." He motioned for Luther to sit in a nearby chair, then went back to sit behind the desk. He ducked his head and looked strangely at Luther. "I heard you were dead, killed at Chickamauga."

Luther raised his eyebrows in surprise, then smiled. "Don't look that way, does it?"

"Nope. Don't have to touch you to know you're real and still among the living."

"War was hell," Luther said.

Ames nodded. "Damned Sherman." He made a pink steeple with the fingers of both hands. "This visit about business, Luther?"

"It is. I understand you been helping my sister-in-law Sharleen. We appreciate that, but now that I'm back, I want to do my duty to her. After all, she's my brother's widow. Family's all that's left after this war, and for lots of folks not even that."

"It was a shame about Will. He was a good boy."

"He was that."

"His widow deserves better than what she's got," Ames said. "What do you have in mind, Luther?"

"A loan for a decent plow my horse can pull, for some irrigation work, a new barn and chicken coop, a well that ain't run dry, and good seed come the spring."

"That's a lot," Ames said.

"Sharleen needs a lot."

"Gettysburg was hell worse than Sherman," Ames said. "Made a lot of Southern widows."

"Northern ones, too."

Ames nodded. "Carpetbaggers are gonna come in here from the North, change this country. Oak River is gonna grow. Guess Sharleen's farm can grow with it."

"You'll help, then?"

"I'll loan you the money, Luther. The work's up to you."

"And I'm up to it," Luther said.

"Just figure out what you need."

Luther drew a sheet of paper from his pocket and unfolded it. "I got it right here."

OAK RIVER GREW JUST as Frank Ames had predicted. And Sharleen's farm prospered. Luther worked hard and became a substitute father for young Samuel, and stayed in the old barn while he built a new one. By late fall the farm had new or repaired outbuildings, but the harvest was meager.

Winter was cold and with more than the usual snow, but Luther kept at his work. Before spring planting, he located water with a divining rod fashioned from a forked branch from a peach tree, a talent that had always been his, and with help from town dug a new well. The spring planting produced a rich harvest that late summer and fall, and Luther and Sharleen began to repay Frank Ames's bank.

At the beginning of their second winter together Luther and Sharleen were married. By that time, nobody was much surprised, and the wedding was a joyful event. The farm became known to the townspeople as the Faver Place.

Both Luther and Sharleen continued to work hard, and when Samuel got old enough he took to farm work. Besides farming, Luther gained a reputation with his dowsing, and the carpetbaggers moving into Oak River paid him handsomely to locate water with his divining rod so they'd not waste time and money digging dry wells.

Frank Ames was soon paid off, and with profits no longer going toward the loan, Luther and Sharleen began to grow rich by Oak River's standards. They replaced the log farmhouse with a fine two-story frame home with a green marble fireplace and a wide front porch.

At the turn of the century Luther had lived longer than he imagined was possible, almost to sixty. But he was healthy and saw more good years ahead for him and for Sharleen.

Samuel had become a tall, handsome man who looked more like Luther than Will, and moved with his young bride to Joplin where they managed a dry goods emporium. One day he appeared at the farm with a fancy carriage pulled by two fine horses, and in his wife's arms was Luther's grandson.

Will's grandson.

"We named him Will!" Samuel said proudly. Then he asked how they liked the carriage and said, "I seen 'em with motors in Kansas City. Nothin' else pullin' 'em!"

"Horseless carriages?" Sharleen asked in amazement. Though graying and thicker through the middle, she was still a beautiful woman, and her eyes widened with the enthusiasm of a youthfulness that would always be hers. The past lived with her and in her.

"So they're called," Samuel told his mother. "I'm gonna talk to a man about a dealership. The carriages might be horseless, but they ain't without profit." He grinned at Luther. "And Dad taught me the value of plannin' ahead."

That evening, sitting before the warm blaze in his marble fireplace, Luther Faver considered that he was one of the luckiest men alive.

The next morning his illness introduced itself, and it never left him. His stomach was never right, and he lost weight until his elbows and knees made sharp angles. Then his hair began to fall out.

Doc Newsner in town didn't know what to make of it. He tried different medications on Luther and bled him with leeches. Nothing seemed to help.

Only Sharleen could comfort him. She stayed awake through the night with him at times, holding his hand while the pain wracked him and caused him to moan and draw up his knees. The nights were the worst time. She would place a folded damp cloth on his forehead and croon softly to him. But the pain persisted.

When Sharleen suddenly came down ill, Doc Newsner figured maybe it was something in the well water.

It wasn't, though. Two days later she died from a burst appendix.

Luther was too ill to attend the funeral. He lay bedridden and alone in the big farmhouse on the Faver Place. Samuel was coming in from Joplin to take him back there to die. Nobody had any illusions about that. They would travel by train to Joplin so Luther could pass while among family.

The night before Samuel was to arrive, Frank Ames paid Luther a visit.

Ames hadn't aged well. He was bent at the waist, walking with the aid of a walnut cane, and his face was deeply lined. His mustache had become gray and scraggly above bloodless lips. As he limped into the bedroom, Luther thought Ames probably wouldn't live much longer than he would.

"Some whiskey in the kitchen," Luther offered.

"Can't drink the stuff anymore," Ames said. His voice had become older than he was, hoarse and so soft you had to listen hard to whatever he was saying.

Luther weakly waved an arm toward the easy chair alongside the bed, and Ames settled into it with a long sigh, his wooden leg extended straight out in front of him.

"Sharleen was buried well," he told Luther. "She was a good woman."

"Always," Luther said. "I hope I did right by her."

Ames drew a briar pipe from his pocket and gave his wooden leg a sharp rap with it. "We came a long ways from Gettysburg," he said, and began packing the pipe's bowl with tobacco from a leather pouch.

"War's a long time ago now," Luther agreed.

"To some it is." Ames struck a wooden match to flame with his thumbnail and held fire to tobacco. He puffed until he got the pipe burning well, then he shook out the match and put the blackened remains of it in the vest pocket of his banker's suit. The room filled with the acrid-sweet scent of the smoldering tobacco leaf.

"Long time ago for everyone," Luther told him. "Time buries everything."

"Sometimes it takes a while, though," Frank Ames said. He reached into the pocket where he'd slipped the burnt match, withdrew an object and laid it on the nightstand alongside the bed where Luther could see it.

Luther raised his head and peered to the side at the glittering object.

"I shined it up for you," Ames said.

"What is it?"

"A locket. Silver. Pretty old now. There's a lock of Sharleen's hair in it."

Something dark and immortal stirred in Luther.

"Your brother Will wore it for good luck in the war. Had it on him when he died."

"Did they send his personal effects to Sharleen?"

"Nope." Ames settled back in his chair and spoke around the pipe stem clamped in his teeth. "I was with Longstreet's troops at Gettysburg, camped near Cemetery Ridge and waiting for morning and the hell it'd bring, when we spotted a couple of Yanks headed for picket duty. The moonlight made them good targets, and some artillery pieces opened fire on them. Killed one of them. The other made it to cover in a peach orchard. I was one of three men sent to capture that lone picket so he wouldn't give information to the Yanks. We didn't know another patrol was sent from Heth's First Corps to capture him. You were in that patrol." The burning pipe tobacco made a soft whispering sound in the quiet room. "I was in the peach orchard and saw what happened that night, Luther. I saw you shoot your brother."

Luther's heart seemed to shrivel. He was having even more difficulty than usual breathing. Possession of the locket was proof of Ames's story. Proof that he was in the peach orchard that night and proof enough of murder. Luther knew that he'd come close to being hanged long ago.

"Why didn't you tell someone?" he heard his own rasping voice ask. "Why didn't you tell Sharleen what happened?"

"I never told her nor anyone else because I knew she needed you," Ames said. "And Samuel needed a father. Me with my missing leg, there was no way in hell I could help her enough, no way I could farm crops and build and be a father to a son not my own. But I loved Sharleen and wanted to do something for her. I couldn't bear to sit and watch her live such a hard life and fall ill and die, or bend beneath her load and become an old woman before her time. You were the answer, Luther. The solution to the problem you created."

"I killed Will so I could have Sharleen," Luther said feebly. There were tears in his eyes. He hadn't cried in decades, not even when Sharleen died.

"That was easy to figure," Ames said. "You always loved her, and you were always jealous of your brother."

"I was a good husband to Sharleen," Luther said. "A good provider, and a good father to her son. Maybe I made it up to her, in a way. Maybe I made amends for what I did."

Ames drew on his pipe and exhaled a cloud of smoke. "I don't think so. I don't think that was enough."

"At least she never found out."

"I didn't say that, Luther."

Luther couldn't lift his head, but he craned his neck painfully so he could see Ames. He didn't like what he saw in Ames's face.

"I told her 'bout a year ago," Ames said. "Showed her the locket."

Luther felt himself go cold from the inside. "She never said anything to me."

"She decided to poison you instead."

Now Luther did manage to raise his head. "Wha . . . ?" The back of his head sank back into his sweat-soaked pillow.

"She's been feeding you arsenic, Luther. Exacting her revenge little by little for what you did to her young husband. Exacting justice. Nothing you can do about it now. It's too late to fix the damage that's been done to you or reverse the process. The poison'll soon have its way."

Luther struggled to speak but could only croak weakly and gasp.

"I thought you oughta know," Ames said, bracing himself with his cane and standing up from his chair with difficulty. "Maybe because I'm a banker and I believe there needs to be an accounting. It's only right. You haven't got much longer and things oughta be settled."

Ames made to leave, then paused and turned. "We were on the losing side, Luther, but you thought you won your own personal war. It took a long time, but you lost just like the rest of us."

Ames limped toward the door. His cane clattered like dry bones as he clumped down the stairs.

Then there was complete silence.

Luther lay with ghosts in the darkening room.

# The Cobblestones of Saratoga Street

## *Avram Davidson*

"Cobblestones to Go" said the headline. Miss Louisa lifted her eyebrows, lifted her quizzing-glass (probably the last one in actual use anywhere in the world), read the article, passed it to her sister. Miss Augusta read it without eyeglass or change of countenance, and handed it back.

"They shan't," she said.

They glanced at a faded photograph in a silver frame on the mantelpiece, then at each other. Miss Louisa placed the newspaper next to the pewter chocolate-pot, tinkled a tiny bell. After a moment a white-haired colored man entered the room.

"Carruthers," said Miss Augusta, "you may clear away breakfast."

"WELL. I THINK IT is outrageous," Betty Linkhorn snapped.

"My dear," her grandfather said mildly, "you can't stop progress." He sipped his tea.

77

"Progress my eye! This is the only decently paved street in the whole town—you know that, don't you, Papa? Just because it's cobblestone and not concrete—or macadamor—"

"My dear," said Edward Linkhorn, "*I* remember when several of the streets were still paved with wood. I remember it quite particularly because, in defiance of my father's orders, I went barefoot one fine summer's day and got a splinter in my heel. My mother took it out with a needle and my father thrashed me . . . Besides, don't you find the cobblestones difficult to manage in high-heeled shoes?"

Betty smiled—not sweetly. "I don't find them difficult at all. Mrs. Harris does—but, then, if *she'd* been thrashed for going barefoot . . . Come on, Papa," she said, while her grandfather maintained a diplomatic silence, "admit it—if Mrs. Harris hadn't sprained her ankle, if her husband wasn't a paving contractor, if his partner wasn't C. B. Smith, the state chairman of the party that's had the city, country, *and* state sewn up for twenty years—"

Mr. Linkhorn spread honey on a small piece of toast, "'If wishes were horses, beggars would ride.'"

"Well, what's wrong with that?"

"'. . . and all mankind be consumed with pride.' My dear, I will see what I can do."

HIS HONOR WAS INTERVIEWING the press. "Awright, what's next? New terlets in the jail, right? Awright, if them bums and smokies wouldn't of committed no crimes they wouldn't be in no jail, right? Awright, what's next? Cobblestones? *Cob*blestones? Damn it, again this business with the cobblestones! You'd think they were diamonds or sumpthin'. Awright. Well, um, look, except for Saratoga Street, the last cobblestones inna city were tore up when I was a boy, for Pete's sake. Allathem people there, they're living inna past, yaknowwhatimean? Allathem gas lamps in frunna the houses, huh? Hitching posts and carriage blocks, for Pete sakes! Whadda they think we're living inna horse-and-buggy age? Awright, they got that park with a fence around it, private property, okay. But the streets belong to the City, see? Somebody breaks a leg on wunna them cobblestones, they can sue the City, right? So—cobblestones? Up they come, anats all there is to it. Awright, what's next?"

His comments appeared in the newspaper (the publisher of which knew what side his Legal Advertisements were buttered on) in highly polished form. *I yield to no one in my respect for tradition and history, but the cobblestoned paving of Saratoga Street is simply too dangerous to be endured. The cobblestones will be replaced by a smooth, efficient surface more in keeping with the needs of the times.*

As the Mayor put it, "What's next?"

Next was a series of protests by the local, county, and state historical societies, all of which protests were buried in two-or-three-line items in the back of the newspaper. But (as the publisher put it, "After all, C. B., business is business. And, besides, it won't make any difference in the long run, anyway.") the Saratoga Street Association reprinted them in a full-page advertisement headed "Protect Our Heritage," and public interest began to pick up.

It was stimulated by the interest shown in the metropolitan papers, all of which circulated locally, "Bluebloods Man the Barricades," said one. "20th Century Catches Up with Saratoga Street," said another. "Beloved Cobblestones Doomed, Historical Saratoga Street Prepares to Say Farewell" lamented a third. And so it went.

And it also went like this: *To the Editor: Sir, I wish to point out an error in the letter which claimed that the cobblestones were laid down in 1836. True, the houses on Saratoga Street were mostly built in that year, but like many local streets it was not paved at all until late in the '90s. So the cobblestones are not so old as some people think.*

And it went like this, too:

*Mr. Edward Linkhorn:* Would you gentlemen care for anything else to drink?

*Reporter:* Very good whiskey.

*Photographer:* Very good.

*Linkhorn:* We are very gratified that a national picture magazine is giving us so much attention.

*Reporter:* Well, *you* know—human interest story. Not so much soda, Sam.

*Photographer:* Say, Mr. Linkhorn, can I ask you a question?

*Linkhorn:* Certainly.

*Photographer:* Well, I notice that on all the houses—in all the windows, I mean—they got these signs, *Save Saratoga Street Cobblestones.* All but one house. How come? They *against* the stones?

*Reporter:* Say, that's right, Mr. Linkhorn. How come—?

*Linkhorn:* Well, gentlemen, that house, number 25, belongs to the Misses de Gray.

*Reporter:* de Gray? de Gray?

*Linkhorn:* Their father was General de Gray of Civil War fame. His statue is in de Gray Square. We also have a de Gray Avenue.

*Reporter:* His *daughters* are still living? What are they like?

*Linkhorn:* I have never had the privilege of meeting them.

MISS ADELAIDE TALLMAN'S FAMILY was every bit as good as any of those who lived on Saratoga Street; the Tallmans had simply never *cared* to live on Saratoga Street, that was all. The Tallman estate had been one of the sights of the city, but nothing remained of it now except the name *Jabez Tallman* on real estate maps used in searching land titles, and the old mansion itself—much modified now, and converted into a funeral parlor. Miss Tallman herself lived in a nursing home. Excitement was rare in her life, and she had no intention of passing up any bit of attention which came her way.

"I knew the de Gray girls well," she told the lady from the news syndicate. This was a big fib; she had never laid eyes on them in her life—but who was to know? She had *heard* enough about them to talk as if she had, and if the de Gray girls didn't like it, let them come and tell her so. Snobby people, the de Grays, always were. What if her father, Mr. Tallman, *had* hired a substitute during the Rebellion? *Hmph.*

"Oh, they were the most beautiful things! Louisa was the older, she was blonde. Augusta's hair was brown. They always had plenty of beaux—not that I didn't have my share of them, too, mind you," she added, looking sharply at the newspaper lady, as if daring her to deny it. "But nobody was ever good enough for *them.* There was one young man, his name was Horace White, and—oh, he was the *hand*somest thing! I danced with him myself," she said complacently, "at the Victory Ball after the Spanish War. He had gone away to be an officer in the Navy, and he was just the most handsome thing in his uniform that you ever saw. But *he* wasn't good enough for them, either. He went away after that—went out west to Chicago or some such place—and no one ever heard from him again. Jimmy Taylor courted Augusta, and William Snow and Rupert Roberts—no, Rupert was sweet on Louisa, yes, but—"

The newspaper lady asked when Miss Tallman had last seen the de Gray sisters.

Oh, said Miss Tallman vaguely, many years ago. *Many* years ago . . . (Had she really danced with anybody at the Victory Ball? Was she still wearing her hair down then? Perhaps she was thinking of the Junior Cotillion. Oh, well, who was to know?)

"About 1905," she said firmly, crossing her fingers under her blanket. "But, you see, nobody was *good* enough for them. And so, by and by, they stopped seeing *anybody.* And that's the way it was."

THAT WAS NOT QUITE the way it was. They saw Carruthers.

Carruthers left the house on Sunday mornings only—to attend at the A.M.E. Zion Church. Sunday evenings he played the harmonium while Miss Louisa and Miss Augusta sang hymns. All food was delivered and Carruthers received it either at the basement door or the rear door. The Saratoga Street Association took care of the maintenance of the outside of the house, of course; all Carruthers had to do there was sweep the walk and polish the brass.

It must not be thought that because his employers were recluses, Carruthers was one, too; or because they did not choose to communicate with the outside world, he did not choose to do so, either. If, while engaged in his chores, he saw people he knew, he would greet them. He was, in fact, the first person to greet Mrs. Henry Harris when she moved into Saratoga Street.

"Why, hel-lo, Henrietta," he said. "What in the world are *you* doing here?"

Mrs. Harris did not seem to appreciate this attention.

Carruthers read the papers, too.

"What do they want to bother them old stones for?" he asked himself. "They been here long as I can remember."

The question continued to pose itself. One morning he went so far as to tap the Cobblestones story in the newspaper with his finger and raise his eyebrows inquiringly.

Miss Augusta answered him. "They won't," she said.

Miss Louisa frowned. "Is all this conversation necessary?"

Carruthers went back downstairs. "That sure relieves my mind," he said to himself.

"THE NEWSPAPERS SEEM TO be paying more attention to the de Gray sisters than to the cobblestones," Betty Linkhorn said.

"Well," her grandfather observed, "people *are* more important than cobblestones. Still," he went on, "*House of*

*Mystery* seems to be pitching it a little stronger than is necessary. They just want to be left alone, that's all. And I rather incline to doubt that General M. M. de Gray won the Civil War all by himself, as these articles imply."

Betty, reading further, said, "*Hmmm.* Papa, except for that poor old Miss Tallman, there doesn't seem to be anyone alive—outside of their butler—who has ever *seen* them, even." She giggled. "Do you suppose that maybe they could be *dead?* For years and *years?* And old Carruthers has them covered with wax and just dusts them every day with a feather mop?"

Mr. Linkhorn said he doubted it.

COMPARISONS WITH THE COLLIER brothers were inevitable, and newsreel and television cameras were standing by in readiness for—well, no one knew just what. And the time for the repaving of Saratoga Street grew steadily nearer. An injunction was obtained; it expired. And then there seemed nothing more that could be done.

"It is claimed that removal would greatly upset and disturb the residents of Saratoga Street, many of whom are said to be elderly," observed the judge, denying an order of further stay, "but it is significant that the two oldest inhabitants, the daughters of General M. M. de Gray, the Hero of Chickasaw Bend, have expressed no objection whatsoever."

Betty wept. "Well, why *haven't* they?" she demanded. "Don't they realize that this is the beginning of the end for Saratoga Street? First the cobblestones, then the flagstone sidewalks, then the hitching posts and carriage blocks—then they'll tear up the common for a parking lot and knock down the three houses at the end to make it a through street. Can't you *ask* them—?"

Her grandfather spread his hands. "They never had a telephone," he said. "And to the best of my knowledge—

although I've written—they haven't answered a letter for more than forty years. No, my dear, I'm afraid it's hopeless."

Said His Honor: "Nope, no change in plans. T'morra morning at eight A.M. sharp, the cobblestones *go*. Awright, what's next?"

AT EIGHT THAT MORNING a light snow was falling. At eight that morning a crowd had gathered. Saratoga Street was only one block long. At its closed end it was only the width of three houses set in their little gardens; then it widened so as to embrace the small park—"common"—then narrowed again.

The newsreel and television cameras were at work, and several announcers described, into their microphones, the arrival of the Department of Public Works trucks at the corner of Saratoga and Trenton Streets, loaded with workmen and air hammers and pickaxes, at exactly eight o'clock.

At exactly one minute after eight the front door of number 25 Saratoga Street, at the northwest corner, swung open. The interviewers and cameramen were, for a moment, intent on the rather embarrassed crew foreman, and did not at first observe the opening of the door. Then someone shouted, *"Look!"* And then everyone noticed.

First came Carruthers, very erect, carrying a number of items which were at first not identifiable. The crowd parted for him as if he had been Moses, and the crowd, the Red Sea. First he unrolled an old, but still noticeably red, carpet. Next he unfolded and set up two campstools. Then he waited.

Out the door came Miss Louisa de Gray, followed by Miss Augusta. They moved into the now absolutely silent crowd without a word; and without a word they seated themselves on the campstools—Miss Louisa facing south, Miss Augusta facing north.

Carruthers proceeded to unfurl two banners and stood at parade rest, so to speak—with one in each hand. The snowy wind blew out their folds, revealing them to be a United States flag with thirty-six stars and the banner of the Army of the Tennessee.

And while at least fifty million people watched raptly at their television sets, Miss Louisa drew her father's saber from its scabbard and placed it across her knees; and Miss Augusta, taking up her father's musket, proceeded to load it with powder and ball and drove the charge down with a ramrod.

After a while the workmen debated what they ought to do. Failing to have specific instructions suitable to the new situation, they built a fire in an ashcan, and stood around it, warming their hands.

THE FIRST TELEGRAM CAME from the Ladies of the G.A.R.; the second, from the United Daughters of the Confederacy. Both, curiously enough, without mutual consultation, threatened a protest march on the City Hall. In short and rapid succession followed indignant messages from the Senior Citizens' Congress, the Sons of Union Veterans, the American Legion, the B'nai Brith, the Ancient Order of Hibernians, the D.A.R., the N.A.A.C.P., the Society of the War of 1812, the V.F.W., the Ancient and Accepted Scottish Rite, and the Blue Star Mothers. After that it became difficult to keep track.

The snow drifted down upon them, but neither lady, nor Carruthers, moved a thirty-second of an inch.

At twenty-seven minutes after nine the Mayor's personal representative arrived on the scene—his ability to speak publicly without a script had long been regarded by the Mayor himself as something akin to sorcery.

"I have here," the personal representative declared loudly, holding up a paper, "a statement from His Honor announcing his intention to summon a special meeting of the Council for the sole purpose of turning Saratoga Street into a private street, title to be vested in the Saratoga Street

Association. *Then*—" The crowd cheered, and the personal representative held up his hands for silence. "*Then,* in the event of anyone sustaining injuries because of cobblestones, the City won't be responsible."

There were scattered boos and hisses. The representative smiled broadly, expressed the Municipality's respect for Tradition, and urged the Misses de Gray to get back into their house, please, before they both caught cold.

Neither moved. The Mayor's personal representative had not reached his position of eminence for nothing. He turned to the D.P.W. crew. "Okay, boys—no work for you here. Back to the garage. In fact," he added, "take the day off!"

The crew cheered, the crowd cheered, the trucks rolled away. Miss Louisa sheathed her sword, Miss Augusta unloaded her musket by the simple expedient of firing it into the air, the Mayor's representative ducked (and was immortalized in that act by twenty cameras). The Misses de Gray then stood up. Reporters crowded in and were ignored as if they had never been born.

Miss Louisa, carrying her sword like an admiral as the two sisters made their way back to the house, observed Betty and her grandfather in the throng. "Your features look familiar," she said. "Do they not, Augusta?"

"Indeed," said Miss Augusta. "I think he must be Willie Linkhorn's little boy—are you?" Mr. Linkhorn, who was seventy, nodded; for the moment he could think of nothing to say. "Then you had better come inside. The girl may come, too. Go home, good people," she said, pausing at the door and addressing the crowd, "and be sure to drink a quantity of hot rum and tea with nutmeg on it."

The door closed on ringing cheers from the populace.

"Carruthers, please mull us all some port," Miss Louisa directed. "I would have advised the same outside, but I am not sure the common people would *care* to drink port. Boy," she said, to the gray-haired Mr. Linkhorn, "would you care to know why we have broken a seclusion of sixty years and engaged in a public demonstration so foreign to our natures?"

He blinked. "Why . . . I suppose it was your attachment to the traditions of Saratoga Street, exemplified by the cobble—"

"Stuff!" said Miss Augusta. "We don't give a hoot for the traditions of Saratoga Street. And as for the cobblestones, those dreadful noisy things, I could wish them all at the bottom of the sea!"

"Then—"

The sisters waved to a faded photograph in a silver frame on the mantelpiece. It showed a young man with a curling mustache, clad in an old-fashioned uniform. "Horace White," they said, in unison.

"He courted us," the elder said. "He never would say which he preferred. I refused Rupert Roberts for him, I gave up Morey Stone. My sister sent Jimmy Taylor away, and William Snow as well. When Horace went off to the Spanish War, he gave us that picture. He said he would make his choice when he returned. We waited."

Carruthers returned with the hot wine, and withdrew.

The younger sister took up the tale. "When he returned," she said, "we asked him whom his choice had fallen on. He smiled and said he'd changed his mind. He no longer wished to wed either of us, he said. The street had been prepared for cobblestone paving, the earth was still tolerably soft. We buried him there, ten paces from the gas lamp and fifteen from the water hydrant. And there he lies to this day, underneath those dreadful noisy cobblestones. I could forgive, perhaps, on my deathbed, his insult to myself—but his insult to my dear sister, that I can *never* forgive."

Miss Louisa echoed, "His insult to *me* I could perhaps forgive, on my deathbed, but his insult to my dear sister that I could *never* forgive."

She poured four glasses of the steaming wine.

"Then—" said Mr. Linkhorn, "you mean—"

"I do, I pinioned him by the arms and my sister Louisa shot him through his black and faithless heart with Father's musket. Father was a heavy sleeper, and never heard a thing."

Betty swallowed. "Gol-*ly*."

"I trust no word of this will ever reach other ears. The embarrassment would be severe . . . A scoundrel, yes, was Horace White," said Miss Augusta, "but—and I confess it to you—I fear I love him still."

Miss Louisa said, "And I. And I."

They raised their glasses. "To Horace White!"

Mr. Linkhorn, much as he felt the need, barely touched his drink; but the ladies drained theirs to the stem, all three of them.

# A House Divided

## Marc Bilgrey

It was a sunny afternoon in late March 1865. My company had been on its way to Richmond, when we were ambushed. I ran for cover in the nearby woods, hoping to circle around the Rebs and take them from the opposite direction. I thought I might bring down an officer or two in the process. But no sooner had I entered the dense foliage, when I was met by a gray who butted me in the head with his rifle. I dropped to the ground like a marble statue. After that everything went black.

When I awoke hours later, I clutched my aching head and looked up to discover a full moon shining in a dark sky. Around me were the bodies of both Union and Confederate men. I can only suppose that both sides had left me for dead.

As I gazed upon this macabre sight I thought about what a grim business it all was. I had agreed to serve my government to the best of my abilities, for I am not a coward. But, just the same, I took no particular joy in it either.

Staggering to my feet I discovered that my Colt .32 caliber revolver, Enfield .57 caliber rifle, knapsack, haversack, belt, and cartridge box were gone. Looted no doubt. After looking in vain for a canteen amongst the corpses I made my way through the trees till I came to a clearing. There I hoped to find a drink of water.

"Good evening, Billy Yank," said a voice.

Instinctively, I reached for my gun but found nothing, not even a holster. I spun around to see a Reb staring me in the face. His gray uniform was ripped in the right arm, and he had dried blood on his upper lip. He looked to be even younger than me, which was twenty. The tiny bugle insignia on his kepi told me he was infantry, same as me. I saw him aim his Smoothbore musket straight at my chest.

"Good evening, Johnny Reb," I said. Without my gun I knew my options were extremely limited.

He came closer. As he did, I heard a cannon blast in the far distance. For a split second he turned toward it. This brief lapse of attention allowed me the time to leap upon him.

He fought fiercely as we wrestled about in the dirt like two dogs fighting over a bone. He was able to land a blow to my stomach. Recovering quickly, I sent an uppercut to his chin, dazing him enough so that I was able to pry the musket out of his hands. I turned the barrel to his head as my finger found the trigger.

"Drop your gun, Yankee!" yelled a voice behind me. "Drop it or I kill you!"

I let the musket fall from my hands to the ground.

"Stand up now!" said the man's voice. "The both of you, and I ain't got all day."

The Reb and I stood up. As we did we looked at the man who was giving us the orders. He was wearing a pair of brown trousers, boots, and a green shirt. He had a long white beard and in his right hand was a C. S. Spiller and Burr .36 caliber revolver.

"Now," he said, addressing us, "step away from the musket."

When we had taken a few steps back, the old man came over, still holding the revolver and staring us down, reached over and picked up the Reb's musket. Then to my amazement, he smashed the musket against some rocks and threw the pieces off into the woods.

"I don't understand," said the Reb, "why are you doing this? We're on Confederate soil. You ought to be helping me take this here Yankee to his just reward, not—"

"I'll thank you to not be giving me any advice, soldier," said the old man, moving his gun just slightly toward the Reb.

"Didn't anyone ever tell you to show a little respect 'round your elders?" The old man pursed his lips and said, "Okay, boys, here's how it's gonna be. You listen to me and do exactly as I say, or I will put some very large holes in you. Nod if you understand me."

I nodded. I was too scared to even look toward the Reb. Being taken prisoner by the enemy was one thing, but what this man had in mind, only the fates knew for certain.

"All right, fellas," said the old man, "now y'all gonna turn around and start walking. You will walk up to that there ridge, and then you will continue to walk till I tell you to stop. And keep in mind that I have the firearm and I ain't afraid to use it. In point of fact, I would be more than glad to use it. It don't matter to me which one of you boys tries anything in the way of an escape attempt. I will kill you where you stand same as I would kill a squirrel for my dinner. Or if you both give it a try, so much the better. I could use the target practice. Not that I need it. I been known to bag a songbird at one hundred paces. Now then, let's start marching."

We began walking. The Reb was next to me. Neither of us said a word. Behind us I heard the old man's footfalls in the twigs. We passed trees and bushes and not much else. I wondered where this old man was taking us. Was it some kind of Rebel trick? Perhaps they were working together and planned to torture me for the purpose of extracting information. I hoped not, since I didn't know a blessed thing. I was a private, not a general.

Here I was, six months into my conscription and thus far luck or providence had prevailed. Though I had seen battle, other than a few minor cuts, I had emerged unscathed. But now I was convinced all was lost.

I was suddenly seized by a severe bout of homesickness. It occurred to me that I would never again witness a sunrise over the Hudson River nor picnic in the bucolic hills of the Bronx with my parents and sisters. The thought of no longer being able to stop in front of Van Horn's Dry Goods Shop, look in the window, and see my father working behind the counter, conversing with the owner or a customer, filled me with a great sadness. How I longed to walk the noisy, crowded streets of Broadway one last time. Odd, the thoughts of a condemned man.

Approximately five minutes later, by the light of a bright moon, I saw a small cabin appear amidst some trees. When we reached the structure (which had boarded-up windows with a few bullet holes in them) the old man told us to stop.

"All right, boys," said the old man, as we turned to look at him, "I want you both to walk inside and each of you to sit down on one of my chairs. And, once again, if you got any ideas of trying to get away from me, give them up now. If a man can't shoot two intruders in his own cabin, ain't no place on this here earth that he *can* do any shootin'. Now, get inside. Get!"

The Reb went in first and then I followed behind him. Inside the cabin we found hardback chairs and each sat down on one. In one corner was a stone fireplace where crackling flames cast a pale yellow glow throughout the room. An oil lamp flickered on a table. The walls were unadorned except for one shelf which held a few books. In the dim light I could not read the titles. Across the room was a door which might have led to another room or a closet. In another corner was a coat rack.

"Move them chairs close together," said the old man. "I want them right next to each other."

We did as we were told.

The old man sat down on a chair opposite us and held the gun pointed in our direction. "How rude of me," he said. "I don't know your names. Mine's Samuel."

The Reb sat up stiffly and said, "I am Private—"

"Stop!" said the man. "Ain't no ranks in my home. I just want your Christian name."

"Owen," said the Reb, reluctantly.

"And you?" he said, looking at me.

"It's Andrew," I said.

"Just like the vice president," he said.

"He ain't no vice president of mine," said Owen, with disdain.

"Oh, no?" said Samuel. "And why is that?"

"Come on, man. You live not twenty-five miles from Richmond and have to ask that question? Are you a traitor? Or just a Northern spy?"

I had to admit he had a valid question, one I had thought of myself.

"I am neither a traitor nor a spy. I am neutral," said the old man.

"Ain't no one neutral in this war," said Owen. "You are either Union or Confederate, and that's a fact."

"You seem to know a lot, boy, how old are you?" said Samuel.

"I'm nineteen," he said, holding up his chin.

"Yup," said Samuel, smirking, "nineteen's about the age when one knows everything."

Now it was my turn to speak. "Sir, I mean you no disrespect, but what do you intend to do with us? Did you bring us to your home simply to have a discussion?"

"You ain't any more polite than your brother, here," said Samuel.

"He ain't no brother of mine," said Owen.

"All men are brothers," said Samuel. "Andrew?"

"New York," I said, "born and bred."

"Dirty Yankee," said Owen.

"I'll thank you not to speak unless spoken to, Owen," said Samuel, tilting his gun at the Rebel. "Now then, would anyone like a drink of water?"

My mouth was parched and so apparently was Owen's. After Samuel gave each of us some water from a tin cup, he sat back down on the chair in front of us and, still holding the revolver, looked us over. I tried to figure out what he would do next. Would he kill me first or Owen? And why bring us to the cabin at all? Why not simply do the deed outside amidst the lost souls I had encountered only moments earlier? Unless he first meant to see if we possessed any knowledge of our superior's plans.

I put aside speculating upon my captor's motives long enough to think about my sweet Bessie. How I longed to see her beautiful brown eyes, her long chestnut hair and feel the touch of her hand again. Why had I delayed in asking for her father's blessing, and postponed my proposal of marriage? The idea that I had wanted to wait till I became a journeyman in order to receive a higher salary seemed so unimportant now.

"Owen, you never told us where you were from," said Samuel.

"I'm from Georgia," he said, "Two days' ride from Atlanta. Or what's left of it after that devil, Sherman, got finished turning it to rubble." Owen looked at me and sneered.

"I suppose Sherman had a hand in Harper's Ferry, Chickamauga, Cold Harbor, First Manassas, and Fredericksburg," I said.

"You can't compare the total destruction of entire cities and thousands of people to—" said Owen.

"That's enough, children," said Samuel. "There's been atrocities on both sides. But that's what war is about, ain't it? Killing as many people as possible?"

"While you sit in your little house out in the forest?" I said.

Samuel squinted at me. "I'll have you know, young man, that I wasn't always a hermit. I was a telegraph operator and a fine one, too, till your army cut my wires."

"I knew it!" said Owen, smiling. "You *are* one of us. Now go on, put the Yankee out of his misery," said Owen.

"Shut up," said Samuel. "I'll do the killing when I please and to whom I please."

This quieted down the Reb, who swallowed and slumped in his chair.

"There's been too much bloodshed," Samuel said, softly. "How many thousands of wives are there without husbands? How many children without fathers? It's gone on long enough. Year after bloody year. This here is a great nation. If the war continues we'll all perish, like that fella in Greece, Pyrrhus. His victory cost him everything. When enough people die, there ain't no winners anymore. Everyone loses."

"That's a right nice speech," said Owen. "How about I take you to meet General Lee and you can recite it to him personally?"

At this, I watched Samuel slowly stand up. *Uh oh*, I thought, *now the Reb's gone and done it. He's opened his mouth once too often and he's going to get us killed for sure.*

Samuel moved away from his chair and took a few steps back while still keeping the gun trained on us. Then he said, "Stand up, both of you."

I stood up as did Owen. *Here it comes*, I thought. I closed my eyes and said a silent prayer. The old man would probably shoot us then toss our bodies outside. Wild animals would undoubtedly devour our remains.

"Strip off your uniforms," said Samuel.

I glanced at Owen and he at me. Was I in some strange morphine dream?

"You heard me," said Samuel. "Take off your uniforms. You can keep on your undergarments."

Neither Owen nor I moved. Samuel held his gun and

took a step closer. I began undoing the nine brass eagle buttons on my frock coat.

"Your brogans, too," said Samuel, pointing at my feet.

I removed my boots. In a few seconds I had my uniform and kepi in my hands.

"Throw them all in a heap on the floor," said Samuel.

My dark blue coat, cap, trousers, and boots landed first, and then Owen's gray ones fell on top of mine. Samuel went over to the uniforms, picked them up, and, with one motion tossed the pile of clothing into the fireplace. The flames immediately began their work and shortly all that remained were ashes.

"All right, boys," said Samuel, reaching for some rope on a nearby table, "sit down on your chairs."

"I don't reckon I understand any of this," said Owen. "What's the idea of burning our clothes?"

"Just be glad it's your clothes I'm burning and not you," said Samuel. "Now, sit down."

We did, as Samuel placed the gun in his left hand, pulled out an Arms D Guard Bowie knife and cut a piece of rope. He threw the rope piece to Owen and said, "Tie Andrew to his chair."

Owen picked up the rope and lashed my wrists to the back of my chair with great vigor. After fashioning what felt like elaborate knots, he tested them a couple of times, then, apparently satisfied with their strength, turned to Samuel.

"Now what would you like me to do?" said Owen. "I could interrogate him regarding troop movements—"

"Sit down on your chair and place your hands behind your back," said Samuel, as he came over with the rope. He cut off a piece and tied Owen's hands to the back of the chair. When he was done he stood up.

"I am puzzled," I said. "First you preach peace, then you have us disrobe and bind us to chairs. You seem as warring as the armies you claim to have contempt for."

"A good observation; however, the difference is, thus far I have only threatened violence while *your* armies are doing far more than that."

"I don't understand," said Owen. "Here you are, living practically within spitting distance of the capital of the Confederacy, and yet you profess to hate both sides. Why?"

I saw Samuel stare at us and then, for the first time since we'd entered the cabin, he looked away, toward one of the boarded-up windows. For a minute or two he said nothing. Then he turned and faced us again.

"I suppose it don't hurt none to tell you. My wife was killed by a Union soldier. We'd just celebrated our thirty-fifth wedding anniversary."

"A Union soldier," said Owen, nodding his head and looking at me with a kind of sardonic smile.

"I had been out of town trying to get some new relays for my switchboard, my telegraph, and when I got back half the village lay in ruins. And my beloved Violet . . ." I saw him blink a few times and wipe his eyes with his sleeve.

"Untie me," said Owen. "You hate the Yankees as much as I do."

"I ain't done yet," he said. "I neglected to mention my son, Clayton. He was about your age when he joined up. They sent him to some godforsaken battlefield. All I know is, he come back in a box. Turned out he was shot by someone in his own regiment. I been told it ain't that uncommon an occurrence. Apparently, the smoke from the gunpowder and cannon fire can turn the landscape into a cloudy white sheet. A man can't see his own hand in front of his face."

"It was an accident?" asked Owen.

"Of course it was an accident, but that don't make him any less dead. That's right, boys, you see, I've had enough of this damn war, of all wars forever. Now, I'm going to go to my bedroom over there and get some sleep. I suggest you try to have yourself a little rest as well."

Samuel went to the front door, locked it, pocketed the key, then walked into the bedroom and closed the door.

I looked back at Owen. He gave me a mean stare.

"We should try to get out of here," I said. "Tomorrow he'll more than likely shoot us. Probably wants to execute us at dawn."

"What do you mean, 'we,' Billy Yank?"

"Listen," I said, "this man is insane, you heard him. His gun doesn't care which of us is blue or which is gray. We've got to work together here."

"Together?" he said, as if he'd just drunk lemon juice.

"That's right, because if we don't help each other we'll both be dead. And it'll be for nothing. It won't be for the glory of the North *or* the South. What are you going to do when you get to heaven and they ask you how you died? Tell them it was on the field of battle as a hero, fighting for what you believed in, or on the filthy floor of some crazy old man's cabin for no good reason at all. Think about it, Owen."

It was the first time I had said his name out loud. It felt unnatural, the way it does when you learn a word of a foreign language and then try to pronounce it. I saw Owen look at the ceiling.

After some time he turned back in my direction. "What'd you have in mind?" he said.

"The first thing we need to do is get out of these ropes. Let's move our chairs back to back and each try to undo the other's bonds."

He nodded and we shifted our chairs around. I felt his fingers on my ropes and then I moved mine upon his. For a few moments we worked in silence. I listened to the sound of our breathing and thought about how hungry I was.

"I sure would fancy some pepperpot about now," I said.

"What's that?" said Owen.

"It's a stew made of tripe and doughballs."

"My mouth waters at the thought."

"I can't say as I'd turn down some sweet potato pie myself."

"My girl, Bessie, makes the best pepperpot in the world."

"Well, my gal, Louisa, can bake a cracklin' bread that just about melts in your mouth. Why the very smell of it alone is enough to send you . . ." Owen's voice trailed off.

I felt his fingers start to loosen the knots of my rope. Even so, the added pressure made the rope burn into my wrists.

"What did you do before you were conscripted?" I said, pulling on his rope.

"I volunteered, but before that I was a farmer. My family owns a small farm. We grow the best corn in two counties, ask anyone. How about yourself?"

"I'm a printer, actually still an apprentice."

I managed to loosen Owen's rope a little. "Now, just so you don't get all kinds of thoughts," I said, "if you get out of your ropes first and decide to leave me and try to break down that front door, the old man will hear you and shoot you for sure. But if we are together I can help disarm him and we can get the key to the door."

"Now you're my helper, Billy Yank?"

"Just for the duration of our imprisonment in this cabin, Johnny Reb."

"Have it your way," said Owen, as I felt him loosening my rope.

As it happened, I was out of mine first. I got up and continued working on his. Eventually, his rope slipped to the floor.

Owen went over to the table and picked up the oil lamp, while I got a small log from next to the fireplace to use as a weapon.

"C'mon," I said, as we quietly made our way toward the bedroom door. When we got there, I put my ear to it and heard snoring. "It sounds like he's asleep," I said, silently testing the doorknob. It was unlocked.

We opened the door swiftly and went inside the room. The old man woke up and reached for the gun which was on his night table, but I got to it first. I dropped the piece of firewood and held the revolver steady.

"So," said Samuel, "this is the way it's going to be, is it?" From under his pillow he grabbed his knife and lunged toward us.

I fired the gun and he clutched his chest and dropped to the floor.

"I guess my plan worked," he said, smiling.

"How's that, old man?" said Owen.

"I wanted you boys to murder me," he said, his right hand over a bloody stain. "I didn't want to live no more. It ain't no life being alone, ain't no life living with this war."

"Why all the political debating?" I asked.

"And why'd you make us take off our uniforms?" said Owen.

"To show you that you're both the same, just boys. Men now. I figured I'd tie you up and then you'd have to put your differences aside against a common enemy. Me. If a couple of young bucks like you can do it, maybe the world's got a chance yet."

"There might be a doctor we could take you to," I said.

"Forget it," he replied. "Besides, I want to die. You two were the answer to months of prayers."

Samuel lay real still and his eyes stared straight ahead, unblinking. I closed his lids. Owen reached into Samuel's pocket and removed his key.

We went into the other room. I took a couple of deep breaths and set the gun down on the table.

"He was a peculiar old man," said Owen.

"Yes," I said, as I noticed the coat rack in one corner of the room. I went over, took a brown coat off a hook and tossed it to Owen. "Here," I said, "no point in running around in our undergarments."

I put on another coat, this one black, and headed toward him. To my surprise, Owen now had the gun in his hand and was pointing it at my heart. "Are you going to shoot me?" I asked.

He stared into my eyes for a long time, then replied, "I don't shoot civilians."

After that, he unlocked the door, stepped outside and disappeared into the night.

I lingered by the open door looking at the shadowy trees. A moment later I walked out of the cabin toward the quiet darkness beyond.

# Blossoms and Blood

## Janet Berliner

T he sun rose over Bloody Pond, promising another hot and humid Tennessee day and heightening the odor of decay and death. Little moved in the stillness of that dreadful morning; little except the shoulders of the slim Union soldier who knelt at the edge of the pond, looking out across the bodies. Thinking how well the night breezes had masked the stench with the heavy smell of peach blossoms from the orchard that lay at the eastern end of what, two days before, had been dubbed the Hornet's Nest.

Next to the soldier lay an open haversack, which held a stack of papers inked with the smudged words of a lengthy war report. Working with deft hands, the soldier transformed the pages into miniature boats, the kind that children construct when they go to the park to feed the swans. They formed a flotilla, which one by one the soldier floated out into the water, watching it until it wedged between bodies, on a sea of mud and caked blood.

When the last boat had been launched, the soldier dug into the knapsack, retrieved what was obviously a journal, and began to read . . .

PETER WAS EIGHTEEN WHEN he first heard the guns of battle. They scared the living daylights out of him. Having for the last few years considered himself a lover not a fighter, the last thing he wanted was to become embroiled in the actual conflict.

By disposition of his birth in Cairo, Illinois, Peter Louis was a Yankee. By disposition of his heart, he was a Confederate. He'd become such in 1860, after spending Easter with his second cousins who lived on a farm in southern Tennessee, in the rich farmlands southwest of Pittsburg Landing known as Shiloh. The entire trip seemed magical. He rode the rivers, up the Ohio to the Tennessee and then south, which fueled a love of riverboats that started when he met a young adventurer named Clemens. On the trip, he saw a countryside so green and beautiful he almost cried, and just before his arrival, the trees burst forth with a profusion of flowers. It was as if the Lord had planned for him to be there during peach blossom season and fall in love with Lucy.

Lucy, the pretty little light-skinned, fifteen-year-old daughter of his family's slaves.

What a time they'd had, rolling around in the fragrant reds of fallen blossoms in the ten-acre peach orchard, in full bloom at the west end of the pond at the edge of his cousin's farm. How they'd laughed, scratching their initials into the trunk of the tree beneath which they had consummated their passion.

How angry he had been when, with the slim and boyish frame he remembered now distorted and heavy with child, she'd escaped and found him and shamed him before his fashionable Cairo family.

"It's your child, too," she'd said, talking like she was white folk. "You got to care for it, Peter."

Care for it? What business did she have even thinking that? He took her to the local hotel, where he made love to her once or twice, then beat her roundly until the baby loosened.

"You murdered your own child," she sobbed.

He put his ear to her bare belly. He could hear and feel nothing.

"Murderer," she said, turning her back on him.

Feeling only relief, he dispatched her back to the South where she belonged and thought about leaving home to board the Mississippi steamboat captained by his old acquaintance, twenty-five-year-old Samuel Clemens.

He thought about it much too long, off and on for more than a year. By the time he'd made up his mind, Clemens had left the river. He had been elected second lieutenant in an irregular unit of fifteen men, whose self-proclaimed duty it was to keep an eye on Grant's men.

Clemens being something of a hero to him, Peter deliberated joining the same unit. Again, he thought too long. Quickly bored by saddle sores, Clemens said the hell with it. Riding an old mule because he'd injured his foot jumping out of a hayloft, he hightailed it back to silver country to take up a career as a journalist.

To Peter, that sounded like the perfect life. He decided he'd much rather be a reporter than a soldier, and he tried to get a job with the local paper. When that didn't immediately pan out, he took a civilian job in the local telegraph office, where he figured he could read and learn from the important papers that passed regularly through his hands.

While Clemens remained his hero, Peter quickly came to detest General Sherman, a red-headed, gaunt man with a grizzled short-cropped ginger beard, wild eyes, and a hungry look. He read that Sherman had recently returned from medical leave for a nervous breakdown. The general was left with fidgeting fingers, his shoulders twitched incessantly, and he was always picking at something, twirling a button, or fiddling with his whiskers. Not wishing to be tarred with a similar brush, Peter made sure that he presented to the world a calm demeanor.

He also adopted General Grant's affect of perpetually chewing on an unlit cigar.

Though Grant was, to his regret, a Yankee, he was worthy, Peter thought, of admiration. This led to a deep interest in the Yankee reports that passed through his hands, many of which came from the pens of Generals Sherman and Grant.

When the papers particularly fascinated him, he took them home to study at his leisure, so that when the war was done—he figured that to be only a matter of a few months— he could make a name for himself by writing about them. He became familiar with the reports, returns, and information that Grant sent to Washington, telling of the strength and position of his command, as demanded by Secretary of War Stanton. Although he was a civilian, the Secretary was said to be as stern and demanding as any man in the military, which helped to earn him the nickname "Old Man Mars."

Since Peter kept the reports, they never reached their destination. Furious, Secretary Stanton complained to General Halleck, who at once suspended Grant from command and ordered him to Fort Henry.

Learning of this, Peter felt pleased with his contribution to the war effort. After all, he had caused it to happen by secreting away the documents. He thought about ceremoniously burning the valuable papers he had kept, but he could not let go of so significant a trophy. Unless they actually saw the orders, Washington Headquarters would never know whether the General had dispatched the messages or failed to do so while in some alcoholic haze. It would forever remain a mystery to which only he, Peter Louis, held the answer.

Peter's pleasure at having changed the course of the war was short-lived. Grant's replacement had received a leg injury; Grant was returned to duty to await first Buell's army, then the arrival of Halleck, who would take command.

By the end of February of the year 1862, Peter was ready to make a new contribution to the war effort. While he did not want to join the regular army and risk being wounded or killed, he had become enchanted by the romance of war and wanted to learn more firsthand. He declared himself a Confederate, packed the papers in a haversack, and took off up the Cumberland River for Nashville, which had become a fast-growing railroad and industrial center. He wanted to see for himself the arsenal of munitions and supplies in the factories there, to learn firsthand about percussion caps and muskets, about sabers and saddles. He wanted to see the looms where the gray cloth was produced for uniforms.

Later, he determined to see New Orleans. He took the railroad south to Memphis, then down the Mississippi where he tied himself to the illicit cotton trade for a while before proceeding to New Orleans. There, because he fancied himself handsome decked out in the dress blues of the Orleans Guards Battalion, he convinced them to take him on as their recorder.

By the beginning of April, Peter found that history had taken him full circle. He was headed for just what he hadn't wanted to experience firsthand, what veterans fondly called the Elephant: Combat. Worse yet, they were marching dead in the direction of the one place he would just as well have avoided, the peach orchards of Shiloh.

On a march, a battery could travel up to five miles an hour on a good road, Peter wrote in his daily journal. He also talked of the fires they built in holes in the ground, of the Confederate belief that food traveled less heavily in the belly than the haversack, so they ate their three-day rations at once and went hungry for the rest of the way. He wrote in the rain and on mud-stained pages of hearing Yankee bugles, of rumors of coughing cured by the application of red-hot pokers, of diarrhea and of nightmares of dead men yelling, "Retreat, retreat!" The only pleasant occurrence, he wrote, was the day they came across Northerners eating a breakfast of hot meat, white bread, and sweet coffee.

Stealing into their camp, he filled his belly with food and his haversack with letters and photos. General Johnston sanctioned the scavenging by acquiring for himself a Yankee tin cup. He would use it to direct battle, he said, index finger hooked through the handle.

Peter endured intermittent showers and steamy sunshine with a certain degree of stoicism. He strangely felt no real fear until he was shot at by fellow Confederates who saw the dress-blue uniforms of the Orleans Guard and, thinking them the enemy, fired upon them. At that, he and the others turned their dress-blues—"graveyard clothes" the Federals called them, when they found out what had happened— inside out and wore them with the white silk linings visible. This to prevent being killed by their own, who naturally assumed that anyone wearing blue had to be a Union soldier.

On April 5, 1862, encamped within a short distance of the enemy army that was going about its normal business, Peter wrote in his journal, unconsciously echoing what Sherman had written to Grant that very day: "I don't believe that anything much will happen today. Some picket firing maybe. Nothing more."

The rain stopped. The moon rose, lighting peach orchards in full blossom reminiscent of the spring of his youth. He took a walk toward the picket line. He would be safe there. It was an unspoken rule. No attacks were made at night on the line. It was a time for the swapping of tobacco and coffee and tall tales, a time for the gathering of firewood and courage.

"Are you not afraid, Soldier?" a muffled voice asked him.

"Yes," Peter said, surprising himself. "Grant is a clever man. He must be prepared for all eventualities."

"One can never be prepared for all eventualities," the voice went on. The face was half turned away, masked by the brim of a cap pulled low.

"I would like to forget about the war for this night," Peter said.

"I have thought of nothing else since we buried fifteen of our dead at Fallen Timbers. Would you walk with me in the orchard, Soldier?" the voice said. "Surely if we decorate ourselves with blossoms we will be protected from harm."

The Union soldier slouched, head averted, while walking awkwardly in a uniform that seemed to be much too big. They walked for a while in silence. Then, stopping several feet before a tree that stood directly in the moonlight, the young soldier pointed at the trunk.

"Look. It's still there."

"Lucy?"

"Took you long enough," she said. "I thought perhaps you had forgotten me." She removed her hat and turned to face him. In the full moonlight her face was etched more with sorrow than with hatred. "I buried him here. Our son. Here among the blossoms. He has been waiting a long time to see you, Peter."

"How could I place you in this context? How could you be a soldier?"

"Why not? After what you did to me, it was easy." She laughed, a hollow, humorless sound. "Besides, do you think I told them that I was a woman? A nigger woman?"

At 8:00 a.m. on April 6, Sherman heard picket firing in his front. Johnston, who heard it, too, hoped to drive the disorganized Federals into the swamps of Snake and Owl Creeks and destroy them.

To the Country Boys of Shiloh, the shots were an overture. They were young and inexperienced volunteers, but what they lacked in experience they made up for in valor. Advancing upon the enemy, they broke silence and sang as they marched to the band playing "Dixie."

The shelling began, every fifteen minutes, red streaks arcing against the sky. By the end of the day, the Federals had been driven back to Pittsburg Landing, but that night, while the Rebels looted from captured Yankee camps and did little to reorganize their scattered units, Grant reinforced his lines with the fresh troops of General Buell and Lew Wallace and at dawn on the seventh launched a counterattack, which, by early afternoon, had the Confederates in full retreat.

After the battle, the dead horses were burned.

Despite the shine of mercury, the odor of ammonia and turpentine, and the promise of chloroform and ether, after the battle, the Hornet's Nest was a tangle of the dead and the dying. Neither arrowroot nor belladonna, mustard or acacia or camphor, could cure their mortal wounds. The volunteers filled the shallows of Bloody Pond, knowing that no amount of quinine, of iodine and opium, could bring them back from the edge of death.

*The sun rose over Bloody Pond, promising another hot and humid Tennessee day and heightening the odor of death and decay. Little moved in the stillness of that dreadful morning, little except Lucy's slim shoulders as she knelt at the edge of the Pond, looking out across the bodies.*

She did not have to look down into the pond for Peter. There was no need. The bayonet was planted too deep. He could not have moved from the tree where she had left him, thinking as she did how well the night breezes would mask the stench of his decay with the heavy smell of peach blossoms.

*Next to Lucy lay Peter's haversack, which held a stack of papers inked with the smudged words of a lengthy war report. Working with deft hands, she transformed the pages into miniature boats, the kind that children construct when they go to the park to feed the swans. They formed a flotilla, which one by one she floated out into the water, watching it until it wedged between bodies, on a sea of mud and caked blood.*

*When the last boat had been launched, she dug into the knapsack, and retrieved what was obviously a journal.*

Holding it in her hand, she stared at a world that was red with bombs and blossoms and blood. Then she began to read . . .

# Whistling Dixie

*Billie Sue Mosiman*

I tried to get Cotton to stay behind when we left for the battle at Crowley's Ridge down by Helena. I expected to find Sergeant Norman Kilpatrick on my own and kill him dead. Norman had first taken our farm away, as he was the loan officer at the Helena, Arkansas, bank before the war, and then the scoundrel bought the place himself for pennies on the dollar. He'd wanted it for years, as the land lay adjacent to his own. Then when the trouble between the states started, Norman joined up with the other side. A traitor to his people! There wasn't a man in my opinion needed dying more. The farm had been all we had after our pa died, a place that was in our family for fifty years. Once Norman foreclosed and moved us out, we drifted to Little Rock, following behind Rebel troops, hearing all the tales about General Holmes, who commanded them, and Sterling Price, his second-in-command.

While living in a tent on the outskirts of Little Rock, I waited for the army to come for me. I didn't want to leave my ma, my four sisters, and Cotton with no one to help them, but I knew it was my time to fight. The battles had been raging for a long time, and I'd neglected to join, knowing my family had

**111**

need of me more. But I'd heard Norman was with the Fort Curtis regiment in Helena, back in the same town he was a traitor to, back as a Union soldier and willing to turn his cannon on his fellow Confederates. I meant to make him a casualty.

It was June 1863 when the infantry recruiter came to our tent flap. He'd come down the line in our civilian tent city, looking for able men, looking to fill the ranks for a rumored plan to take back Helena. I watched him approach on horseback and the way he took off his cap at each tent as he called out the old men and the boys. Once he got to me, I was waiting, the hot sun in my eyes. Right behind me in the shadows, Cotton listened, and before I knew it he'd stepped up to my right, smart-saluted the officer, and said, "Me too, I'm going, too."

Cotton was twelve then, tall for his age, but just twelve and my only brother. I pushed him behind me and grinned nervously at the captain. "He's not right in the head, sir. He's just a boy. He won't be going."

"He's big for a boy," said the weary officer, slapping his Rebel cap on his dusty horse's flank. "We got boys with us littler than him. We got boys his age who just volunteered."

"Yessir!" Cotton said, whipping his arm from my grip so he could sidestep me and get up front again. "I'm big and I can shoot the eye from a red turkey at a hundred feet."

The captain's lips twitched into a bitter smile. "We need some sharpshooters like you, son. And you there," he said, pointing his cap at me. "How old are you now?"

"I turned seventeen this month, sir," I said, standing straight as a willow reed.

"Well, we can use both of you. Come on over to the garrison and we'll get you outfitted with caps. There ain't no uniforms to be found in the state of Arkansas. Bring what weapons you got at hand; we're short on rifles, too."

I stood staring after the captain as he rode away, his hat back on his head, a dust cloud raised in his wake that obscured him finally, and then I turned on Cotton.

"I'm taking you out to the woods and I'm bringing Daddy's razor strap." Ma had made me head of the family and look what I'd just let happen. I wanted at that moment to whip Cotton raw.

Cotton cringed at the idea. He hung his head and said, "J. T., Daddy would've let me go."

"No, he wouldn't! Who's going to stay with Ma and the girls? Who's going to keep them safe now if we both go to war? You should have stayed here."

Cotton reached into his pocket and brought out his wing-bone whistle. He put it to his lips and blew some sad melody. He'd carved the whistle from the bone of a robin and always said it was a lucky piece, but here he was blowing it on the day he offered to go get himself killed and that meant to me it wasn't lucky at all.

"God dangit, Cotton, put that away and go get your musket. Maybe they've got powder and lead, 'cause if they don't, me and you are gonna be shooting air at the Feds."

They drilled us for a month, supplied us with plenty of powder and chunks of lead that we made into balls. All the while I watched Cotton closely to make sure he was learning what he had to know. It was true he could shoot so well he could bring home supper every single night, but what would happen when the prey was shooting back? I didn't know how I was going to protect him from grapeshot and artillery bombs. I didn't know how things had gotten so bad these last years. Why all of Arkansas was in a perpetual startled state that the Union army had occupied Helena, seventy miles south of Memphis, one of our strongest agricultural and commercial centers, while the rest of the state was controlled by Confederates. How had we let them sneak in and take it over that way?

I'd heard the soldiers garrisoned down in Helena were from places like Iowa and even from way north in Pennsylvania. I heard they hated Helena's cold winters and stifling, disease-ridden summers, that they called it "Hell-in-Arkansas." I would turn my head away when I heard those tales, remembering hanging from Muscatine grapevines over deep cool ravines, remembering the rising and falling of the Mississippi behind the levee and how we swam and fished in the waters. It was my town. My home. And I'd been cheated out of it and seen it taken over by strangers.

From fifteen hundred souls, Helena once swelled by another twenty thousand when General Prentiss brought in his troops. Now I heard the twenty thousand was down to four thousand, due to the rest being sent to Vicksburg to fight.

It was rumored all around the camp that we'd take back Helena. Whispers ran from cook to drummer, from captain to private: Helena would not stand, not with most of their troops away on the march.

Cotton said one night late in June, "I'm not scared, J. T."

I scraped the last of the beans from my tin plate with a corner of cold cornbread before replying. Cutlery had been in short supply and most meals we couldn't find a spoon to save our lives. "You ought to be. If you ain't scared when we get down to Helena, you'll take the first shot."

"I just mean I won't let you down."

I looked over at him in his gray cap pulled jauntily over one eye, his dirt-encrusted clothes, and saw the little boy hiding behind the man's words. He was really scared, despite the protest. Maybe I could knock him out during the attack, just roundhouse him in the chin and then I wouldn't have to worry about him taking a gut shot or a head wound. We'd both heard how bloody these battles could be. We'd seen relatives come home missing arms and legs, hands and fingers. And now they were saying there might be a paddlewheel steamer down on the Mississippi at Helena, just waiting with its big old guns to blow us all to kingdom come. It floated on the muddy water, gun turrets poised and at the ready.

"It's not me you need to worry about letting down," I said. "It's Ma and the girls. If you don't come back from this campaign, they'll be mighty damn let down."

"What about you?" he asked. "What if . . . ?"

I waved away his worry. "Nothing's going to take me down, Cotton. I know it, somewhere down in here." I pointed to my gut. "I'm coming out of this like Old Glory after cannon fire. I'll be waving in the wind, a hero. I wouldn't be surprised if they make me a captain."

I didn't believe that, didn't really have any gut-feeling, but I had to make Cotton believe it. If he feared he'd be fighting on alone without me at his side, he'd surely collapse before we ever entered the fray. I looked around the camp and saw too many other boys who were surely as young as Cotton. Men grouped around them like hens over chicks, giving them courage, telling them tall tales of heroic deeds done in other battles and those about to commence down in Helena. If they could not impart real protection for the youths, they at least could bolster their faith, the way I was doing for my brother.

We were all on pins, sleeping restless, dreaming and waking with nightmares. The orders were forming and the battle plans were being consolidated. Holmes commanded us and Price was his man, then came Fagan, all three figuring what troops to lead against Helena and how to position them in attack. On July 2 the thousands of us were called out to parade in full summer sun and Holmes spoke from a platform raised in the center of his men. Those of us who could not hear were told in whispers by the men in front, the word passing back through the ranks like a whispering wind.

Cotton and I caught the whispers and sent them on behind us. "We're nearly sixty-two-hundred strong," Holmes shouted and the cheers went up. "The Union in Helena is smaller in number, and that's our advantage. But they have the terrain in their favor, men, and I want you all to know, those of you not from that area, that it won't be easy to overrun it. There are hills and deep ravines. There's Fort Curtis to take, and I am sure they have made fire pits, earthworks, to hide in like dogs to shoot us as we approach. If I know Prentiss, he's still smarting from defeat at Shiloh, so he'll be bound and determined to put the fire to us. But that city is our city, men! They've held it long enough. If we hit them while the battle of Vicksburg is going on, we can scatter the bastards and run them straight into the mighty Mississippi!"

The message was halting, coming as it did in bits and pieces from those in front of us, but it sounded good to me. I wanted everything back the way it had been. And I wanted to find and face the scalawag, Norman Kilpatrick. I'd stick my long blade knife through his black heart. Some way, after the war ended, I'd convince the bank to let me try to catch up on the taxes. I'd point out the ruthlessness of Norman and how he just wanted my land for his own.

It galls me now to think how I stood before him, all dejected and sad, tears coming to cloud my eyes. I'd mentioned the problem of the slaves running off and how I was doing all the work of ten men trying to save the crops. I demeaned myself before him with my begging and pleading. I promised once we got the cotton and corn to market, I'd give every single penny to the bank, but that man just sank back in his big leather chair and laughed like there was no tomorrow. "We're not waiting," he said finally in a dark voice. "We're taking that farm, and we want you off it in a fortnight."

He certainly did. And in a fortnight he had made up the papers in his name, too.

Ma cried the entire month, selling off some of her best dishes and quilts because we couldn't carry them with us. My sisters, Janie, Sugar, Marly, and Ruthanne, all looked on me with betrayed eyes as if it was my fault the slaves had absconded and the fields had gone to ruin. It wasn't my fault even if I did tell them to go if that was what they had to do. I was no abolitionist, exactly, but I'd never seen the slaves happy a day in their lives and that pulled me down, too. It was better to try to till and hoe and harvest with only Cotton and the girls to help me than to see those dark faces giving me sidelong looks of woe.

I had not come to fight against the men who would steal and set free our slaves. They'd already done that with their posters and with the war. The Emancipation Proclamation had been issued a year already, and it was said a company of free Negroes were standing fire in Helena and another company had been trained there and sent south. No, I was going to march on Helena for an altogether personal reason, and no one but Cotton had to know it.

"We leave for Helena tomorrow, men," Holmes was shouting and his words were carried back and back until they reached us. "We strike them on the Fourth of July! At the coming of the day!"

The cheers and stomping feet of the assemblage sounded like a great swell of thunder going up to greet the sky. I stomped, too, and Cotton cheered, and neither of us thought about dying, not even for a second. In our minds we had already won the battle and were mighty victors, proud to wear the Grey.

OUR ARMY REACHED THE Allen Polk house, five miles from Helena, on July 3. By that time the troops had lost some confidence in Holmes's competency to command. Here he was taking us against what was apparently a formidable defense that would take Armageddon's forces to breach. Holmes commanded Price and, Marmaduke with the Calvary, to take their units, and together it would be a three-pronged attack. Holmes told Marmaduke to take his 1,750 dismounted Calvary to Rightor Hill northwest of town. On his left a Calvary brigade under L. M. Walker, a West Pointer from Tennessee, was supposed to prevent any Federal reinforcements from reaching the hill. Fagan's 1,339 men would move on Hindman Hill, southwest of town. But the main thrust would be made by Price, with 3,095 men against Graveyard Hill near the center of the defensive perimeter. "We all attack at daylight," Holmes said.

Cotton and I were under Fagan's command, and we were going to have to take a well-fortified hill. I knew the treacherous Hindman Hill, had climbed it a thousand times as a child. It was pocked with sudden drops into ravines; the hillsides were steep, densely wooded, and gloomy as a place this side of Hell could be. I had hoped we'd be with Price, for I trusted him more, but this was our orders, and I'd get up that hill if it was the last thing I ever did.

The last five miles to our rendezvous against Prentiss's batteries in Helena was a morbidly silent march. Men walked softly and glared around at the night, fearing the Union knew we were coming and might be lurking along the way. A half-mile from our position, Fagan halted us, and his officers waved their arms for us to hunker down right where we stood. We were waiting for first light. I pulled Cotton over close to my side and cupped my hand around his ear. "I want you to drop to the rear when we move on them."

Cotton jerked away his head and then caught my own ear in his cupped palm and replied, "I'll be damned if I will. I'm no yellow belly!"

I whispered to him again, this time gripping the top of his shoulder so hard I knew it would leave marks. "You do what I say or when we get through here today I'll take the hide right off your ass."

Again Cotton tore away from me and then scooted a few feet distant. Damn him, he was going to disobey me. He seemed to court jeopardy and I had to find a way to keep him alive. I shivered in the dew damp night, glancing fearfully at the dog star. We all watched the eastern sky, staring at it as if Christ in heaven was going to rise with the sun. Fog coasted along the ridges and down in the low places, hanging from tree limbs like ghosts, wrapping itself around the troops as if to swallow us.

Our muskets were primed and ready, our lead and powder hung in rawhide bags securely at our sides. I didn't have a bayonet, but I had my hunting knife strapped against my leg inside my boot. I could smell the fear rising from those thousand and more men, their sweat coming despite the early morning chill.

The light broke, struggling through milky fog like the brow of a god almighty ship sailing out of the night. It wasn't sunrise yet, and I wondered if Holmes had meant to wait till sunrise, but evidently Fagan thought he'd meant true first light. I hoped he was right, Lord, I prayed for him to be right. Before I could muster my thoughts, we were all on our feet and those in front of me were running forward. We were like a thunderous pack of wolves descending on the city's stronghold, and when we closed on the hill, the shouts and yells went up that sounded like a battalion of banshees let loose from the bowels of hell. I screamed, too, running alongside Cotton, keeping him always in my sight. I screamed in misery and disappointment that life had been so cruel, I screamed in frustration that it was still too foggy dark to know exactly where I was going, and I screamed in fury, hoping to kill the men who would keep Helena from me.

The first thing we encountered were fallen logs spread across the approach to the hill. Our men stumbled and fell, crawled and stood again only to strike up against another impediment and tumble headlong. The Feds knew we were coming now and must have been alert because artillery began to boom and the battlefield lit up with fiery blossoms of death. As I ran, my nostrils stinging with the scent of gunpowder, I wondered why Price wasn't also attacking Graveyard Hill and why we were the only troops under fire. Hadn't Price seen first light? Were we going to do this all alone, take all the fire, be wiped off the face of the earth without any help whatsoever?

"It ain't daylight!" someone screamed, and the cry was taken up even as we hurried forward under rifle fire that seemed to come from ground level, and from artillery bombs raining down overhead. "We're too early!" men shouted, and then we all understood Fagan's mistake. There were precious minutes between first light and sunrise. On this fateful day it was a discrepancy of half an hour. But there was nothing to do now but race forward and beat the terror that chased through our veins.

The rifle fire was coming from earthworks, rifle pits dug in the ground just at the ascent of Hindman Hill. I could still see Cotton, though now there were towers of acrid smoke and the fog was thick as gray velvet all around us. The sky was raining with lead and my shoulders were hunched against it. Fire burst over and over from the pits, and it was like entering the gates of Hades to go there. But the pits kept us from the hill and we would have to take them. At the zenith of Hindman Hill, cannons spewed iron balls of death at us, tearing up great gouts of dirt that sent men flying and broken bodies into the sky to mix with the falling lead.

I was breathing like a cow giving birth. My feet stumbled over Rebels lying in my way, and my face and shoulders were splattered with the blood of men caught in cannon fire. "Oh, God," I cried, never having imagined it would be this horrible. My mind fell back and my body kept going, rushing toward the rifle pits. I could see a pit in front of me now looming out of the fog and smoke. There were men in it, three firing and four or five of them reloading their weapons. "There!" I screamed to Cotton, "Shoot there and take the pit!"

Cotton slowed, brought his rifle to his shoulder and taking aim, shot one of the Feds square in the face. I had run closer, for I was not as good a shot as Cotton, and I raised my own musket and took down a second Fed. Troops behind us converged and together we fell into the pit, fighting with rifle butts and fists, kicking and screaming, our nostrils flared, our lust to kill paramount.

I had lost sight of Cotton in order to survive the next minute and then into the next, but it was over fast, the Feds falling under our attack. I pulled my knife out of the man's ribs where I'd buried it and twirled around, looking for another to attack. I saw Cotton on the far side of the bloody pit, going hand to hand with a man double his size. Before I could reach him another Rebel soldier stuck a bayonet through the big man's back and Cotton pushed him down into the pit, stomping on his head as if it were a venomous snake.

We had taken the pit, and looking to our right and left we saw our soldiers had taken the other pits, too. A victorious swell of cries went up, whoops and hollers, as I stepped on top of dead men to take Cotton into my arms. We had crossed a continent and dropped into a bower of death, but we were still whole.

All around me soldiers who had taken the pit scrambled out again and pressed forward. "Stay here!" I yelled at Cotton above the rifle shots and cannon fire. "Don't move!"

Cotton wrestled away from me, scowling, and began to fill powder into his musket. If I hit him I reasoned he'd be out long enough to escape the worst of it. I stepped to one side of him and swung the butt end of my musket against the side of his temple. The hard wood stock connected loudly with his head. He went down like a heavy sack of feed, dropping on top of the big dead man who had tried to kill him.

I checked the pulse in his wrist and then leapt from the pit. I had to move forward and get into Helena and find Norman Kilpatrick. I could taste the sweet revenge on the back of my tongue and it sung a siren song in my head. I would get back our farm. I would save my family's future.

Between the earthworks and the hill there was more impediment, more fallen logs strewn about like kindling. The fire now from the cannons on the hill came like clockwork, booming so loud my ears rang and went near deaf. I saw our men crawling into hollows and behind logs to reload.

Sunrise exploded like no day before it. My feet began to slip in the blood. The ground was littered with our men, groaning and dying, calling out for their mothers and for God's mercy. I took little sips of air through my mouth, unable to stand the stink of death everywhere around me. I fired and fell to the ground, grabbing for my powder and lead to reload my musket. I stood and ran a few feet closer and fired again, toward the blooms of fire I'd seen coming from the hillside. They were coming out to meet us! They were coming down the hill in droves and I saw our troops falter, turn back, and begin to scatter. I saw men climbing under logs and searching for deeper ravines throughout the dense woodland, this time to hide instead to reload. I heard Fagan's command to fall back, and then in just one minute more I heard his command to raise the white flag of surrender.

Now I could see it clearly. Hundreds of us were splayed out on the killing grounds, bleeding and taking last breaths. Four Feds came out of the last scraps of wispy fog, rifles pointed, and told me in excited voices to throw down my gun. A dozen men behind me did as they were told, tossing their weapons, and when I saw that, I let go of my musket to let it clatter at my feet. I worried they'd find Cotton and think him dead or bayonet him to make sure. "My little brother's back in the pit behind me," I said as they rounded a group of us up. "He's got a bruise on his temple but he's still alive."

A captain with the Feds heard me and told me he'd check for him, "Now git your Reb ass moving before I shoot it off for you, you sonovabitch."

My heart, so long beating fast and under pressure, thundered to a slow sad beat that seemed to thump right up against my ribs. We were defeated, and it was unbelievable. We'd lost so many, hundreds of us instantly shattered by artillery. By now Price might be waging a furious attack on Graveyard Hill, but that didn't help us now. Hundreds of the living and wounded were laying down guns and being rounded into groups to be marched into Helena. What they'd do with us there I could not imagine, not knowing if they had a stockade built or not.

"Have you a Sergeant Norman Kilpatrick?" I asked one of the Feds prodding me in the back with the bore of his rifle.

"He's the Orderly Sergeant up there on that hill, manning the cannon," the man said proudly. "He broke all you Reb bastards down!"

Up on the hill. Straight up Hindman Hill stood Kilpatrick with his torch for the cannon, the murdering fiend.

Sunrise had broken in the east hours before, but the light here in the near woods was still grim and smoke-filled. More Rebel soldiers lay in sorry disarray all around and it made my eyes tear up again until I took my fists and rubbed my eyes clear.

"Move on!" the Fed behind me said, burying his rifle bore deeper into my back ribs.

I couldn't even look back for Cotton.

I DIDN'T SEE MY brother until I'd been boarded on the USS *Tyler*. It was a massive paddlewheel, a hundred eighty feet long and forty-two feet wide. There was a hastily built five-inch oak bulwark over all the top of the deck to protect it from attack. It carried a thirty-pound Parrott gun and six eight-inch smoothbore cannon. This monster alone could have defended Helena for many hours.

We had heard Price and Holmes and Walker had been repulsed. They were already straggling back to Little Rock under defeat. I counted it Holmes's fault, telling his officers something so vague as to "attack at daylight." Some did attack at first light, like Fagan, but the more experienced Price, it was said, waited until sunrise. With all our troops so divided on time of attack, how could we expect our courage to win the day?

Price was the only commander to take the opposition. Twice repulsed, he tried a third time and took the battery, but when he turned the guns on the retreating Feds he found the guns disabled. When Holmes joined him, as the commanding officer he gave such confusing orders to the men that some of them tried to go to Fagan's aid and others moved to attack Fort Curtis. Finally, they were all attracting fire so fierce that the bodies piled on top of bodies and Holmes called for the retreat.

Cotton was in the hundreds of captives put aboard the *Tyler* for a trip up to Memphis. They'd kept us all garrisoned only one day and then we were marched to the river and caught first sight of the warship on the dawn of July 5. Throughout the night the Feds had celebrated their awesome victory, taunting us with the fact they had held off an army much greater in number.

"You Reb bastards couldn't fight your way out of a string-tied bale of hay," they said to us.

That was not the truth, of course, for we'd fought like the insane, moving toward nearly certain death from cannon and rifle, bombarded by artillery so hard it made the earth move. We died brave and fought hard, but we'd never be given proper credit when it was known we had to surrender and when the rest of Holmes's troops, battered by *Tyler*'s cannons and fire from the four batteries Prentiss had set up around Helena, turned back in retreat.

Cotton, thank God, was sitting against a wall of the ship, his head in his hands when I found him. When he looked up at the calling of his name, his eyes teared and he stumbled like a lame calf to his feet. "J. T.," he said, holding on to me hard, "I thought you were dead."

And then he cried, giving out hard gasps, as I held on to him tightly. "Why did you hit me?" he cried. "I was fighting good as anyone, so why did you do it?"

"I couldn't face losing you on the hill," I said. "That you got as far as the rifle pits was due to God's grace."

He saw other men watching him before turning away in shame and embarrassment, so he wiped down his grimy face and took in a big breath. "They say we're going to Memphis, to a prison there until the war's over."

"That's what they say."

"I heard Lee was routed in Gettysburg on July 3 and yesterday while we fought, Grant took Vicksburg."

I had not heard the news so that it was a slap in the face, causing me to jerk suddenly, like a man going into convulsions. The war . . . the war was finally nearing an end. And we had lost it. "Lee was beat?"

Cotton nodded and began to cry again. I put my arm around his shoulder and said to him in a low voice, "The war's 'bout over then, Cotton. You won't be long in Memphis. You'll be out and back to Little Rock before you know it."

My words sank in and Cotton raised his face, streaked with soot and the tracks of his tears. "What about you?"

"I'm getting off this tub. You won't know when or how, but I won't be aboard when she pulls into Memphis."

"But J. T., where you going? What are you going to do? Take me with you!"

"You know I can't do that. If two of us go, it will be twice the danger. And you can't swim as good as me."

Cotton knew I was right. One man might slip away, given sufficient stealth and intelligence, but two would surely be spotted. And the last time the two of us had swum across the Mississippi at Helena, when the summer had dried the riverbeds behind the levee and caused the river to shrink to no more than a large creek, he'd almost drowned before he reached the other side. He had to wait an hour, breathing heavy, his arms trembling, before he could attempt the crossing back again.

"But why are you doing this, J. T.?"

"I'm going after Norman Kilpatrick. He's back in Helena. He commanded the cannon atop Hindman Hill, and he killed all those men you saw lying over our green earth."

"He's the man took the farm?"

"Yes, and he almost took our lives, too, and he needs a killing more than any Fed ever drawed breath."

The rest of the morning Cotton tried to talk me out of my plan, but I was not to be moved. When he wasn't whining at me, I was watching the Federal guards and noting gaps in their security. They didn't have enough ropes or chains to bind us, so they stood over us with rifles and frowned in the heat, swatting away flies and scratching at flea bites.

We were the sorriest bunch of soldiers I think I'd ever seen. Our skin and clothes were so black with powder and dirt and soot that we looked like poor Negroes beaten unmercifully.

Before we'd gone far, I knew it was time to depart. "I'm going now," I whispered to Cotton. "You stay put and don't cause a row. I'll be back when the war ends, so you tell Ma, and you hug her real tight, you hear? And you tell our sisters that I love them and that they must stay away from the Federal men, especially if the rascals win the war."

Cotton clawed at my shirt sleeve when I rose, but he stayed put like I told him. I bumbled over sitting and reclining men, coughing and hacking like I had a burr in my throat. One guard looked me over and then back to his charges as I passed him by and headed for a four-foot square opening in the bulwark at the ship's side. Men, Reb and Yank alike, had been using it for pissing into the river. Beyond the opening rushed white waves stirred by the paddlewheel, and beyond that was the far shore. I would have to leap out, dive under to avoid rifle fire, and wait for the ship to slide past so that I could make for the near shore of Arkansas. It was a desperate plan, but no more than the taking of Hindman Hill, I thought, and for a much clearer ideal.

I could not stop to think, for if I mused on the liberal expanse of the opaque water I might turn back and accept my fate as captive. I glanced once behind me, saw the guard was paying no attention to me, thinking I was there to relieve myself. And then I grabbed the oaken rail with both hands and leapt up, landing with both boots there to teeter only a moment before I had flung myself over the side and down into the rolling whitecaps.

I heard men yelling immediately on reaching the surface again and I felt the tug of the ship as its wake tried to bring me back under. I had to swim toward the wrong shore first in order to free myself from the horror of being sucked beneath the boat and chewed up by the paddlewheel. Shots rang out, though I didn't hear them at first, only noting birds taking flight suddenly from trees on the opposite shore. I dived down, kicking with all my might for the bottom and for the far shore. When I could hold my breath no longer and the hard tug of the ship's wake had lessened, I broke the surface for air.

That's when I saw Cotton. He was floating like a sawmill log toward the ship's stern and the great turning wheel.

"No!" I screamed, flailing at the current, trying to swim back the way I'd come so that I might grab hold of Cotton before he went under for good.

The ship had not slowed and now it was turning another bend of the Mississippi, its hungry wake trailing out behind it like a rippling skirt. The force tugging Cotton's body toward the wheel let it go and now it turned in eddies, swirling round and round, face down in the muddy waters.

The *Tyler* was not going to slow to pick us up or to make sure we were dead. It was what I'd banked on. It was nearly gone finally, smoke from its stacks filling the sky above it. A shot rang out now and again, but they were too far distant to hit me.

My heart was a stone in my chest as I paddled closer to Cotton. I had stopped hurrying, wasting what strength I had left, for I knew what had happened and there was to be no aid or help in my hard swimming. Cotton must have followed me, coming just behind as I leaped, and they were on him, shooting at him no doubt before he ever broke the river, our skim of safety. In the end he had never listened to me, not when I asked him not to volunteer for Holmes's army, not when I told him to stay behind in the ranks, and not when I wanted him to remain in the rifle pit on the battlefield. Now he had disobeyed me for the last time, thinking that if I was going back to Helena, he would, too. He would be a hero, like his older brother. He would show the Feds what a boy could do to their plans.

I reached him and took hold of one arm, pulling on it so that his head bobbed up. I got hold of his shoulder and then his face and while kicking furiously to keep my own head above water, I pulled him closer. I flinched seeing that a shot had entered the back of his brain and exited his left eye.

I let him go immediately, throwing my arms back in the water and crying out in a shout that heaven could have heard if it had been listening. I turned my head away so that I did not have to see my brother so disfigured, and then knowing I could not let him go to the river's depths as his grave, I turned back again and hooked my arm around his bloody neck.

Finally on the Arkansas shore, I hauled Cotton over the muddy bank. I lay on my back, arms spread, gasping for breath, my eyes closed. Here we were then, Cotton and I, one of us dead and the other brokenhearted. Ma would say, in the end, that at least she had not lost us both. But this loss, the one I'd tried so hard to prevent, was too great for me.

It was all the fault of Norman Kilpatrick. If he'd been less a demon and if I'd been less bent on revenge, Cotton would have been alive.

I would bury my brother along the bank this side of the levee where we had played so many summer days. I searched and found his wing-bone whistle and stuck it into my pocket. "You can get this back later," I said.

It was dark before I had scratched red dirt deep enough to keep Cotton safe from predators. I had used my knife in one hand, a sharp river stone in the other. I gently lifted Cotton and lay him in the depression, crossing his hands on his chest. *I'll miss you forever*, I thought, and then I told God to hold on to him tight.

In the deep night I washed my face and arms in the Mississippi before I climbed the banks of the levee and slid down the other side stealthily into the city. I had buried my Rebel cap with Cotton and now looked no different from any other Helena citizen. I walked right into the streets as if I belonged there, which I did, and searched every male face as I passed it by. The Yanks were drinking and having their way with some women, victors savoring triumph.

I made my way past Graveyard Hill, where a company of men were digging graves for the Confederate dead. I pushed up Hindman Hill, carrying a pail I'd found along the way, filled with water. If asked, I would say I was sent for drinking water and if they didn't believe me, I'd pretend to be an idiot, unable to make sense. No one cared what you did if you were light in the head.

Without any incident at all I found Kilpatrick in his private tent, lying in a cot with an arm over his eyes. There was no guard posted, as the threat, he believed, had been dispatched.

Kilpatrick raised his head at my entry. "Get out of here, boy, I gave orders not to be bothered."

When I didn't move to leave, he swung his legs to the ground and fumbled for the lantern. I wanted him to see me. To know. To taste the same fear I had as I'd made my arduous way to him during battle.

Once the light was hissing, he turned to me and frowned. I watched his face carefully for signs of recognition.

"What do you want? Who are you?"

He didn't know me! It had been just over two years and he had forgotten me forever. My family and I had been nothing but victims to him, gnats to swat aside for his pleasure.

"I am J. T. Halsworthy, Sergeant. You took our land, you killed my brother, and you are a turncoat against the Southern Confederacy."

Some slight bit of understanding dawned in Kilpatrick's face just as he rose from the cot to reach for his pistol.

"I'll have none of that," I said, kicking the holster across the ground so that it landed in a corner of the tent.

"I don't know what you want, young man, but you're going to be strung up at dawn for assaulting an officer."

"No, sir." I came toward him, showing the blade of my knife as I twisted it back and forth in the lamplight. "I'll not suffer for this murder, sir. It's a venture of war. I am a Confederate soldier, and this is my land you've stolen and my people you've massacred."

He lunged for me, but his arms missed catching hold and the blade of my knife sank deeply into his chest where I brought it up and up against bone and sinew until it would rise no more.

He clutched me to stand, but as his blood spilled over my trousers and boots the look in his eyes dimmed and his hands loosened as he fell to his knees.

When I had him off the ground and back in his cot, I took out Cotton's little whistle made from the wing of a robin and I placed it carefully in his lips. When they found him dead they would wonder what he was meant to whistle, but I would know the tune, and so did Kilpatrick. For eternity, or until Cotton found him to retrieve his favorite toy, Norman Kilpatrick would whistle "Dixie."

I gently blew out the lantern and slipped from the tent flap.

It was time to walk back to Little Rock. We'd all be coming home to Helena one day soon . . . my mother, my sisters, and me.

# Behind Enemy Lines

## John Helfers and Carol Rondou

**M**ary walked into the oak-paneled dining room and surveyed the mess before her.

The cream of the Rebel army had just met here to plan the defense of Richmond, the capital of the Confederacy. The officers had left the normally stately room a cluttered mass of scrawled notes, maps, dirty dishes, and cigar butts. Smoke hung in a pallid haze above the long table, and Mary knew she'd have to beat and air the drapes again. She saw the mud tracked into the room by the generals' boots and, sighing to herself, made a mental note to have the carpet cleaned as well.

Setting down her waste bucket, Mary crossed the room, pulled open the heavy gold curtains, and opened a window. While she began collecting ashtrays, she scanned the table, sorting through the piles of maps and notes. As she worked, her eyes lighted on a neatly folded sheet of paper. Carefully unfolding it, she began to read, keeping an ear cocked for any noise outside. The paper contained a list of dates, locations, troop movements, army strengths, just the kind of information she was looking for.

131

The sound of bootheels clicking in the nearby hallway broke her attention. Mary quickly refolded the paper, thrusting it under the stinking pile of ashtrays, then continued her work, wiping down the table with a rag.

"Mary, what are you doing?" It was Lieutenant Martin Williams, President Jefferson Davis's new aide, immaculate in his spotless uniform. She could feel his suspicious grey eyes on her as he surveyed the room.

Rearranging her face into the mask of bovine placidity she wore whenever soldiers were around, Mary looked up and exclaimed, "Sir, the Confederates done won the war! I just cleanin' the room after they left." She gazed stupidly at the young lieutenant and waited.

Williams relaxed and smiled as if he were addressing a child. "Perhaps not yet, Mary, but soon enough. Continue with your work." He left the doorway and Mary didn't breathe until she heard him on the stairs heading to the president's office.

For Mary Elizabeth Bowser, black servant in the Confederate White House and Union spy, it was one close call too many since the lieutenant had arrived. He was always watching her, ready with his insinuating questions and surprise inspections. *That man's harder to shake off than a pack of coon dogs after a fox*, she thought.

Mary's tenure at the White House had been relatively quiet until recently. With the army drafting any able-bodied man, even blacks, for labor, the capitol had been short-staffed for months. With fewer eyes watching her, Mary's spying had been much easier. At least until the lieutenant had arrived. *I can't scarcely round a corner without him popping up somewhere*, she thought.

So far, Mary had managed not to attract any attention to herself. If Williams had suspected anything, she would either be dead or sold into hard labor by now, free woman or not. Slipping the paper into her apron pocket, she forced herself to continue working. The dining room would be needed for the family's evening meal.

As she worked, Mary shivered and pulled her shawl tighter over her shoulders, glancing at the cold, empty fireplace. January of 1864 was a time of shortage, and even the White House had limited supplies of coal and wood. With the Union Army driving General Lee farther and farther back, the South was suffering hemorrhages of men, supplies, and support.

Richmond couldn't hold on much longer, and hopefully the information she sent through the lines would hasten the city's fall. Day after day the wagons rumbled through the streets bearing their grisly cargo of dead and dying. Every building that could be commandeered became a hospital or a morgue, and often the former turned into the latter. If the war didn't end soon, there would be no one to come home.

The sound of a throat clearing made Mary look up again. Standing in the doorway was Burton Harrison, President Davis's personal secretary. Harrison was an energetic, self-contained man who prided himself on anticipating President Davis's needs. The long war years had taken their toll, etching deep lines of worry and overwork into his face. He was not an unkind man, but he was a staunch supporter of the Southern cause and had profited from the South's "peculiar institution." As such, Mary was always on her guard around him.

"Can I help you, Mr. Harrison?" she asked. *Just take whatever you need and go*, she thought.

"Mary, have you seen a stack of letters on the table?" He asked as he scanned the room, taking note of her wastebasket and brush. "President Davis needs them. He brought them in here for the meeting."

"No, sir, I haven't seen anything like that," she said.

"Why Mary, they're right here," Harrison said, shaking his head as he snatched the letters off the table and headed out. He paused at the door and glanced back at her. "Don't be concerned, Mary, everyone is overworked."

"Yessir, we certainly are," Mary replied with her wide smile. As she went to the kitchen she thought about Lieutenant

Williams, and how much he may have seen since coming to the White House. Mary had never heard of him until his arrival a month ago. He was a young graduate of West Point, and she assumed he had family connections high in the Confederate government to be the president's aide. While other young officers clamored to go into battle to protect the sacred soil of the South, he seemed content to stay in the capital and wait. Perhaps he was here to uncover the spy ring that had operated in Richmond since the beginning of the war. Perhaps they had captured one of the runaways the ring had helped, and discovered that the Confederate White House was being used as a way station for escaped slaves traveling to the North. Maybe he suspected her of passing information and was planning to catch her and her allies, perhaps leaving the papers she had found to lure her into revealing herself.

Mary watched the flames dance as she burned the trash and thought about her next move. The information had to be sent to Elizabeth Van Lew, the Union spy master and her girlhood mentor. She couldn't risk not sending this information on, it was much too important. Heading back into the kitchen, she took a deep breath to steady her nerves.

Mary reached for the egg basket and the hollow egg that would contain the message. Carefully folding the paper into a small cylinder, she slid it into the egg, sealed the hole with a paste made from flour and water, and placed the egg in the basket among the others. She would pass the false egg to one of Miss Van Lew's servants as she took the basket, by the order of the president's wife, to the military hospitals for the wounded. She cleaned her hands and was whipping them dry on her apron when Lieutenant Williams strode into the kitchen.

"What do you have there, Mary?" he asked and glanced into the basket, picking up an egg.

Mary's blood froze in her veins as he reached into the basket, but the years of living her double life helped her to stand still as stone, her face betraying none of the fear raging inside her. She showed no emotion of any kind when he selected a true egg.

"Eggs for the wounded, sir. Mrs. Davis told me to take them to the hospital for the boys," she said.

"Of course. President Davis would like some coffee. Send Liza up with a pot. Continue on your mission of mercy, Mary." He carefully replaced the egg and left the kitchen.

Liza was one of the few remaining servants in the mansion. Mary hid a smile, of course he would ask for her. *Like he wasn't haunting her steps,* she thought.

Liza was a pretty young woman about twenty years old. She had fine features, large, melting brown eyes, and mocha-colored skin. The well-spoken daughter of a planter and a mistress, her father had educated her as a house servant and had only sold her to appease a new wife. Many gentlemen who had visited the Confederate White House were taken with her beauty, but the Davis's refused to consider selling her. She had been the children's nurse since the war began, and they were devoted to her. A deft hand with pencil or ink, the children often clamored for her to sketch them or other people. Of course, she now had other duties since the war had affected the staff, but she always tried to find time for drawing. She was not free, but was part of the cell, and tomorrow night would be the next one sent through the lines to freedom.

Just then Liza entered the kitchen from the cellar, staggering under a heavy load of firewood. "Hello, Mary. I think I brought enough to last through the afternoon at least. How do people live in cold like this?" she said, placing the wood in the storage bin, then crossing over to the washbasin and scrubbing her hands.

"Don't worry, you'll get used to it," Mary said. "Lieutenant Williams has ordered a pot of coffee for the president's office, and requested you to bring it. Watch out for him, there's more to that man than he seems."

"I intend to stay as far away from him as I can. Mary . . . ," she began, only to be cut off by the chiming of a bell. "I have to answer that. Mary, I found some important papers. I'll give them to you when you get back from Miss Elizabeth's." The bell continued to chime as Liza took the coffee pot from the stove, transferred the contents into a carafe, placed it on a tray with cups and spoons, and small pots of cream and sugar, and went up the back stairs.

Mary watched her leave, tempted to wait for her but knowing if she didn't leave for the Van Lew home now, her absence would be noticed and she wouldn't make it back to the mansion by curfew. Placing her heavy wool cloak about her shoulders, Mary made sure she had her pass, then started the long walk through the city streets to the Van Lew mansion.

Winding her way through the mostly deserted city streets, Mary came to the bottom of Church Hill, which was crowned by the Van Lew mansion. The stately home commanded one of the best views of Richmond. On a clear day, one could see all the way to the Tredegar Iron Works and down to the James River.

Going to the Van Lew mansion was a return home for Mary. She had been owned by the family, but as soon as old Mr. Van Lew had died, Mary and the others had been given their freedom, and Miss Van Lew sent her to live among the Quakers in Philadelphia to be educated. She wouldn't have returned South, except Miss Elizabeth had asked for her assistance in what seemed to be a mad scheme at the time. However, the chance to help others escape to a life of freedom as she had was something she couldn't ignore. Only Elizabeth Van Lew could have convinced her to return to the danger of the South and to become a spy on top of it. *Once this war is over*, Mary thought, *I'll never come this far south again.*

AT THE MANSION, MARY knocked on the kitchen door and was greeted warmly and hustled into the cozy interior. The Van Lew household had been looked upon as eccentric since the early days of the war. Miss Van Lew was referred to as "Crazy Bet" because of her habit of whispering to herself and skipping down the street. "Crazy Bet" made it easier for her to gain access to the Union prisoners in Libby Prison and assist in their escapes.

Regardless of how she did it, Elizabeth Van Lew was playing a desperate game and some people were becoming suspicious. Last year an editorial in the *Richmond Dispatch* criticized her for visiting Federal prisoners at Libby Prison, even claiming she was giving aid and comfort to the enemy while Southern boys languished in hellish Yankee prison camps. When President Davis declared a national day of fasting, the Van Lew house dined in sumptuous fashion. During General McClellan's 1862 campaign against Richmond, Miss Van Lew and her mother had set aside the best bedroom in the house for him when he conquered the city. They called it "the McClellan room."

"Sit yoself down chile', and warm up," Nancy, the Van Lew cook, insisted, taking her cloak from her shoulders and hanging it on a peg by the fire. She was a mulatto woman in her mid-fifties, dressed in a calico dress with a starched white headscarf. She poured Mary a hot cup of tea and set a huge slab of pound cake before her. "Ain't dos Davis's feeding you none? You ain't nothin' but skin and bones. And you always was such a lil' bit of a thing."

Mary gratefully sat at the table and clasped the teacup in her hands to warm them. "Thank you, Nancy. It was a long walk today. I never remembered Richmond's being so cold."

Nancy nodded in agreement. "It won't git no better either. If de weather holds der'll be another food riot. Member de Bread Riot dis pas' April?"

Mary nodded. The harsh winter coupled with the crippled economy had seen the cost of a barrel of flour climb to $100. The desperate population had reached their breaking point in early April. A mob of over one hundred women had marched to the business district and begun smashing shop windows, grabbing whatever they could carry. The mayor had called out the city militia and ordered the crowd to disperse or they would be fired upon. The soldiers had been reluctant to fire upon a crowd of mostly poor women who were the wives, daughters, or sweethearts of their comrades at the front. Finally President Davis arrived and, in desperation, took money out of his pockets and began to throw it to the crowd. He then took out his pocket watch and gave the crowd five minutes to leave or he would give the order to fire. Fortunately, the crowd dispersed and the crisis ended as suddenly as it had begun.

"If the North carries on as it has been, the war should be over by spring," Mary said between bites of pound cake. "Tennessee has been under Federal control since November, and Vicksburg surrendered in July, which gave the Union control over the Mississippi River. Last week General Cleburne proposed freeing some slaves and training them to fight. If that doesn't mean the end, I don't know what does."

Nancy chuckled, "Dat jist puts 'em a year behind da Yankees. I wonder when we gonna see dem colored Yankee troops. What dey say about dat?"

"They refused to listen," Mary said. "Called the idea revolting and said it would demoralize the army. If the idea of their families starving isn't demoralizing, I don't know what is."

Nancy took the false egg from the basket, cracked it open, and removed the paper. "Miz Elizabeth be happy to git dis. You best git movin' or dose Patrol boys will git you."

Mary rose from the table and put on her cloak. "The last thing I need is a run-in with them. I still need to visit the hospital before I go back. There's just so much to do, even now.

"That reminds me; Liza said she found something important. I have to get back to see what it is," Mary said as she took her basket and let herself out of the kitchen.

The walk to the General Hospital Number 9 was uneventful, but seeing the wards, filled to capacity with the wounded and dying, always distressed her. She quickly made her delivery and hurried back to the White House.

MARY ARRIVED HOME AS the hall clock struck four. Hanging her cloak next to the fireplace, she looked around the quiet kitchen. *Odd,* she thought, *Liza should be here preparing the children's afternoon tea.* Mary called for her, but no one replied. A draft from the open cellar door caught her attention. Usually the door was always kept shut, especially during cold weather. *Another oddity,* she thought.

Mary pushed the door shut as Rebecca, the Davis's cook, came into the kitchen bearing a tray. She was an elderly black woman with a sour temper and a reputation among the other servants for carrying tales to the mistress. Mary had always treated the older woman with care, but she knew that Rebecca would have sold her out to Lieutenant Williams in a second.

"What you gawkin' at?" she demanded, glaring at Mary. "Mus' be fine to gallivant all over town while Ise doin' yo' work." She set the tray down with a clatter.

"Do you know where Liza is?" Mary asked.

"Iffen I knew, do you think Ise be haulin' dat tray fo' her?" she grumbled, walking across the kitchen to the stove to check the contents of a stewpot. "Why don't you do sumpin' useful and get some mo' firewood?"

Mary was happy to escape the kitchen and Rebecca, so she opened the cellar door and was surprised to see a light at the bottom of the stairs. Normally anyone going to the cellar brought a lantern and took it out when they were done. She continued down the stairs, concerned about the odd light.

When she reached the bottom of the stairs, she saw Lieutenant Williams kneeling by the woodpile, his back to her. He had taken his uniform jacket off, and hadn't seemed to hear her on the stairs. He appeared to be stacking wood on the pile. She stopped her descent and the stair creaked as her weight shifted. The lieutenant whirled around, and

Mary saw that his shirt was torn and there was a scratch on his cheek. Rising to his feet, Williams pulled on his jacket and stalked to the stairs.

"What the hell do you mean sneaking up on me like that?" he demanded of her.

"Cook needed wood . . ." she began, and he cut her off with a wave of his hand.

"Fine, but get it from the other end of the stack. That end is piled wrong; it could collapse if you're not careful," he said, looked at her for a long moment, his arms crossed. "Well, what are you waiting for?"

Realizing he wasn't going to leave, Mary walked over to the woodpile and gathered an armload of logs. While she worked, she stole a quick glance at the wood Williams had been crouched over. She thought she saw a piece of cloth sticking out from between the logs.

"Damn it, Mary, hurry up!" Williams said. "All of Richmond society will be here tomorrow, and I will not have it said that the food wasn't ready because a servant couldn't get the firewood fast enough!"

"Yessir. Sorry, sir," Mary said, standing up with a large armload of wood. The lieutenant stepped aside to let her pass, then followed her up the stairs.

The two emerged into the kitchen, Mary dropping the wood into the woodbin and going to a basin to wash her hands. After that she went to a table and began peeling potatoes. Williams stood in front of the cellar door and watched Mary work. Rebecca kept her head down and continued chopping vegetables, shooting venomous glares at Mary when she was sure the lieutenant wasn't looking.

After a few minutes, Williams stalked out of the kitchen. The second he left, Rebecca whirled on Mary.

"What you do to get him all riled up like dat? I'se got enuff problems without him standin' over us," she said.

"I just didn't get the firewood fast enough to suit him, that's all," Mary said.

"That kind o' trouble I don' need. Hard enough to cook tomorrow's dinner as it is. You best keep that bin full, I cain't have the stove dyin' down," Rebecca said.

"You're absolutely right," Mary said, going to the cellar door. "I'll be right back."

Once back downstairs, Mary walked over and examined the woodpile. It appeared normal in the dim light. Taking the lantern down from its peg, she brought it over to the far side of the pile. The light revealed a dark red stain on the brick wall about a foot off the ground. Bringing the light closer, Mary realized it was fresh blood. She looked for the piece of cloth she had seen earlier, and spotted a scrap of muslin sticking out from underneath a chunk of wood. Removing it revealed the sleeve of a dress with a hand sticking out. A small woman's hand. Mary jumped backward and screamed involuntarily.

"Mary? What's y'all doin' down dere?" Rebecca called from the kitchen.

"Oh—oh nothing. A mouse jumped out from the wood-pile, that's all," Mary said after a moment.

"Well, kill it and get up here wit' dat wood," Rebecca said.

When she had gotten control of herself, Mary removed a few more logs. It was Liza, dead, her hair sticky and clotted with blood. Her dead brown eyes gazed into Mary's in mute appeal. Mary rocked back on her knees and gazed down at Liza's dead pale face. Choking back her revulsion, she searched Liza's apron pocket and clothing looking for the papers, shuddering whenever her fingers came in contact with Liza's cooling flesh, but found nothing. She noticed that Liza's hands were stained with ink.

*Either Williams already found whatever Liza had, or else she hid it somewhere in the house,* Mary thought. *If he had found it, he probably wouldn't have been so angered by me finding him in the basement.* Perhaps he hid her body so he could search her later. Speculation was pointless now. Liza was dead, and she had to find the documents and send them through the lines. There was nothing she could do for Liza but try to provide her with a decent burial. The poor girl had been so close. Tomorrow night, during the reception, she would have started on her journey to the Northern lines and freedom.

*Liza's dead and I can't even accuse her murderer,* Mary thought. She knew that, even with her position in the household, no one would take her word over Lieutenant Williams's about what had happened. He could make up any story he wanted, and would get away with it. *Not if I can help it,* she thought.

Murmuring a quick prayer for the dead girl's soul, Mary carefully replaced the firewood covering Liza. She then loaded one arm with logs, picked up the lantern and, with leaden legs, climbed the stairs.

MARY CONTINUED THE REST of her duties in a mechanical fashion. She was dimly aware of a search of the house being conducted by Lieutenant Williams for the missing Liza. When asked about Liza's whereabouts, she answered dully, saying she hadn't seen Liza since that afternoon, before she left for the hospital. Mr. Harrison was almost finished questioning her in the dining room when Lieutenant Williams entered and coolly announced that Liza had run off. Mary noticed him staring intently at her, and she kept her face unmovable as she returned his gaze, noting with satisfaction that his eyes dropped first. It was late when Harrison finally dismissed her to the servant quarters and the room she shared with Liza.

The bedroom was simply furnished, with two beds, a bed stand, wardrobe, two small trunks, and bare wood floors. Liza's half of the room was in disarray, as if someone had prepared for a sudden trip and left whatever they hadn't taken strewn about the room. What meager possessions she had were gone except for a few stockings, an apron, and a torn skirt.

Mary looked over her half of the room and found that her possessions had been gone through and an attempt made to replace them. Blowing out the lamp, Mary lay on her bed to prepare for an uneasy sleep. She had no way of contacting the ring to inform them of Liza's death and no idea where the documents were hidden. Assuming she could find them, the only way to deliver them would be to pass them to the contact, who was expecting to meet with Liza during the reception for top government officials being held at the mansion tomorrow.

*How am I going to find the documents and get them to the courier in a house full of high ranking Confederate officials? Not to mention Lieutenant Williams, who will be watching me like a hawk on a titmouse,* she thought. *Well, let's start with what I do know; the documents aren't in this room, they weren't on the body, and they weren't in the woodpile.* Beyond that, the situation seemed hopeless. Mary lay awake pondering her problem well into the early hours of the cold, gray dawn.

THAT MORNING MARY WAS assigned Liza's duties as well as her own, so the search for the missing information became much more difficult. She was able to conduct a hurried search for clues in the cellar on several trips to gather wood, but found nothing. She also searched Lieutenant Williams's office during a pretext of cleaning, on the hunch that maybe Liza had hidden the information under Williams's nose, but came up empty there as well. Mary knew Liza never would have hidden anything in the kitchen, that was the sharp-eyed Rebecca's domain, and the abrasive woman knew every hiding place like the back of her hand. She had searched everywhere in the mansion she could think of, all to no avail.

Coming out of the kitchen with a platter of smoked meats for the dining room, Mary almost stumbled over a small boy in the hallway. Looking down, she saw Joseph Davis, the youngest of the Davis children, standing before her.

"Where's Liza?" the child asked.

"Oh . . . she's away visiting kin for a few days, she'll be back soon enough," Mary said with a forced smile, hating to lie to the boy, but knowing she had to.

"She promised to fix my horse yesterday, and she hasn't yet," Joseph said, stomping his foot.

The horse was a stuffed patchwork animal loved by Joseph, and as such was often in need of repair. Every few days Liza would have to sew a limb back on or mend a seam torn from vigorous play. Of course, the toy was the boy's favorite, and he was never without it. Mary looked down and saw a trail of sawdust behind the boy leading up the stairs.

"I'm sure that's the first thing Liza will do when she gets back, child. Why don't you run upstairs and play?" Mary said.

Joseph stomped up the wide staircase towards his room, leaving another trail of sawdust in his wake. Mary watched him go, shaking her head, and went to get a broom. She finished sweeping the hallway and stairs just as the clock struck six, and Mary bustled into the dining room to put the finishing touches on the food for the reception.

When the guests began to arrive, Mary was kept busy circling among them, refilling wineglasses and bearing trays of meats and cheeses. She heard snatches of valuable conversations, but she was no closer to the lost information.

During a pass through the library, she saw Lieutenant Williams in an intense conversation with Joseph Mayo, the mayor of Richmond.

". . . and she said to me, 'Massa, the 'federates done won de war.' I wish I could have such simple faith." Lieutenant Williams and the Mayor laughed heartily and each took a glass of wine from her tray, ignoring Mary as if she wasn't there. She passed from group to group, offering drinks from the tray and soaking in the information being passed around her, all the while trying to think of where Liza might have hidden those papers.

AT A QUARTER OF eight, Mary slipped out the back door to meet Liza's contacts. Jeremiah and Joshua Clifton were a father and son from a farm outside the city, both of whom had worked with the Van Lew family since the beginning of the War.

"Where's Liza?" the older one asked.

"She was murdered last night by Lieutenant Williams, President Davis's new aide," Mary said. "Liza said she had some important information for me to send out, but she hadn't given it to me yet. I think Williams found out about her mission and killed her when she wouldn't tell him what she knew."

"Murdered? Pa, we best go away now 'afore we gets arrested," Joshua said.

"Hush, boy! Let me think," Jeremiah said as he thoughtfully stroked his beard.

"Please, I need your help. Liza died for those papers and I've got to find them," Mary pleaded. "She also needs a decent burial, if you can manage it. It's the least we can do."

"Where is the bod—where is she?" the old farmer asked.

"Pa . . ." Joshua began.

"In the cellar, this way," Mary said before the elder Clifton could change his mind.

"Hold a minute, Mary," Jeremiah said. "We can't wait forever. We can bury Liza on the farm, but we have to meet our contact in two hours. Can't you bring the papers to Missus Van Lew during your weekly drop?"

"Williams murdered Liza because he discovered she was spying. I think he suspects me now. I could be next."

"I'll give you one hour, Mary. Joshua, let's see to the poor girl. We will meet you in the barn out back in one hour. Agreed?"

"Agreed. We have to hurry." Mary led the two men down to the cellar and watched as they carefully uncovered Liza and gently wrapped her body in a blanket. She was light enough for the younger man to carry alone up the stairs.

"We meet in the barn in one hour," Jeremiah said, reaching for his pocket watch. "I have eight o'clock. If you ain't there at nine, we'll have to leave."

"If we could create a distraction to clear out the mansion, I could search without being discovered, and you and the boy could wait in the barn for me," Mary said, looking at the pile of firewood and at the lantern the old farmer was holding. He caught her meaning and a slow smile crossed his craggy face.

"You head upstairs and I'll start a fine blaze," he said. "Once I'm outside and I see smoke, I'll raise the alarm. How much time do you need?"

"Give me a few minutes before you start calling out and wait fifteen minutes after," Mary said.

"Done, but get out if the smoke gets too thick," Jeremiah replied.

Mary nodded as she dashed up the stairs.

Once she was gone, the farmer searched the cellar until he found the stores of oil. Stacking several pieces of wood in the middle of the basement, he soaked the pile and tossed the lit lantern onto it. The wood burst into flames as he escaped up the stairs.

Mary continued moving among the crowd, offering refreshment. Her eyes would often travel to the mantelclock, watching the minutes tick by. Suddenly a sharp cry split the air. It was Rebecca screaming from the kitchen.

"Fire! The cellar's on fire!"

Mary ran behind President Davis and Lieutenant Williams to the kitchen. When the door was open a cloud of thick black smoke rolled out.

"Mary, get my children out of the house," the president commanded. "Williams, organize a bucket brigade. I'll see to the guests."

Mary saw Lieutenant Williams eye her with suspicion as she rushed up the rear stairs to the top floor where the

Davis children slept. She could hear Williams commanding the remaining servants and the house guards to fight the flames.

The children were asleep in their large airy room on the mansion's top floor. The room was a sanctuary for them, filled with toys and games, far away from the hustle and bustle of life in a capital city at war. Mary shook the oldest boy awake first.

"The house is on fire. You have to help get the rest of the children out," she said. The youth sprang from his bed and helped her wake his remaining siblings and get them into their coats. By now the smoke had wafted up the stairs and was filling the room. Mary swept the youngest child out of his bed and carried him, screaming and crying, down the stairs. She led the children down the stairs through the front door to their grateful mother waiting for them in the street.

"Mummy, Mummy. Where's my horse!" Joseph Davis cried as he clung to his mother's neck.

*The horse! Liza must have hidden the documents in the horse,* Mary thought. *That had to be it!* "I got it!" she shouted as she ran back into the house. She could hear Mrs. Davis ordering her to come back, but she ran on.

The smoke filled the first-floor hallway, almost forcing her back, but she struggled up the stairs to the third floor. The smoke was now thicker in the nursery but she still could breathe fairly well. The stuffed horse was lying on the floor in a small pile of sawdust on the far side of the room. Running to it, Mary picked it up and saw new stitching along the toy's back. Picking the stitches apart revealed folded hand-drawn maps of the defenses of Richmond and Petersburg.

"I'll take those, Mary." Lieutenant Williams's voice came from behind her, on the top of the landing.

Mary whirled around, dropping the horse but keeping the maps in her hand as she did so. "Take what, sir?" she asked, trying to think of a plan.

"Don't insult me, Mary," the lieutenant said. "Although I will admit, you fooled me for a while. If I hadn't seen Liza with ink on her hands after she had left my office and the maps of the city out of order, you might have gotten away with it. Now you will be hung as a traitor and a spy."

Mary raised her head proudly, placed the papers in her apron, and stood there as the smoke continued to fill the room. "She and I will be replaced by a hundred others," she said.

Lieutenant Williams smiled. "Don't be foolish, Mary, there is nowhere for you to go. These stairs are the only way out. I promise you will die quickly." He stood ready for her at the top of the staircase.

"Like Liza?" Mary said.

"She refused to give me the documents," Williams said. "I knew hiding her death would bring her accomplices into the open. If you continue to resist me, I will shoot you where you stand. Without your help it will take longer to break up your ring of spies, but I will do it. Regardless, without you I am willing to bet there will be no more information coming from the White House."

Mary silently said a prayer for forgiveness for what she was about to do. Raising her hands as if surrendering, she walked towards Lieutenant Williams. She stopped in front of him.

"The maps are in my pocket," she said.

Lieutenant Williams's eyes flicked downward to her apron, then reached for her pocket. He brought the papers out and began to unfold them.

At that moment, Mary shoved him with all her strength. The lieutenant flailed, trying to regain his balance, grabbing for her arm to try to hold himself up. Mary twisted away from his grasp and watched him fall down the stairs, his body tumbling and twisting as it slid to a stop on the second-floor landing.

Mary picked up the papers from where the lieutenant had dropped them. She tucked them away again, then

came down the stairs, coughing at the thick pall of smoke
rising up the stairway. Lieutenant Williams lay sprawled on
the landing, his head twisted at an odd angle. Carefully
stepping over him, Mary poked his body with her foot.
There was no response. Kneeling down by him, she leaned
over and listened for the sound of his breath. The man was
dead.

Mary felt sickened by what had happened. The smoke
was growing thicker, and she gagged on both the smoke and
the knowledge of what she had done. Rising to her feet, she
continued down the stairs, heading for the kitchen. She stag-
gered for the back door, the smoke stinging her eyes and
blinding her, her chest bursting with lack of oxygen. Throwing the door open, Mary rushed to the barn, her lungs
greedily drinking in the cold night air.

"Mary, did you find what you needed?" Joshua asked.

"The fire spread faster then I thought," Jeremiah
explained. "I didn't think you would get out in time."

"Here are the papers. Go quickly," Mary gasped, pressing the maps into the older man's hand.

After the Cliftons were safely away, Mary left the barn
to mingle with the crowd of servants and Southern aristo-
crats outside the mansion. By the time she got there, the
fire had been put out and the Confederate White House
had been saved. She saw the president, his face smeared
with sweat and smoke, and Mrs. Davis comforting their children. Young Joseph saw her and started to struggle out of
his mother's arms.

"Horsey! Horsey!"

Mary took a deep breath and walked over to the Davis
family. "I'm sorry, ma'am. I couldn't get Master Joseph's horse."

Mrs. Davis smiled kindly at her, "Thank you for trying,
Mary. It was a very brave thing to do, although I don't see
for the life of me why you went back. We can always get
Joseph another horse."

"It doesn't matter now, 'cause it looks like they got the
fire under control," Mary said.

Burton Harrison rushed up to President Davis, slightly out of breath. "Sir, everyone has been accounted for except Lieutenant Williams. After the fire was put out in the cellar, he ran back into the mansion yelling something about the nursery."

The president frowned, and the two men exchanged suspicious looks. Before anyone else could speak, Mary addressed Harrison.

"Mr. Harrison, sir. The lieutenant came to the nursery to help me out of the house, and while coming down the stairs, I'm afraid he slipped and hurt himself quite severely. I ran down the stairs to get help, but in all the smoke got turned around and found myself in the kitchen. I came out the back door, and ran to find you."

"Thank you, Mary," the president said, breathing heavily. "Burton, get some men and see to the lieutenant. I think this has been quite enough excitement for one evening, don't you agree, dear?" he asked his wife.

*Amen*, Mary thought as she looked at the smoke-filled house and thought of the maps Liza had bought with her life, the maps that would hopefully bring a swift end to this terrible war. *Amen.*

# The Unknown Soldier

## *Kristine Kathryn Rusch*

He finds himself in his own nightmare. Cold deeper than any he has ever felt, wind whistling through the makeshift barracks, hunger eating away at his stomach. His feet are wrapped in ripped cloth—his shoes long worn down by marching, marching, marching. He doesn't remember throwing them away, even though the soles were gone. Perhaps someone stole them on the long train ride to this prison camp on the outskirts of a Wisconsin town.

Other men huddle around him, some clinging to thread-bare blankets, others clustered together for warmth. The fire in the stove is not as bright as before, now only a little more than glowing coals—the guards will not build another until morning. He sits as close to the stove as he can, a prime position won because he can still fight. The warmth coats his left side, making the right even colder. He stares through one of the chinks in the wood, seeing the large white flakes drift down to earth. He has heard of snow, has seen it now, day after day, week after week, but he still does not understand it. How can anything so cold be so fragile?

He asked one of the guards once, but the guard just laughed at him. *I'm assigned here same as you,* the guard said. *Only I didn't turn traitor from my country.*

Traitor. He doesn't consider himself a traitor. He is a soldier, a man called to serve, not by Jeff Davis, not by the Confederate States of America, but by his family, people who lived in New Orleans through one regime after another, who fought to protect bayous and cypress trees and warm sunlight falling on the backs of their necks. People who believed not in a cause, but in a place. A place he might never see again.

He slides closer to the stove, so close that a slight movement would cause him to burn his left arm. He doesn't know what he believes in. Used to be he believed in himself, in his future, in his own powers as a human being. But his powers disappeared along with his shoes, and his future disappeared when he took his father's horse and rode off to enlist. He has no dreams left. Only nightmares. One particular nightmare that may or may not come true.

HE FIRST HAD THE nightmare as a young boy. It was a hot July night. The shutters were closed, letting in only a slight breeze to disturb the oppressive air. His overstuffed mattress felt damp, and sweat ran off his small body. He wished himself cold, wished for cold, and dozed . . .

*. . . seeing the rags on his feet, the torn gray pants made so lovingly by his mother. The heat from a fire touched his left side, but the rest of him was cold—so cold he never thought he would be warm again. He wrapped his body into a ball, shivering. Then the wooden door opened to a world of white—and slashed across it, blood . . .*

He woke up, a scream buried in his throat. Then sat, realizing that no one was coming to him. He was in his room, safe and alone. Only when he touched his skin for reassurance, the left side was too hot, and the rest too cold.

NO ONE SPEAKS IN this godforsaken place. They all stare straight ahead, as if they are looking backward at their lives. He can see forward for some of them—a sometimes gift his mother denied. His grandmother never did. She called it "the sight," and she used it. Only after he enlisted, she would never again use it on him.

He glances around the room, sees things that are going to be: the too-thin man in the corner, dead, placed in the ice-house with the other bodies to be buried come thaw; the man asleep on the only bunk, walking home to a magnificent plantation in Georgia, finding nothing but ash-covered Doric columns; the man beside him, face hidden behind a white hood, whipping his horse near-death chasing a black man across a field.

Sometimes he spends hours with these future visions, but they all end the same. Used to be when he turned the sight on himself, he saw a myriad of things: sitting, as an old man, in front of a tumble-down shack, children playing around him; a book about the "old South," held in a woman's gnarled hand, his name in gold leaf on the spine; standing beside his mother in the house of his birth as blue-clad soldiers clatter in, leaving muddy tracks on the polished wood floor.

The last time he saw any of those dreams, he still lived in the New Orleans house. His father's near-lame horse remained in the barn. He called on the sight the day his grandmother introduced him to a red-haired girl, and saw even more futures: a burned Great House; their bodies, naked and entwined; a red, squalling infant; another woman, long black hair trailing to her waist. He tried to call up those images after he enlisted, but could not. When he took his father's horse and rode toward war, all those dreams disappeared. Now, when he turns the sight to himself, he sees nothing. Nothing at all.

EXCEPT HIS PAST:

"YOUR grandmother wants you to marry." His mother took her lemonade into the garden and sat on the wrought-iron chair, her skirts falling across her legs like a fan. A carriage rumbled past the gate, then there was silence. He always thought of the garden as a green sanctuary in the middle of the city. "I do not."

"But, Mama." He protested more out of duty than desire. He was not in love, but he wanted to do what his grandmother bade him. He gazed at the shuttered windows of the house, willing her to come outside and defend him. Since his father's death in Mexico, his mother had wielded too much power. His grandmother appeared on the porch as if she had heard his summons. She nodded once and started down the stairs.

"You don't care for this girl, and you're much too young. You have plenty of time—"

"He doesn't have time." His grandmother stopped just short of the bench. She stood on the path, the sculptured hedges behind her. "A man is remembered by doing great deeds, creating beautiful things, or having a family that lives beyond him. He has no time to do great deeds nor to create beauty. He only has time for a family."

His grandmother's words chilled him—and with the cold came the memory of the nightmare, the rags on his feet. He had had that dream every night since his father's death.

"The war will end soon," his mother said.

"Wars never end," his grandmother replied.

HE CAN'T EVEN REMEMBER the girl's name, nor her face, only the softness of her bosom against his chest as they danced. He hasn't married, hasn't had a family. Before the occupation, his mother left New Orleans to live with friends in Atlanta, and his grandmother—his grandmother died the night he left. He has heard rumors of the burning of Atlanta, and his dreams lead him to believe his mother is dead. He is the last, the keeper of his family's lives, guardian of the future. And he has created nothing of beauty, done no great deeds.

This morning, he woke up believing today is the last day of his strength. The last day of conscious choice, before he becomes as vacant as the men around him, surviving only by sheer luck or fortitude.

Perhaps the vision he has left is not a nightmare. Perhaps it is his great deed, the thing that will make him remembered.

He has been thinking of this for some time. If he can get the others to rebel, they might be able to escape, to find their own ways home. The barrack guards are strong, but the rest are mere German bumpkins, pulled in from the fields. The train station is a short ride away, and the trains are still running regularly. He can hear the whistle at the usual intervals, speaking to him of safety, of freedom, of warmth. Of home.

Great deeds. All a man needs is one. One will last him his lifetime, give him the home and family, and make him remembered. One act . . .

THE DOOR DOES NOT open until the barracks are nearly dark, the stove almost cooled. As soon as the cold air drifts in, he launches himself toward it, hitting the guard full across the chest, butting his head against the guard's chin. Blood gushes out the guard's nose and spatters the snow. A small feeling of victory rises in him, followed almost as rapidly by a sense of disquiet. There is more to the nightmare than he can remember.

The other men watch with disinterest from the door. He yells to them, "Come *on!*" and begins to run before he notices whether they respond. He imagines them rising on stiff legs to follow him toward freedom.

His own legs are stiff, but they move well enough. The air is cold, colder than any he has ever breathed, so cold it freezes his lungs. The snow has finished, but he can feel its remnants, wet and soggy against the rags on his feet. He will worry about that later, when he is free, when he is on the train.

He runs down a well-worn trail, past other barracks, some with light in the windows and thin curls of smoke rising from the chimneys. Not cells, surely, not anything more than guard quarters for the Northerners who keep the Southerners imprisoned.

As he passes them, another shiver of victory captures his chest. All he has is the poorly guarded gate to cross, and then he's in the open. He can hear no footsteps behind him—no guards or other prisoners tracking him. Only his own harsh breathing. The breath plumes before him like the steam from a locomotive. Free. Free. He is free.

Too late he sees one of the bumpkins beside a building. The lump isn't even wearing a uniform, just the wide homemade pants and heavy jacket of a farmer. The bumpkin raises his rifle—and he leaps to avoid the shot. In that split second, the sight comes to him, and he sees his mother recoiling as a soldier slams a rifle butt into her face. The soldier sets the house on fire, and as it burns, his mother lies unconscious on the floor.

"No!" he cries, and then a burning pain scrapes into his chest. He is still airborne. On the snow beneath him, the familiar bloodstain pattern blooms, the one that has haunted his dreams, and he remembers the part of the nightmare he has always forgotten upon wakening:

*The pattern ends against a man's body twisted and half-buried in snow. The eyes are open, lifeless, and the skin almost blue with cold. This man is cold, as cold as a man ever gets. The body gets moved to the icehouse, to wait for the thaw, when it will be buried in a mass grave with a hundred others, all unknown.*

"No!" he cries again, and lands so hard that the breath escapes his body. His arms cross, his legs bend at odd angles, and pain like he has never felt shoots through him before numbing into nearly nothing.

*Soldiers,* his grandmother said once about his father's death fighting Santa Anna in Mexico, *fools who die for another man's folly.*

He now knows why she wouldn't touch him, why she only used the sight on him once. He was given vision so that he could make choices. He didn't look; he didn't see. The choice he made was the one he was supposed to avoid.

Cold. He is so cold.

And alone. He wants the bumpkin to come over, anything to give him one last chance at making an impression. But no one comes. He tries to close his eyes, but his strength is gone. The last thing he sees is something he has seen before, but never understood—the zigzag pattern of his own blood on freshly fallen snow.

Cold.

He will never be warm again.

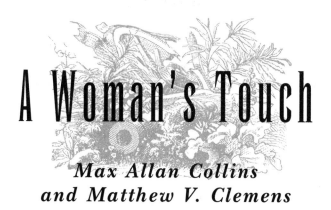

# A Woman's Touch

## Max Allan Collins
## and Matthew V. Clemens

T he unmistakable click of a cocking pistol told
Sergeant James Harley he'd just made a terrible mistake. On his haunches, bent over the narrow creek,
Harley knew he'd never reach his holstered Remington in
time. With the sun retreating, and the dense forest all
around, he may not have made a perfect target, but apparently good enough a one for that Reb—somewhere on his
right, on the opposite bank—to draw a bead on him.

His voice low and tight with tension, Harley said, "Not
very neighborly, shootin' a man while he's wettin' his whistle."

The Reb said nothing.

*Smart,* Harley thought, fingers edging ever closer
toward his holster. Though the flap was unsnapped, it still
covered the pistol butt and he knew the odds were long that
his revolver would even clear his holster, let alone get off a
shot. Sweat beaded his brow, though the promise of a cool
evening hung in the September air.

Chickamauga Creek—as Harley had heard Lieutenant
Patterson of Company E call it two days before—had turned

into a bloodbath for the Federals, especially Harley's outfit, the 100th Illinois Infantry. Though General William Rosecrans's Army of the Cumberland had succeeded in driving the Rebs out of Chattanooga—and forced them east of Chickamauga, Georgia—the Confederates had, in the last two days, mounted a slashing counterattack that had left Rosecrans's command in tatters, sending Harley and the boys of the 100th running in any direction where they didn't see Johnny Rebs.

That was how Harley had gotten separated from his unit in the first place. When the line broke, two of Harley's best chums—Matthew Bush and Albert Deal—had been cut down right before his eyes, dropping like so much kindling. The next thing Harley knew, the entire Federal army sprinted past in full retreat, and Rebs were everywhere, separating him and his fleeing comrades-in-arms.

He'd found a good place to hide in a small swale in a stand of pines. Pulling the body of a dead Reb over him as camouflage, Harley waited for the fighting to move far away.

The Reb smelled of gunpowder, blood, and death. The body's weight pressed like a grain sack on his back, but Harley gritted his teeth, steeled himself and stayed under the corpse as long as he could, his face mashed to the earth. Still, he felt those lifeless eyes boring a hole in his head, and he wondered if ever he would be able to wash the stench of death off of him.

Now that he'd finally tossed off the foul-smelling corpse and gingerly moved to the creek bank from his hiding place— thirsty, yes, but mostly wanting to clean that smell off of him!— it seemed he'd have to pay for his impatience with his life.

"You don't have to kill me, friend," Harley said, fighting to keep his fear under control. "I'm separated from my boys. Hell, for all I know, I'm the last one. You fellers whupped us good today." As he spoke, his fingers inched ever closer to his only chance.

"Yeah, we did," came a drawl from slightly farther upstream than Harley had anticipated. "An' now I'm gonna whup you, Yank."

"No need, Reb. You got yourself a prisoner!"

"Provisions are short enough for our side, 'friend.'"

"Not even goin' to give me a chance, Johnny?" asked Harley, easing his fingers nearer the grip of the pistol.

"You're havin' your chance right now," the Reb said, a grin in his voice.

*Shit!* Harley thought. The Reb had been playing with him the whole time, reeling him in like a big flapping trout.

No time for further conversation; no more verbal parries and thrusts, no waiting for the Reb to say anything else, because that Reb had said everything he had to say, already . . . .

Harley drove off his haunches, and dived into the creek. Just before he splashed into the water, something drilled through his right shoulder and spun him in mid-air. As he broke the surface, his mouth opened to scream, but instead of sound coming out, the frigid creek water rushed in.

Sputtering for breath, Harley exploded out of the water, his Remington in his left hand. The Reb who had stepped out from behind a tree had only enough time for a look of shock to register before Harley—praying God or luck was with him, and that the water had not silenced his weapon—squeezed the trigger and, yes, the roar shattered the stillness of the forest as a bullet tore into the Reb's chest, a pinkish cloud puffing from the hole as he sank to the ground, sat there looking confused for perhaps a second, perhaps two—and died.

"Damn Johnny Reb," Harley muttered as he spun around looking for friends of the slain Confederate.

But as he slowly scanned the trees and foliage, he saw no one—not even a bird, the shot having scattered them—and he realized that the Reb must have been separated from his outfit as well.

"Just my damned luck," he said (already forgetting how fortunate he'd been that his Remington had fired), as he gently probed the hole in his shoulder. It didn't really hurt, at least not like he thought it would. While the skin burned, especially right around the wound, his arm felt surprisingly cold, and heavy, and useless. His stomach began to churn, his eyes burning as sweat dripped from his lank blond bangs, and his balance wanted to betray him, his head spinning.

*Can't go down,* he thought. If he passed out here, well, that'd pretty much be the end of the trail for him. Unsteadily, he holstered his pistol, untied the kerchief from around his neck and used it as a compress on his wound. He knew he needed a tourniquet, but didn't have anything to use and didn't know if he could tie it with one hand anyway. Maybe the dead Reb had something he could use.

Crossing the creek as quickly as he could, Harley plopped down next to the man who'd plugged him—a fellow in his late twenties with flaxen hair and sky-blue eyes, staring eyes, which Harley thumbed closed. He considered saying a brief prayer for his late opponent, then thought, *To hell with it.*

The Reb had been an officer—his uniform said so—a lieutenant . . . a lieutenant who had somehow lost his belt and replaced it with a length of rope, which Harley stripped off the corpse. He tied a slipknot at one end, then gingerly slid the loop up his arm; picking up a stick nearby, he slipped it through the knot and cinched it down tight. Biting his lip against the pain, he grabbed the Reb's pistol and jammed it into his waistband.

Darkness closed around him on every side, but he didn't feel safe. The sound of the shots could have been heard by anybody for half a mile. Harley figured it wouldn't be long before greycoats were swarming all over this spot.

Ignoring the sweat running down his face, the ringing in his ears, and the cold hard throbbing in his shoulder, he pushed himself to his feet, wobbled, nearly went down, caught himself, then stumbled off into the night. Moving slowly in the pitch blackness, blundering into low-slung branches, tripping over exposed roots, Harley tried to stay within earshot of the creek without getting too close to it.

Not long after he started out, he heard thrashing from the creek and Harley pressed himself against the trunk of a tree.

"Jesus, Lucien, what the hell are you doin'?" a voice drawled.

The answer was more nasal. "Sorry, Sarge, a piece of the bank slipped away."

A third, deeper voice said, "You keep makin' noise like that, Lucien, you gonna get us all killed. Take better care."

Sliding silently to the ground, his pistol drawn, Harley tried not to even breathe until he could no longer hear the voices from the creek. He had to get away from here. He needed to head north, get back to Chattanooga, where he'd be safe. The cloudy night sky gave him no stars to navigate by and if he stayed here, sooner or later, the Rebs would find him.

Harley was fairly sure the creek ran sort of east and west, so if he just walked away from it he'd be . . . He froze. *Which side of the creek had he ended up on, north or south?* He didn't remember. During the retreat he thought they'd crossed the creek two or three times, or was it different creeks? Harley had no damned idea.

*Shit*, he thought. Forcing himself back to his feet, he turned his back to the stream and moved away from it. Right or wrong, north or south, he had to move . . . .

What seemed like a lifetime later, the first hint of light appeared on the eastern horizon—on his left.

Dropping to his knees in the tall grass, he didn't know whether to laugh or cry or pray or just scream until the Rebs came and got him: he had spent the whole night walking south. The only thing that made him feel anything other than utter dejection was knowing that the going had been so difficult, he knew he couldn't have got very far.

The only other good thing was that the dense woods had given way to smoother footing and these fields of long grass. As the sun crept slowly into the sky, Harley found himself on the edge of what appeared to be someone's farm property. In front of him the grass had been mowed down and he could see several small buildings, chicken coops he guessed, and beyond those he could make out the outline of a wide, two-story house. To his right, fields stretched as far as he could see. To his left, the same. Hunkering down just within the confines of the tall grass, he looked for signs of life.

The morning breeze carried sounds from the coops that told him there were indeed at least a few chickens over there. The clucks from the chickens were nearly drowned out by the rumbling that issued from Harley's stomach. He couldn't remember the last time he'd eaten and knew he'd lost a lot of blood.

If he didn't do something soon, he'd be a goner.

Looking around, he knew that even though the place seemed deserted, someone had to be caring for those chickens. He decided to sit tight a while, and see who came to tend the birds.

A quarter-hour passed, then another, and a third before Harley heard the chickens rustling in their coops. Easing the pistol out of his belt, he crawled forward, careful to keep the coop between himself and whoever fed the creatures. He expected that he'd find a slave dishing out grain. Maybe, just maybe, he could enlist the black man's help in getting some food, a fresh bandage, and a place to hide till nightfall. Then, he could begin making his way back to his own lines.

Excitement welled in Harley's gut as he crawled painfully to the side of the coop. He still couldn't see anyone else moving around either outside the house or through the first-floor windows. Pushing himself to his feet, his back plastered against the coop wall, Harley side-stepped to the corner and carefully peeked around the edge. He saw a flash of white muslin, then it was gone.

*A female*, he thought. He'd caught a glimpse of a dress before she moved to the second coop. Going back the way he'd come, Harley moved around the back of the first coop, checked between the buildings, then slipped up the side of the second coop. At the corner, he again peeked around searching for the slave girl. As she worked, she hummed a melody he didn't recognize. She had her back to him, tossing grain on the ground as the chickens gathered around. It seemed like a nice enough backside to Harley. He just wished she didn't have a bonnet covering her head so he could see her hair.

Stepping from the shadow of the coop, he approached her silently and stuck the barrel of his pistol into the small of her back.

"Don't move," he whispered.

She let out a little gasp, but stood still.

"Turn around real slow. I don't wanna have to shoot you."

She turned—real slow—and Harley felt his mouth go slack as he looked into the bluest eyes he'd ever seen.

"I thought you were a slave," he said numbly.

"Have you ever seen a white slave?" the woman huffed.

"No, ma'am. My apologies—how was I to know, from behind, that you were a servant girl."

The blue eyes flared. "I'm nothing of the kind. My name is Rachel Farris—Mrs. Benjamin K. Farris—and this farm belongs to my husband and myself."

Harley's eyes darted first toward the house, then toward a barn farther to his right—a building he hadn't seen earlier, because the coops blocked his view.

"You can look all you want, brigand, but you won't see him."

"Ma'am?"

"My husband." She stood up a little straighter. "Captain Benjamin Farris of the 60th Georgia Infantry."

"An officer!"

"That's what a captain is, yes." Her eyes blazed at him and a wisp of cornsilk blonde hair escaped from the edge of her bonnet.

"And where is the good captain now?"

Looking away, she said, "I haven't seen Benjamin for two long years."

"If you're lying . . . if he's in that house . . . or off getting supplies . . ." Harley raised the pistol even with her heart-shaped face and cocked the hammer.

"I am not lying," she said. "The last letter I received from my husband said he was in Virginia. That was months ago."

"Who else is here?" he asked, the pistol still leveled between her eyes. "Kinfolk? Children?"

"I have no living kin, nor any children," she said, then added, with a note of pride in her voice, "I work the place by myself."

"No slaves?"

"Benjamin and I do not believe in keeping slaves."

Harley gave her a long appraising look. "Then why does your husband fight for the Southern cause?"

Face growing pink with anger, she said, "Just because we don't keep slaves doesn't mean that we accept the North's idea of how we should live."

"We should get into the house," Harley said almost absently, as he tried to digest what she'd said. "No telling who might wander by."

"Must you have to point that awful thing at me?" Mrs. Farris asked.

Harley looked at the Remington curiously, as if he'd forgotten the weapon was in his hand. Slowly, he lowered it, gesturing with it at the same time. "Start movin'."

"Would you be so kind as to allow me to finish feeding my chickens first?"

He shook his head. "No. You be so kind as to get your pretty self inside that house . . . ma'am."

The house had looked better from a distance. As he drew closer, Harley could see chipped paint, loose boards, and a roof that looked tired from years of wear. The chicken coops and barn lay in similar disrepair, and Harley realized these facts should have told him there was no man around.

*Gonna have to be more alert,* he told himself, if he was going to get back to his lines alive. As they neared the house, Harley heard the sound of hoofbeats.

"Damnit," he said, scouring the area for cover.

Mrs. Farris looked from his wounded arm to his face. "You can hide in the barn. I'll shoo whoever it is away."

"I can't do that, lady! You'd give me up . . . !"

"Do you think I want my farm shot up, for the likes of you?" she said, the blue eyes wide and flashing. "No time to argue. Go—now!"

Feeling like he was surrendering without a fight, Harley did as she told him. He crept into the shadows of the barn just as several Confederate soldiers came around the corner of the house. Two of them—officers—rode horses, while a dozen or so infantry men followed.

"Morning, Mrs. Farris," the leader said, tossing her a casual tip of his hat.

Watching from the barn, his pistol still in his good hand, Harley wondered how long it would take the woman to betray him.

"Why, good morning, Lieutenant Pettigrew," she said melodically, butter-wouldn't-melt. "What brings you fine gentlemen out this way, so early on this lovely morning?"

Looking around the area as he dismounted, the lieutenant handed the reins of his mount to one of his soldiers. "Have you noticed anything—or anyone—out of the ordinary this morning or last night, perhaps?"

Mrs. Farris tilted her head to one side, apparently perplexed. "Out of the ordinary? How so, Lieutenant Pettigrew?"

"One of our officers was killed near the creek last night."

"Oh, my. Hostilities all around us—is there nowhere safe in the entire South?"

"Well, it wasn't safe at that creek last night." Lieutenant Pettigrew sighed gravely. "About four miles from here, it was. We figure if it was a Yank he'd have taken off north, but we're checkin' out all the local homesteads, just the same. You see, he may have been wounded and taken refuge."

Leveling his pistol at the officer, Harley watched, waiting for the woman to turn him in.

"And how have you ascertained that the Yank may have been wounded?"

"A trail of blood."

She touched fingertips to her mouth. "Oh my! Did it lead here?"

"No—it barely led anywhere . . . he must have bandaged himself shortly after the altercation. Have you seen anything, Mrs. Farris?"

Harley silently thumbed back the hammer.

She seemed to think about the question for a long moment before saying, "No, Lieutenant, nothing out of the ordinary."

Though the officer nodded, he didn't seem satisfied. "As I say, he may have taken refuge. We'll just have a look around anyway. You have no objection, certainly . . ."

Keeping the pistol pointed in the general direction of the yard, Harley desperately searched the shadowy barn for a hiding place. Two stables in one corner stood empty, mounds of hay littering their floors. Next to the nearest stall a sharp-looking pitchfork leaned against the wall. Harley played out the scene in his mind and rejected the stalls. On the back wall he saw a ladder that led to the hayloft above. It might not be any safer up there, but at least he'd have the high ground.

"Of course not!" the woman was saying. "I appreciate these efforts to assure my safety . . . but I haven't seen anyone—Yankee or one of our boys—in over a week."

Harley quit listening to their conversation and as stealthily as he could he made his way to the ladder. The thing creaked as though it might give way under his weight, and he worried that the noise might be enough for the soldiers to hear. He tucked the pistol back in his belt, feeling naked as he slowly hauled himself up the ladder with his one good hand.

Harley had just slid down behind two stacked hay bales when he heard the voices.

"Leonard, you and Heyward check out the barn."

"Barn, yes, sir," Leonard drawled.

Pulling the Reb pistol from his belt and resting it on the floor in front of him, Harley unholstered his Remington and prepared to make his final stand. Beneath him, he heard the two Rebs moving around.

"Mrs. Farris sure is a fine-lookin' woman," Heyward said.

"You better get that thought right outta your head—she's married to an officer!"

"He ain't been around in nigh on two years. If I had me a woman that pretty, I wouldn't be off fightin'—I'd be right at home takin' care of what was mine."

"Be quiet, you fool, and check the damned loft."

Harley's breathing stopped as he heard the creak of the ladder as Heyward stepped on the first rung. Upon the third creak, Harley cocked the Remington.

A voice Harley didn't recognize said, "You boys findin' anything?"

"Nope," Leonard replied. "Nothin' here but hay and manure."

"C'mon then—we got lots of other places to check out."

"All right."

The men talking had drowned out the sound of Heyward on the ladder, but Harley fully expected to find the man there when he raised up. He took a deep breath and prepared to start the fight.

"C'mon, Heyward!" Leonard called from below. "We're headin' out!"

Harley froze.

"I'm on my way," Heyward answered, his voice sounding very nearby.

Then the ladder groaned several times as the Reb climbed down.

Not daring to believe his good fortune, Harley crawled on his belly to the wall that faced the yard and peered between the boards. The lieutenant was back on his horse and leading his men away from the house.

"You know you're always welcome, Lieutenant Pettigrew," Rachel Farris said as she waved to the departing column.

Pettigrew tipped his hat in her direction then led his troops back to the road.

Harley rolled over on his back, let out a long breath, and shook his head. He couldn't believe his luck!

"Are you in here?" she asked, her voice barely above a whisper.

He said nothing.

"Yankee, I asked, are you in here?" she repeated, almost yelling.

"Up here!" he answered, finally.

He heard her climbing the ladder, crossing the whining boards of the loft, then he looked up to see her peering down at him.

She asked, "Are you all right?"

"Fit as a fiddle."

"You look tired. You look as if you might pass out any second."

He swallowed. "I am tired."

"How is your arm?"

Biting his lip, he said, "It burns like hellfire."

She frowned in sympathy. "Can you manage getting down the ladder?"

"I . . . I think so."

She helped him to his feet, led him to the ladder, then went down first. He followed slowly, his arm throbbing and still hanging uselessly at his side. By the time his boots touched the floor, sweat drenched his shirt, he felt wobbly, and he wondered if he had the strength to reach the house.

Allowing himself to slip to a seated position on the floor, Harley groaned. "Need to rest."

She looked toward the yard, then at him. "All right—for a minute or two . . . then we'll move you inside the house."

"You didn't turn me over to them," he said, his eyes searching hers.

"No."

"You easily could have."

"You might have shot me."

"No. You could have screamed and scurried out of range. Why didn't you?"

"Scream and scurry?"

"Turn me over."

"I . . . I'm not entirely sure. Maybe because you're hurt. Maybe because you didn't hurt me when you could have. Maybe because I would hope some other soft-hearted, soft-headed woman might do the same for my own wounded husband . . . Maybe it's the brown of your eyes . . . or maybe I don't really know, exactly."

"Maybe you figure there's been enough killing."

"May well be."

"Well . . . thank you," he said. Awkwardly, getting a lift from her, he rose.

Her eyes locked on his.

"Did you . . . did you kill that man by the creek?"

"Yes I did."

"And he's the one who shot you?"

Harley nodded. "That's what soldiers do, in war—shoot at each other."

She shivered at the thought. "Well, let's get you inside the house and I'll bandage that arm properly. You seem to have lost a great deal of blood. Can you walk?"

"I believe so."

She ducked under his good shoulder, tucked one arm around his back and held his left hand in hers at her shoulder. "I'll help you."

Harley inhaled her fragrance. She smelled of spring flowers and soap. Such a simple combination of scents, and yet he couldn't remember anything ever smelling so sweet.

He told her so.

Blushing, she said, "Thank you."

They got into the house and she helped him ease into a chair at the kitchen table. Sweat ran down his face and he felt as though he had a fever.

"I'll fetch a pail of water, then I can dress that properly."

"Thank you, ma'am." He didn't know what else to say.

She went outside and he looked around the kitchen. The yellow room reflected the sunlight streaming through the windows and reminded him of the parson's house back home. Dishes lay stacked neatly on shelves on one wall. A stove stood against the opposite wall, a small pile of wood in a box next to it. On a counter opposite him a loaf of freshly baked bread cooled next to a jar of preserves. The aroma made him homesick.

Though he had no wife back in Illinois, his mother would come over and bake bread in his stove. He loved the smell of freshly baked bread. The room reminded him of his mother's kitchen—it too had a distinct woman's touch to it.

When she returned with the pail of water, Harley rose to take the bucket, but she motioned him back to his chair. "You just sit down. I can handle this. I've been hauling water for two years now, I'm plenty used to it."

He watched as she filled a basin, moving with the easy confidence of a man, and the grace of the beautiful woman she was.

Then she turned and said, "Let me help you upstairs."

"I can walk, ma'am."

"Not without my help."

The basin cradled in one arm, she slipped the other around his waist, and they made their way down a short hallway into the parlor. A maroon velvet chaise sat against one wall, three wing chairs in various colors and materials were scattered around the chaise and the low table that squatted in front of it. This room carried the scent of Rachel with just the faintest hint of old cigars to tell Harley that she hadn't been the only one living here.

Struggling up the front stairs, the pair paused halfway so Harley could catch his breath.

Sweat poured down his cheeks now, his head swam again, and the wound in his shoulder burned down to the bone.

"Are you all right?" she asked, huffing some herself from the exertion of holding him up.

Gritting his teeth, Harley nodded.

She led him up the rest of the stairs, and turned into the first room on the left, the master bedroom. A tall oak armoire stood against the wall next to the door, a small writing desk and chair perched under the room's large window. Sunlight filtered in through gauzy curtains, haloing the large four-poster bed.

"Sit down," she said, helping him to the edge of the bed.

Harley did as he was told. "You've been running this place alone for two years?"

She nodded. "Are you surprised by that?"

He shrugged. "A mite, I guess."

"Because I'm a woman?" she asked, trace of a smile at the corners of her mouth.

"Well . . . there's no denying you're a woman."

Looking him square in the eye, she moved in front of him, lifted the Reb pistol from his belt and laid it on the writing desk behind her. Then she unlatched his belt and holster and placed them on the desk as well. Stepping close, she began unbuttoning his blue wool shirt. "Women can do a lot if they're given half a chance."

He glanced around the room, suddenly unable to meet her eyes. Harley felt warmer than he had even a minute ago, and now he was pretty sure it wasn't just fever. She leaned in close to help him pull his injured arm out of the uniform shirt. Her bouquet filled his head with thoughts he knew he shouldn't be entertaining this far behind enemy lines, the swell of her bosom just inches away, inviting sweet surrender.

"I'll be back shortly," she said.

Woozy from both the wound and her scent, Harley managed only a nod.

Soon she returned with a white bedsheet. She removed his makeshift bandage, tore the sheet into strips and scrubbed his wound clean. His fingers throbbed as the pain worked its way down his arm. Tearing more of the sheet, she fashioned him a new bandage and wrapped his wound.

She asked, "How does that feel?"

Harley mumbled something, felt his eyelids growing heavy, his body turning to stone. His feet were lifted and he felt himself fall back for what felt like an eternity before he landed gently on fluffy pillows. He wondered if he'd landed on clouds, then suddenly remembered he was on a bed.

"It's going to be fine, just fine," she said, her voice soothing but faraway now. "You merely need a little rest."

He tried to reply, but the words wedged behind the thick brick that his tongue had become.

Easing a cool towel onto his forehead, Rachel said, "Don't try to talk—just calm yourself."

Again, Harley felt his lips move but heard no words come out, and his eyelids lowered, like a curtain on a play's first act.

When he awoke, sunshine still poured through the window and he figured he'd slept perhaps an hour. He had just managed to sit up, when she whirled through the door in a calico dress.

"How do you feel today?"

He tried to smile. "Mite better . . . that little nap sure helped . . . Today? What do you mean?"

"That 'little nap' lasted you just over twenty-four hours."

Gaping at her, he said, "You're joshing!"

She shook her head.

Harley looked around the room as if there were some way to see the passage of time on the articles scattered around. Everything looked the same, though. His guns still lay on the desk across the room, the curtains still hung the same way, nothing had changed. "Twenty-four hours?"

"Hmmm hmmm." Rachel bent over him to check his dressing. "Looks better . . . nice and clean . . . not red a'tall."

"Doesn't hurt much," he lied.

"Such strong arms," she said idly, trailing a finger over the biceps of his left arm. "I like strength in a man."

Harley's pulse pounded in his ears and finally his eyes settled on hers and locked. He saw the desire there, the same passion he felt. Pulling her to him, he pressed his lips to hers.

The urgency of her response told him he'd made the right decision. Her tongue jabbed into his mouth, hot and probing, making him forget any pain in his arm.

Then she gazed at him, breathing heavily, the cornsilk hair tousled, and said, "There are things a woman . . . a woman alone can't do for herself . . ."

They undressed each other, beside the bed, and it was by turns graceful and awkward, measured and rushed, and Harley was stunned by the beauty of the body hidden beneath the white dress and petticoats. He cupped her round, full breasts in his hands as his mouth eagerly sought the pink tips. As if doing their own bidding, his fingers traced the lines of her ribs, her hips, her thighs.

As he eased her onto the bed, her moans sounded like a choir to him as she threw her arms around his neck. Pulling his head up to her face, she kissed him and whispered, "Please, please . . . please . . ."

Needing no further encouragement, Harley slipped inside her and any thoughts of the war, the Rebs, or any world outside the two of them vanished in a whirl of desire.

Their tryst completed, each reverted to modesty and dressed quickly. Harley, discreetly turning his back as Rachel finished repairing her appearance, glanced out the window to look down upon a Confederate on horseback coming up from behind the chicken coops, just where he had approached now so long ago.

"Shit," Harley hissed. "Another damn soldier!"

"Lieutenant Pettigrew must have sent a rider back for something," Rachel said, and then looked over his shoulder, out the window, then turned toward the desk where Harley's pistols lay.

"Am I safe up here?" he asked, one eye still on the approaching rider. "You can go down and deal with that soldier, surely?"

She didn't answer.

For the second time in less than twenty-four hours, he heard the ominous sound of a pistol being cocked. He turned to find Rachel aiming the dead Reb's pistol at his chest.

"This time," she said, not unkindly, "you're not safe, and you can't hide."

"What are you saying? That you've had your tumble and now you're turning me over to them?"

Her reply was a squeeze of the trigger, and the world exploded, something hammered him in the chest and he found himself on his back, on the floor, at the foot of the bed, looking up at the ceiling. Surprisingly, he felt no pain. His brain registered what had happened and his ears rang from the sound of the shot, but no pain, no pain . . .

Her words sounded distant and didn't really make sense; she seemed to be speaking to herself, not him: "Your kind pillages and rapes . . . every soldier understands that . . ."

Trying to speak, Harley gagged on his own blood. Were those bootheels on the stairs, or some distant drum? Her final words were whispered, or seemed to be whispered; at any rate, he barely heard them before slipping into blackness.

"You see, my love, that Reb is my husband—and that makes you just another damn Yankee."

# Ghost

### Bradley H. Sinor

After three years of war I thought I had seen everything.

The last thing that you expect to see on a hot afternoon in Richmond is a ghost. And certainly not one standing in the front door of the Capitol Building of the Confederacy.

Well, I saw one.

I tied up my horse at a hitching post on the southeast corner of the building, in an area away from the main door. I had arrived a quarter-hour early for my appointment with General Morgan Girard, my commanding officer. A soldier, obviously on guard duty, approached me, his rifle carried low in his left hand.

"Excuse me, sir. This area is restricted to army officers only."

"As well it should be," I said. "Which is exactly why I'm leaving my horse here."

"Sir," he said. "It's for *army* officers only. The civilian areas are around the corner." He put a special bit of emphasis on the word *army*.

Because of the nature of my work, I've been more often out of uniform than in one. There are places where a uniform would stick out as much as Abraham Lincoln walking the streets of Richmond.

I held my identification where he could see it.

"Sir, I'm afraid I can't . . . read," he said.

"That's all right, son. I'm Captain Adam Thorne, military intelligence."

He eyed me for a moment. Then he snapped to attention, his rifle sliding down to rest at his side in the proper manner.

"Sir, sorry for bothering you. I've been ordered to stop any civilians from leaving their animals here."

"Not a problem. You just keep on doing your duty. I wish more of our people were as adamant as you."

"Do you have a match, Private?" I said as I pulled a cheroot from my inside coat pocket. He passed a Lucifer match to me. I had just dragged it along the bottom of my boot when I saw the ghost.

She was standing at the top of the stairway, looking off in the distance. Jenny, a vision in blue, her long red hair hung loosely on her shoulders, the parasol in one hand, to protect her from the sun.

"Jenny?" I muttered, unsure of even the sound of my own voice. Not that I expected her to hear me.

"Captain? Are you all right, sir?"

The guard was looking at me with the uncertainty that a lot of enlisted men seem to have when dealing with officers. Before I could do or say anything, pain shot through the tips of my fingers. I realized that the match had burned down and was attempting to steal a few seconds more of life by using my flesh as its home. I dropped the burning ember and stamped on it with my foot.

"Captain?"

"I'm all right. My mind was elsewhere." When I looked back, she was gone. If she had ever been there in the first place.

The memory of the headstone bearing her name was as fresh as the first time I had seen it three years before. No, it had to have been my imagination, it couldn't have been Jenny.

Yet . . .

"RIGHT ON TIME. NOT that I would expect anything less than that from you, Thorne."

Brigadier General Morgan Girard stood up from behind his desk. He was not physically a big man, standing barely five feet, eight inches tall, yet he always seemed to fill whatever room he occupied.

Girard had recruited me within a week of when the war for independence had begun. As a graduate of West Point, I had expected to serve our new country in the regular army. Instead, I found my talents being put to use in other ways. Our office was attached to the Secret Service, but they preferred not to talk too loudly about the connection.

"It's always good to see you, sir," I said. "I was sorry to hear about Mrs. Girard. I know her death must have taken a great toll on you."

"Thank you, Adam. These last few months have been very hard. But thankfully, I've had the boys, George and Derrick. They've been a source of great strength for me," he said.

"I've been told it was her heart?"

"Yes, I came into the bedroom one morning and found her. She had slipped away in the night. She just lay there, peacefully. I sat with her for an hour, before I kissed her cold blue lips and found the strength to summon the rest of the house," he said.

There were few things, outside of his job, that I had seen Girard care passionately about. His wife, Allison, had been one, his two sons the others.

"Well, I'm not the only one to have lost loved ones in this war, so enough about me. Let's talk about what you're going to be doing next. I think you'll find it not nearly as big of a problem as that matter in New Orleans," he said.

That would be a relief. I preferred not to dwell on the New Orleans matter any more than necessary. There were, at times, things a soldier had to do in service for his country. You didn't have to like them, but they had to be done. New Orleans had been one of them.

"I'm putting you in charge of security for Lord Anthony Case-Jones."

"I take it this fellow isn't your average traveler on a grand tour over here instead of in Europe."

"Far from it. He's a special representative from Prince Albert sent here to prepare recommendations on the question of diplomatic recognition."

Girard didn't have to explain the significance of that move. Diplomatic recognition would be a godsend for this country. It could bring us aid and allies, which we desperately needed. I had come to the conclusion a few months earlier that shy of a major miracle there was no way that we could win this war.

This might be that miracle.

"You'll meet his lordship tonight. He's staying with an old family friend of mine, James Collins," said Girard.

"So how does his lordship feel about having a shadow?"

"It doesn't really matter what he wants or doesn't want. He will be protected," said Girard. "I'll send a carriage for you tonight at eight. We dine at nine."

I knew when I had been dismissed.

"CAPTAIN THORNE! CAPTAIN THORNE!"

I was just fastening the last button on my waistcoat when someone started pounding on my hotel room door. My watch indicated half past six.

"Captain Thorne! Captain Thorne!"

"A moment," I answered. After slipping on my jacket I picked up a small pistol from the table. Just because someone knew my name and where to find me didn't mean that they had my best interests at heart. There are certain things that you have to do to stay alive. Better to do them and not need them than to lay bleeding and regretful minutes later.

"Yes?" I said, standing to one side of the door.

"Captain Thorne. General Girard sent me. My name is Cole Masterson," he said.

Cole Masterson turned out to be a lanky man in his thirties. He had an odd accent, one that I couldn't place.

"I wasn't expecting anyone until eight."

"I understand, sir. However, something has happened and the general wants you to come to the Collins house as soon as possible. He sent me with a carriage and orders to bring you there straight away."

"Can you tell me what happened?"

"No, sir. The general said he would brief you upon your arrival," said Masterson.

That sounded like him. I dropped the pistol into my coat pocket, picked up my hat, and motioned Masterson to follow me.

THE COLLINS FAMILY HOME was an elegant three-story affair, built at the turn of the century on the south edge of Richmond. Several rooms on the first floor were so brightly lit that they fairly glowed in the fading July sunlight.

We were met by a man in his fifties, balding with a fringe of iron gray hair, whom I presumed to be the family butler. He was accompanied by a young nigger boy who took charge of the carriage, without a word.

"If you gentlemen would come with me, you're expected," said the butler.

I didn't know too much about the Collins family. The great-grandfather had emigrated to the United States just after the first war for independence. They had extensive mine, manufacturing and farm holdings.

Girard was waiting for us in the entrance hall. He wore his usual grim expression, an unlit cigar in his mouth.

"Good evening, sir," I said.

"Ah, you made good time, Thorne. Masterson, I need you to take this to the naval office." He handed an envelope to Masterson, who promptly saluted and left without a word.

"Well, Thorne, I had hoped that this evening would be a pleasant interlude for the both of us. So much for those hopes," said Girard. He motioned for me to follow him through a pair of double doors into what proved to be the library. It was a big room with floor-to-ceiling bookcases and a fireplace at one end. Two oil lamps were the only sources of light.

The general gestured toward a wing chair in one corner. Someone sat there; a man in his late forties with heavy sideburns and a dark tropical tan. His eyes were milky gray stones sunk deep into his face. Only, now that I looked at him, it wasn't his face that caught my attention. What looked like a long red sash ran across the front of his jacket, up over his shirt, and onto a deep gash in his neck.

"Do I take it that this might happen to be the gentleman who you wanted me to keep alive, Lord Anthony Case-Jones?"

"Indeed."

Well, so much for that assignment. I glanced around the room and in a dim mirror on the far side of the room I saw the ghost again. Just for a moment, peering out from a booklined alcove on the other side of the room. Only this time it was wearing the black dress and white-collared uniform of a maid. It was Jenny! She was gone just as quickly as the first time I had seen her.

"Well, I don't know what recommendations his lordship had in mind, but I would say that someone did not approve of it," I said.

"Then you agree with me that this is very likely the work of Yankee agents," said Girard.

"Possibly," I said. "Who all is in the house?"

"Just Collins, his lordship's traveling secretary named Rodney, and us. The rest of the Collins family has been living on one of his plantations near Florida for the past six or seven months. There are several hired servants, the butler who you met, a cook along with a couple of general handyman types," said Girard.

"What about slaves?"

"Amazingly, none. The handymen are niggers, but they've both been manumitted. I honestly hope that we find out it is a personal thing, rather than a political one. That will make it far easier to explain," muttered Girard. "But whatever the reason, I want answers as soon as possible."

"If you would get everyone in the living room, I think we can begin there," I said. "I want to have a closer look at a few things about his lordship, here. Shall we say in fifteen minutes or so?"

"Agreed," said Girard.

After he left I gingerly slid my hands into the dead man's pockets. There was little there of interest; a handful of coins, a pencil, and several peanut shells. My manipulations caused him to slump to one side. That was when I noticed an inch or so of chain sticking clear of his shirt collar. It was a medallion of some sort. I thought at first it was one of those religious ones, but when I drew it free I could see a single letter engraved on each side.

"Don't you think it's about time that you came out," I said.

There was no response, certainly not from his lordship. But he wasn't who I had been speaking to.

"I saw you in the mirror. I'm going to presume you've been listening and watching since then," I said.

To my left I heard the slightest sound of metal creaking and hinges at work. Out of the corner of my eye, I caught sight of one of the bookcases swinging back into place.

"Can I get you a drink?" said the ghost. She looked every inch the proper ladies' maid. Her red hair had been wound beneath a white mob cap. At first glance it would have been hard to recognize her, but this close there was no mistaking my sister, Jenny.

"Yes. Scotch," I said.

She poured me two fingers of amber liquid from a bottle on a table near the fireplace. Then poured herself a twin of my offering.

"I hope you don't mind drinking with the hired help," she said.

"As if you were really the hired help," I said. "I imagine the only reason that you are employed on these premises is because you wanted to be."

"A girl has to earn a living," she said defensively.

"Are you saying that Davis Walker doesn't pay his spies well enough?"

I've always enjoyed being able to pull a rabbit out of my hat and surprise my sister. The astonished look on Jenny's face was enough to prove that I had not lost my skill.

"Not bad, little brother, not bad at all," she said.

Major General Davis Walker was Girard's opposite number on the Northern side. I had encountered one of his men in Cuba six months before. We had gone to West Point together and considered ourselves friends still, in spite of political differences. Besides, our particular assignments at that time did not conflict, so we spent the evening drinking and reminiscing. It was somewhere past the second bottle of rum that he mentioned to me that Jenny had gone to work for Walker.

"Looks like there are two Thornes in the spy business now," he had said.

"So, do you like working for the enemy?" I said.

"Adam, I don't consider what I do as working for the enemy. I'm working for the country that we were both born in. But let's not get started on any political discussions. I had enough of them with Father. How is he, by the way?"

"Still as hardheaded and stubborn as ever. You know that he considers you to be dead. He even went so far as to erect a headstone for you in the family plot."

I'd been there the day that he had it set in place. I suspect he would have held a formal funeral service for her, but my mother, and the local parson, had said no to that idea.

He and Jenny had disagreed on things for most of my life: slavery, politics, the proper way to respect one's parents. Their shouting matches were legend in our family. It had been her falling in love with Nathan Jackson, a Northerner, and wanting to marry him that had driven our father and her to the breaking point. It had stormed the night the two of them drove off together, four years ago. That had been the night my father had announced that as far as he, and the family, were concerned, his daughter Jennifer was dead.

So I suppose, from my father's point of view, I was talking with a ghost.

"You heard about Nathan?" she said.

"Yes, a botched bank robbery, and he was in the wrong place at the wrong time. Was that what drove you to work for Walker?"

"Among other things," she said quietly.

"You responsible for this?" I gestured at his lordship.

"Hardly. We learned he was coming, and I was sent to keep an eye on him. A dead envoy will not help the United States' relationship with Great Britain. It might even be enough to drive them into recognizing you.

"Besides, it is my understanding that he was going to file a report saying that the English should stay neutral in the whole matter. Something to the effect of letting us settle our own internal matters," she said.

"THIS IS HARDLY THE way you normally investigate a murder," said Girard. "However, you all must realize this is not a normal murder. Otherwise, we would have summoned the local police at once."

Girard was pacing back and forth in front of the leather couch that took up most of the main living room of the Collinses' house. Our host, James Collins, was a man in his mid-fifties, but seemed older. He stood near the large bay window that dominated the room. Seated near the door was Alexander Rodney, the late Lord Case-Jones's traveling secretary.

"Sir, why are you wasting your time here?" said Rodney. "It's obvious that a Yankee agent murdered his lordship. You should be pursuing him. The fiend is no doubt halfway to Washington by now."

I didn't like Rodney's tone and his presumption.

"We are pursuing all avenues of investigation, Mr. Rodney. Not just in this house, but elsewhere, as well," I said. "Do you have a particular reason to believe that the North even knows that you are in this country?"

The secretary's face burned red with anger. "Of course they know we're in this country! I have no doubt that detailed reports of our every move are making their way to Abraham Lincoln's desk in each morning's mail.

"Are you aware, sir, of the delicacy of our trip here? There are members of the government who do not want to grant the Confederacy diplomatic recognition. They want us to formally ally with the United States against you."

"The general has seen fit to brief me on your mission. I only wish I had been brought into the matter sooner. Perhaps we could have prevented this murder," I said.

"I doubt that," said Rodney.

"Mr. Collins, where were you and Mr. Rodney earlier this evening?" I asked.

"Business kept me away from the house for most of today. I had barely returned home when Morgan discovered his lordship's body. I last saw him this morning at breakfast. In fact, that's also the last place I saw Mr. Rodney," said Collins.

"Don't go trying to accuse me, sir. It was Northern assassins!" said Rodney. "In the last fifteen years I've traveled to many countries with his lordship. But this is the most vile one I think I have ever encountered!"

"General, the stories you told us of this country were enough to frighten any sane man. But all they did was make his lordship want to come here all the more," said Rodney.

"You had met Case-Jones before, General?" I asked. It was a fact that he had not mentioned.

"Yes, Allison and I spent a year in Europe and England before the war. I believe we met him at the Burton estate in Sussex," said Girard.

"Enough of this!" said Rodney. "You must stop gibbering like old women and find the killers. They are getting farther away with each passing minute!"

"Oh, I think not?"

"Really? Would you care to explain, Thorne?" said Girard.

"Actually, gentlemen, I know who killed his lordship. I have only one more matter to confirm before settling this entire matter," I said.

THE SITTING ROOM AND bedroom that had been assigned to Case-Jones was midway down the hall on the house's third floor. It wasn't locked; there was no need. So I let myself in. If the whole thing were the work of Yankee assassins, then no doubt they were, as Rodney seemed so convinced, long gone.

Everything in the room was as neat and orderly as if the maids had just finished cleaning up the room. I opened the closet and found each of Case-Jones's suits perfectly arranged. Three pairs of boots, which I suspected were shined to within an inch of their lives, sat on the floor.

I was about to inspect one when something struck me hard across the back of the head. The blow didn't knock me out, but I had to grab onto the door frame to keep on my feet. Whoever my attacker was followed with a swift kick that connected to my hip and almost sent me down.

Somewhere in that process I realized that I still had one of Case-Jones's boots in my hand. I threw it at my opponent, missing, of course, but that bought me time enough to get back on my feet and face him.

Without really thinking I threw myself against him, sending both of us tumbling down. What I presumed to be a knife went clattering to the wooden floor. My own pistol was in an inside coat pocket and caught between the two of us, essentially unreachable.

"I'd suggest that you boys call this whole thing off right now!"

Jenny! She was standing with a gun of her own in one hand. The expression on her face as cold and unfeeling as any I had ever seen.

"Are you all right, Captain Thorne?" she asked. Better not to acknowledge each other.

"Aye, and very grateful to you."

I looked down at the familiar face of my opponent. Morgan Girard.

"YOU'RE INSANE, THORNE," SAID Girard.

I'd had the butler summon the two nigger handymen who were now standing on either side of Girard. He hadn't really wanted to come back to the living room, but the barrel of the gun I had taken from Jenny and held in the small of his back provided a powerful argument in favor of doing what he was told.

Jenny had excused herself, claiming to feel close to fainting now that it was all over. Officially, she had been passing by the room, heard the scuffling, and went in to investigate. Actually, I had left her hidden in the hallway, waiting to see who might come along.

"See here, Captain Thorne, I hope that you know what you're doing," said Collins. "I've known Morgan Girard since we were both small children. I cannot conceive of the idea that he is a killer."

"Then perhaps you had best learn," I said.

"So, what is it you're claiming? Is he a Yankee spy and killer?" asked Rodney.

"Killer, yes. But I doubt he is a Yankee spy. I have no doubt of his loyalty to the Confederacy," I said. "He just wanted us to think that a Yankee spy was behind the murder. It would keep people from realizing that it was actually a matter of jealousy, revenge, and, more than likely, double murder."

"Double murder?" said Rodney and Collins at the same time. "Who?"

"Yes, I'm fairly certain that in addition to murdering Lord Case-Jones, Girard also killed his wife, Allison," I said.

"Thorne, you have become a monster. You know Allison died of a weak heart," said Girard.

"Indeed, I attended her funeral," said Collins.

"But do we know that? We have only his word and the word of a doctor who no doubt made no close examination. This morning Girard told me about discovering Allison's body. He mentioned that her lips were cold and blue. It strikes me now that that may well have indicated death by either poison or suffocation," I said.

"But why? And why kill Case-Jones?" asked Collins.

I took out the medallion that I had removed from his lordship's neck and held it out where the others could see the disk. On one side was a stylized *A* and on the other an *M*. But the *M* had been obliterated.

"This is significant?" asked Rodney.

"It is, indeed," answered Collins.

"You know?" I said.

"I was there when Morgan had those made. They were his wedding present to Allison, one for her, one for him." Collins's face had grown still, showing no emotion.

I didn't have to look to see that Girard still wore his, under his shirt. I had seen it on several occasions before.

"I would suspect that during their sojourn in England, Allison Girard and Case-Jones began an affair. That was no doubt when she gave him the medallion. At some point Girard found out about it, but opted to do nothing. Perhaps he felt having an ocean between the two lovers was enough. That was until he heard that his lordship was being sent here as a special envoy. That was when he made up his mind to have his revenge, on them both," I said.

I had wondered why he had gotten me involved in the whole matter. The only reason I could conceive of was that he thought my loyalty to him would let him conceal anything that was too incriminating.

"This is a fine tale you've spun, Thorne," Girard said. "But it is nothing but pure fantasy. It's obvious to me that you've gone over the edge, pressure of the war. I've seen it in others who've worked for me. Trust me, son, I'll see that you get the best medical treatment."

"Morgan, shut up," said Collins. "He's right. You told me yourself that you knew Allison had had an affair. You know the hidden passages and panels in this house almost as well as I do. We spent many hours prowling them when we were children. So I would say that the best thing to do right now is to keep quiet."

I expected Girard to do something. But not what he did. Instead of making a grab for a weapon and trying to escape, he reached into his coat pocket and brought out a small enamel snuff box. With a slow dignified manner he administered several pinches to himself.

I don't know exactly what was in it, but the reaction came a few seconds after he set the box down. He went stiff for a moment and then his head slumped forward on his chest. I didn't bother to check; if he wasn't dead, then it was only a matter of a few minutes. Perhaps this was better than the gallows or a firing squad.

Still, the whole matter left a foul taste in my mouth. I didn't say a word to Collins or Rodney as I excused myself, went out into the hallway and lit a cheroot.

A few minutes later Jenny came up beside me. "Not the most pleasant circumstances for reunions, big brother," she said.

"No, no it wasn't," I said.

Jenny reached over and plucked the cheroot out of my hand. She lifted it to her lips and took a long puff from it, then blew the smoke out in a slow series of rings.

"I know you looked up to Girard. He was a good man who went wrong, somehow," she said.

"I think we all have that potential, little one," I said.

"You know, you're a pain, but I definitely like having you around. Be careful, and don't you go wrong," she said as she passed the cheroot back to me.

"I'll try." That I was speaking to empty air didn't surprise me. My little sister is good at what she does.

"Is there a problem, sir?" The butler came from the direction of the kitchen, looking at me rather oddly.

"No, no, nothing that won't eventually right itself," I said. "I was just standing here thinking."

"Very good, sir, although I did think I heard you speaking to someone a moment ago," he said.

"Actually I was. One of the maids, the one with red hair," I said.

"Red hair? You must be mistaken, sir, we have no maids with red hair. Besides, both of them have been working in the kitchen for some time," he said. I could see the slightest sparkle in his eye.

"Perhaps I was mistaken, Who knows, maybe I was chatting with a ghost," I said.

"Quite possible, sir," he said.

# The Last Day of the War

## James Reasoner

The rider rode hard through the South Texas chaparral. It was a hot, humid day in May, and both man and horse were sweating. The rider shifted the strap of the leather pouch he carried. The wax-sealed documents inside it were bound to be something important, he supposed, but carrying the pouch over his shoulder was uncomfortable.

He was thinking about that when the bullet struck him in the back, knocking him out of the saddle to sprawl lifeless on the sandy ground. The horse, spooked, galloped on down the narrow trail in the low, thick brush.

The rifleman stood up from the place where he had crouched in hiding until the rider passed him. He levered another cartridge into the chamber of the new Henry rifle he carried and walked forward to check the body, nodding in satisfaction when he had made sure that the man was dead.

Like the man he had just killed, the rifleman wore the uniform of the Confederate Army.

"WAKE UP, SHERIFF."

DAN KELLER stirred and lifted his head from the desk in front of him. "Wasn't sleeping," he said as he rubbed a hand over his face. "Just resting my eyes. What do you want, Dobie?"

Keller's long-nosed, big-eared, overeager little deputy jerked a thumb over his shoulder and said, "There's a fella outside with a dead body."

Keller frowned. "What's he bringing a body here for?"

"Well, you're the law, ain't you, Sheriff?"

Keller snorted. Being the sheriff of Cameron County, Texas, in the month of May and the year of Our Lord 1865 didn't amount to a whole hell of a lot. Not with Confederate troops under the command of old Rip Ford occupying Brownsville, Union troops squatting on the sandhills of the spit of land known as Brazos de Santiago to the east, and the gamblers and saloon owners and smugglers who populated Brownsville, Matamoros, across the Rio Grande, and the port city of Bagdad on the Mexican coast to the southeast really running things. Keller knew good and well the only reason all those folks allowed him to stay in office was because they figured he wouldn't rock the boat. They knew him pretty well, he supposed. He liked to drink a bit, and it was easier just to go along and get along.

"I really think you ought to take a look at this dead man, Sheriff," Dobie went on.

Keller sighed. "And why's that, Dobie?"

"Well, for one thing, he was shot in the back. And for another, he's nekkid."

That made Keller frown. Not the back-shooting part; with all the rivalries amongst the denizens of the red-light districts on both sides of the river, bushwhackings were common. But the corpses usually had clothes on when people found them.

Keller heaved himself to his feet. He was a big man, over six feet, with broad shoulders, a massive torso, and a belly that showed the results of too many bottles of *cerveza*. His curly, reddish-brown hair was beginning to show some gray. He followed Dobie to the door and snagged a broad-brimmed Mexican sombrero from a peg in the wall beside the opening. He preferred it to an American hat because it shaded him better.

The dead man lying face-down over the back of a mule was definitely naked. Keller winced, partially from the brightness of the sun and partially from the view. A Mexican farmer was holding the mule's halter. Keller went around to the other side of the animal, being careful to stay out of range of the hooves in case the jughead decided to kick, and looked at the corpse from that angle. The man had a bullet hole in his back, all right. The wound hadn't bled a lot, which meant the bushwhacker's shot probably had found the victim's heart.

The dead man had blond hair that dangled below his head. Keller grasped it and lifted so he could see the man's face. Probably early twenties, Keller judged, and definitely a stranger.

"That ain't nothing to be putting on display in the street," Keller said to Dobie as he dropped the dead man's head. "Take him on down to the undertaker's."

"What you going to do about this, Sheriff?"

"Spread the word, I guess. If anybody's missing this gent, they can go to the undertaker's and have a look at him, see if they can identify him." Keller grimaced. "If they do it early enough in the day, that is. I reckon by this evening, he'll be better off in the ground."

"You're not going to try to find out who killed him?"

Keller turned to the farmer who had brought in the body and asked in Spanish, "Where did you find this man?" The farmer answered, and Keller turned back to Dobie. "He stumbled over him out on the Laguna Espantosa trail. You know how thick the chaparral is up there. Anybody could've ambushed him, and you couldn't ever track 'em through there."

"No, I reckon not." Dobie sounded disappointed.

Keller patted him on the shoulder with a meaty hand. "Go on along, Dobie. We ain't responsible for every dead man in the world."

As he turned back toward the office door, Keller frowned again. He supposed the oath he'd sworn as sheriff sort of made him responsible for the dead men found in Cameron County, anyway. But it was hot, and he'd never been one to beat his head against a wall for no reason, so he went back inside.

"GREAT MEN HAVE TO do great things, Colonel. It's their destiny."

Colonel Theodore H. Barrett, commander of the Union garrison on Brazos de Santiago, leaned back in his chair and looked almost hopefully at his aide-de-camp, Lieutenant Dermot Pierce. "Do you really think so, Lieutenant?" Barrett asked.

"Absolutely, Colonel," Pierce replied without hesitation. "And this may be your last chance."

Barrett frowned, torn by indecision. He knew quite well that the War Against the Southern Rebellion was coming to a close. So far, Barrett had seen no action whatsoever, and his recent posting to this obscure command in a Texas backwater did not auger well for his chances of leading men into combat, especially in light of the news he had received a few days earlier.

The voters loved a military man, especially one who had been victorious against the enemy. Barrett closed his eyes for a moment, seeing visions of himself standing on a platform draped with red, white, and blue bunting, basking in the cheers of thousands of admirers whose fondest wish it was to propel him into higher and higher offices until . . . dare he think it? . . .

Barrett sat up straight and thumped a fist on the desk. "Order the men to prepare to march, Lieutenant," he said. "By God, we're going to take Palmito Hill, whether General Brown wants us to or not!"

"Seventy-five thousand dollars in gold, I tell you," said Enrique Castillo.

Colonel Flornoy shook his head. He was a medium-sized man with close-cropped, iron-gray hair. "Where would Juarista rebels get that kind of money?"

"From the British and French cotton merchants. The Union blockade has hurt them, Colonel, you know that. They must have cotton for their mills, and if the only way to get it is to smuggle it across the Rio Grande, they will do so."

Flornoy was well aware of that. The traffic in contraband cotton had been going on for several years now. But it angered him that *French* cotton merchants would buy bales from the rebel smugglers who were trying to overthrow Maximilian's glorious empire. Did they not see that they were hurting the cause of their own nation? Did they care only about money?

Flornoy knew the answer to that, of course. And he could understand it, he supposed. Was he not on the verge of making an arrangement with one of the treacherous Mexicans himself? Castillo had no more loyalty to his supposed leaders in the revolution than . . . well, than Flornoy did to his own leaders in the Emperor's army. It was a hard thing for a man to admit, even to himself, that he would exchange his beliefs for nothing more than gold.

But still, seventy-five thousand of the American dollars! With his share of that, Flornoy thought, he could vanish into the mountains of Mexico and live well no matter who won, Juarez or Maximilian. He could have a little empire all his own.

"You say they are taking the gold across to Brownsville?"

"*Si*, tomorrow."

Flornoy nodded. "We will be ready."

LIEUTENANT PIERCE WAITED UNTIL the troops had left Brazos de Santiago before saying to Colonel Barrett, "I think I ought to scout ahead, sir."

"What if you run into Confederate skirmishers?"

Pierce smiled. "I'm not afraid of a motley bunch of Rebels, Colonel."

"A commendable attitude, Lieutenant. Would you like to take a couple of troopers with you?"

"No, sir," Pierce shook his head. "I won't be gone long."

Barrett gestured for the younger officer to ride ahead. "Good luck, son. Come back quick if you spy any Rebs."

"Oh, I will, sir, you can count on that."

Pierce spurred his horse and left the column of marching infantry behind him. He could already see the low rise of Palmito Hill up ahead, although the land around here was so flat that distances were deceptive. Pierce figured it would take most of the day for the column to reach the hill.

That would work out perfectly. At least, Pierce hoped so.

He rode for a half-hour, getting well ahead of the Union troops. He didn't stop until another rider reined his horse out of a thicket of brush and raised a hand.

"Right on time, Pierce," the second man called. Like Pierce, he wore a lieutenant's uniform—only instead of blue, it was Confederate gray. "I reckon everything's going all right?"

"Just as planned," Pierce replied. "Did you take care of your end, Blaine?"

"Damn right," said the Rebel lieutenant called Blaine. "We don't have a thing to worry about."

"What about Enrique?"

"He was supposed to talk to Colonel Flornoy today."

"You think he'll go along with it?"

Blaine snorted. "For a share of that gold? That Frenchy'll cooperate, all right."

Pierce took a deep breath and asked the question that was worrying him the most. "What about the messenger from Galveston?"

Blaine took a stub of a cigar from his tunic pocket, put it in his mouth, and said around it with a smile, "You don't have to worry about him. I burned the pouch and all the documents in it. Good thing you let me know he was on his way down here. It could have ruined everything if ol' Colonel Rip had got his hands on those papers."

"Well, then." Pierce stuck his hand out. "Here's to being rich men."

Blaine shook with him. "Rich men," the Confederate repeated, relishing the sound of it.

IN THE LATE AFTERNOON, Sheriff Keller heard hoofbeats in the street outside and hoped they would go on past the office. He'd been about to go over to one of the cantinas for some supper.

The horses stopped outside, though, and after a moment bootheels rang on the boards of the porch. A tall, rangy figure in a black hat and Confederate jacket came into the office. Colonel Rip Ford had a short white beard and a craggy face that had been leaned down by illness in the past year or so. The old Ranger hadn't let being sick stop him, though. There had been a time, a couple of years earlier, when the Yankees had controlled the whole blasted Rio Grande Valley all the way up to Eagle Pass. Then Rip Ford, who wasn't even officially a member of the Confederate Army, had formed what was variously called the Cavalry of the West and the Rio Grande Expeditionary Force. It was an irregular cavalry battalion that thought of itself as fighting for the Confederacy, and the members even outfitted themselves in whatever pieces of Confederate uniform they could get their hands on. But they took orders from the Confederate Army only when it suited them, and they got damned little support in return from the Confederates.

But that hadn't stopped them from rolling right down the valley and driving the Yankees out of town after town, including Brownsville, until the only Union presence in far South Texas was the little garrison on Brazos de Santiago. Rip Ford had done that, riding at the head of his makeshift cavalry.

Keller stood up. A fellow like Ford made other men want to get to their feet. He nodded pleasantly and said, "Hello, Colonel. Something I can do for you?"

"I heard that a dead man was brought in to you this morning, Sheriff," Ford said. "I was wondering if I could take a look at him."

Keller scratched his head. "Well, uh, I'm afraid he's already been planted, Colonel. What with it being so hot today and all."

"Are you going to try to find out who killed him?" Ford had been a Texas Ranger before the war started, and Keller supposed that once a lawman, always a lawman.

"I've been asking around . . ."

"What did he look like?"

Keller could answer that question. "He was a young fella, maybe twenty-two or twenty-three, with blond hair. I never saw him before."

"You mean he was a stranger around here?"

Keller nodded. "Yes, sir, absolutely."

"And I heard as well that he was . . . unclothed."

"Naked as a jaybird," Keller said.

"That makes me wonder—" Ford began, but then he stopped as a man came into the room. Ford looked around and asked, "What the hell is it, Sergeant?"

"Beggin' your pardon, Colonel, but a rider just come in from out at Palmito Hill. Cap'n Giddings and his men are tradin' shots with a bunch of Yankees."

Ford's eyes widened in surprise and anger. "I parleyed with General Wallace myself! We agreed there would be no more fighting until we got word from back east about the disposition of the war."

"Well, I reckon the Yankees must've changed their minds, Colonel. What're we goin' to do?"

"Send out riders to call in all the cavalry units. We're going to fight, damn it!" Ford started toward the door, then stopped abruptly and looked back at Keller. "I was about to ask you, Sheriff, why a bushwhacker would steal all of a man's clothes."

"Uh . . ." That was all Keller could manage.

"Think about it," Ford snapped, and then he was gone.

Keller didn't want to think about it. He wanted to think about a big plate of beans and peppers and tortillas, washed down by a few mugs of beer. That was all he wanted on his mind.

But despite himself, as the evening went on, he found himself trying to figure out the answer to Colonel Ford's question.

GENERAL SLAUGHTER, THE OFFICIAL commander of the Confederate forces in Brownsville, wasn't as eager as Rip Ford to fight. In fact, he had already ordered that wagons be loaded with supplies for an evacuation, and he was in the middle of packing his personal belongings when Ford found him at Confederate headquarters. The old Ranger realized what was going on, and his face twisted in a grimace of disgust. "Running out, eh?"

"I plan to order a general retreat," Slaughter replied stiffly. "At this point in the war, I have no intention of provoking a major battle."

"The damn Yankees are the ones doing the provoking," Ford snapped. "You can retreat and go to hell if you want! These are my men, and I'm going to fight."

"Colonel, you can't—" Slaughter began, but Ford had already turned on his heel and was stalking out of the general's quarters. It was too late.

Too late for a lot of things, Slaughter supposed.

SEVERAL TIMES DURING THE night, Keller thought he heard gunfire in the distance. *Could be the Yankees and the Rebs still skirmishing with each other out yonder at Palmito Hill,* he thought. Sound could sometimes travel that far, especially on a calm, quiet night. If there was a real battle, though, it wouldn't come until the next day. Rip Ford was still in town, waiting for all his scattered cavalrymen to join him.

Keller rolled over in the bedroom of his little house and sleepily patted the rump of the Mexican woman who was his mistress. She stirred and turned toward him, but he wasn't interested in that right now. Instead, to his intense disgust, he found himself sitting up in bed and thinking about what Ford had asked him.

Why *would* a bushwhacker strip his victim down to the buff, especially when the dead man was a stranger?

*Because maybe,* Keller thought, *if the man had been wearing his clothes, he wouldn't exactly be a stranger anymore.*

BY THE MIDDLE OF the next morning, enough of Ford's men had shown up for the colonel to move out from Brownsville. He was riding at the head of the troops as they galloped out of town and headed for Palmito Hill to fight the Yankees.

Keller stood on the porch in front of the office and watched them ride out. When the cavalry was gone, Keller stepped down into the street and walked toward Fort Brown, down at the end of the street. It wasn't much of a fort, but it served as the official Confederate headquarters in Brownsville—just as it had been Union headquarters when the Yankees were in charge. Keller had seen it change hands and never really cared either way.

Now he was interested in talking to General Slaughter. To do that, he had to go through the general's aide, a lieutenant named Blaine. The lieutenant asked him curtly, "Why do you want to see the general?"

Keller had taken off his sombrero when he came into the office. He held it in one hand and used the other to scratch his head. "I was just wondering if the general was expecting anybody to show up yesterday."

Blaine frowned. "What are you talking about?"

"A messenger, an army courier of some sort. Or anybody else who's in the army."

"Not that I know of," Blaine said without hesitation. "And I would know if a courier was expected, so I don't see any reason to bother the general with this, Sheriff."

"You're sure?" Keller asked.

"I'm positive," Blaine answered, an edge of impatience creeping into his voice now. "What's this all about, Sheriff?"

"Well, there was this dead fella brought into town yesterday, and he didn't have any clothes on. So I got to wondering if maybe he was in the army, and the hombre who bushwhacked him took his clothes all the way down through his longjohns so nobody'd know they were army issue."

Blaine looked confused. "That seems rather far-fetched, doesn't it, Sheriff?"

"Well, yeah, I reckon it does. And I couldn't figure out any reason why a killer would want to keep it a secret that the gent he shot was a soldier. But if you weren't expecting anybody to show up . . ."

"We weren't," Blaine said firmly.

"I guess I'll have to keep pondering on it, then."

"You do that, Sheriff."

Keller left the fort and walked back to his office. Blaine waited until the sheriff was gone and then left as well.

THE TWO AMERICANS, A couple of rawboned men who'd brought several wagons full of cotton bales down from central Texas, went into a saloon called *El Cabeza de Javelina*—the Head of the Boar. The owner of the saloon was an Englishman called Whitson who had named the place after the Boar's Head Tavern back in the little English village where he'd grown up. It was a little reminder of home, the only such reminder in this hellishly hot and dry place.

In the middle of the afternoon like this, the saloon wasn't very crowded. In fact, there were no customers at all, only Whitson and a single bartender. People were inside somewhere sleeping if they had any sense. The Texans nodded to Whitson, who gestured them toward the back room. Whitson was being paid to provide some privacy for this meeting, and that was all he cared about since he was not an overly ambitious man. Otherwise, he supposed he would still be in England. The Mexicans who had arrived earlier, two of them carrying a wooden chest that was evidently heavy, were already waiting in the back room to conclude the deal.

Whitson sauntered toward the doors, intending to close and lock them behind the batwings to give his visitors even more assurance of privacy. Behind the bar, the bartender lazily polished the hardwood. Whitson reached for the knob of the right-hand door. Something blocked the light coming in from outside. He looked up and saw six men shouldering through the batwings. They were all dressed in dark suits.

"Sorry, gents," Whitson said. "Closing up temporarily. Come back in an hour or so."

The man in the lead of the odd group reached under his coat. Whitson thought he was probably reaching for a wallet. The man brought out a knife instead and thrust it into Whitson's chest as hard as he could. Whitson had time to gasp in surprise before he died.

Behind the bar, the bartender saw Whitson sag and fall. He said, "Hey—"

Pistols came out from under coats. The bartender turned pale, lifted his hands, and backed against the shelves behind the bar. One of the men covered him while the other five marched toward the back room, guns drawn.

DOBIE CAME INTO THE sheriff's office and looked around. Keller wasn't there. Dobie grinned slyly. This was his chance to go behind the desk and sit in the sheriff's chair and pretend that *he* was the sheriff. He liked to do that whenever Keller wasn't around.

But Dobie stopped short as he rounded the corner of the desk and saw the bulky form sprawled on the floor behind it. Keller was lying face down, and there was a dark stain on the back of his vest.

Dobie started to back away. His mouth opened and closed but no sound came out. He heard a sound, though, and wondered where it was coming from since he knew he wasn't making it.

After a second, he realized that Keller had let out a groan. Dobie gathered up his courage and rushed forward. Keller was moving around, trying to push himself up on hands and knees. Dobie grabbed his arm to help him, and Keller heaved upright and swung his left arm in a back-handed blow that knocked Dobie all the way across the office onto the rundown couch with its broken springs. Dust puffed up from the padding as Dobie landed on it.

Keller lumbered to his feet and said, "Stab me in the back, will you!"

"I didn't stab you, Sheriff!" Dobie cried as he held his hands out, palms toward Keller, as if that would hold off the enraged lawman. For all of his slow-moving ways, Keller was sort of like a bear when he was aroused. "I didn't stab nobody!"

Keller stopped, swayed on his feet a little, blinked a few times. "Dobie?" he finally asked.

"Yeah, it's me, Sheriff. What happened to you?"

Keller frowned and shook his head. "Somebody came in the back door. I heard it scrape on the floor. I was, uh, resting my eyes again. Started to turn around, but whoever it was stuck me with a knife."

"How come you ain't dead?"

"Good question." Keller started to reach behind him, then stopped and grimaced. "Hurts like hell, I know that much. Blade must've missed anything too important."

"I reckon it helps to carry a lot of meat on your bones."

Keller glowered some, but he said, "Yeah, I reckon." Then he said, "That son of a bitch!"

Dobie swallowed. "Who?" He hoped the sheriff wasn't talking about him. Keller looked mad enough to tear somebody's head off.

"The only one who had any reason to stab me." Keller started toward the door.

"What reason?"

"Don't know," Keller said as he grabbed his sombrero and clapped it on his head. "But I reckon he knows, and I aim to find out." He went out of the sheriff's office, the bloodstain on the back of his vest slowly spreading.

BLAINE WAS WAITING IN the alley alongside the Head of the Boar. He slid up the pane and went in the window of the back room as Colonel Flornoy and four French soldiers came in the door. Of course, the colonel and his men weren't in uniform, since they were no longer representing the Emperor Maximilian. They were out for themselves now, just like Blaine.

The Mexican rebels, who were also cotton smugglers, and the two Texan wagonmasters were caught flat-footed. One of the Mexicans was holding open the lid of a wooden chest filled with gold coins. None of the men moved as Blaine and the French renegades leveled pistols at them. Blaine grinned in satisfaction. Everything was working perfectly. He would have to split the gold with Flornoy, but they'd be long gone by the time that damn fool Pierce could get here. Pierce had actually believed that Blaine would keep his end of the bargain. That was a Yankee for you.

"Y'all just sit still, and nobody will get hurt," Blaine said to the Mexicans and the Texans. "We'll be taking that chest."

One of the Texans said quietly, "Damn you. How can you betray the Confederacy like this?"

Blaine laughed. "I got news for you, mister. There isn't any—"

He was still standing close to the open window. An arm came through it, a hand grabbed the back of his uniform coat, and he was jerked backward violently, crashing out through the window in a shower of broken glass from the upper pane.

"Stab me in the back, will you!" Sheriff Keller roared.

Inside the saloon's back room, the Texans took advantage of the distraction to grab for the revolvers holstered on their hips. Colonel Flornoy opened fire, as did his men, but even though one of the Texans fell over backward in his chair, the other put a couple of slugs in Flornoy's chest. The Mexicans had gotten guns out and were shooting, too, and the whole back room was nothing but smoke and flying lead.

In the alley, Keller reached down, grabbed the stunned Blaine, picked him up, and slammed him against the wall of the building on the other side of the alley. "It had to—uh!"

Keller drove Blaine against the wall again. "Had to be you! Uh!" Another crashing impact. "You're the only one I talked to—after I figured out why that fella was naked—You must've lied to me—He was a Confederate courier, wasn't he?"

Blaine was in no shape to answer. His jaw was broken, for one thing, from one of the half-dozen times Keller had slammed him against the wall. He was only half-conscious, too, but somehow he had managed to hold on to his gun. When Keller finally let him go, Blaine sagged against the wall and started to slide down it before he caught himself. He knew now he would never get his hands on that gold, and his fury over that fueled his need for vengeance. He turned around and started to bring up the gun. If nothing else, he would kill that fat bastard of a sheriff.

One of the bullets being blasted inside the back room of the saloon hit the thin boards of the wall, punched through them, whipped past Keller's left ear, and hit Blaine in the center of the forehead. Blaine's gun was still pointing toward the floor of the alley as he fired it involuntarily in the moment of dying. He fell back against the wall in a heap.

Keller became aware of more slugs buzzing around him and went diving for the ground. He'd been mad enough at Blaine for trying to stab him that he'd gone looking for the lieutenant. But on the way to Fort Brown, he'd glanced down this alley and seen a gray-clad leg disappearing into a window. Figuring that Blaine was a likely choice to be skulking around an alley, he'd taken a look through the window, and sure enough, there was the man who'd tried to kill him.

But whatever was behind that massacre going on in the saloon's back room . . . *that* was none of his business.

He was only the sheriff, after all.

RIP FORD'S CAVALRY OF the West reached Palmito Hill and found the Union troops under Colonel Barrett still engaging the Texan pickets under Captain Giddings. Ford promptly flanked the Yankees, tore into them from the side, and sent them scurrying back toward Brazos de Santiago in a full-fledged rout. Several times along the way, Colonel Barrett tried to rally his men, but to no avail. The Yankees were beaten.

As the battle turned, Lieutenant Dermot Pierce was furious. Blaine, that damned Confederate, had assured him that regular Union troops could defeat Ford's makeshift army. Ford had been the only threat to their plan, according to Blaine, so it had been necessary to provoke this battle and get him out of town, but from a military standpoint, Ford was no threat, Blaine had assured him. It was just that the man was a former Texas Ranger, and if he'd been around when Blaine and the Frenchmen stole the gold, he probably would have said to hell with the war and come after them—especially since that gold was supposed to find its way into Confederate coffers and help the Texans prolong the war.

A war that these stupid frontiersmen didn't even know was over, had been over for more than a month. Blaine had taken care of that by killing the courier who was bringing the news from Galveston to Brownsville.

If everything had gone according to plan, the Federals would have defeated Ford's cavalry, marched on into Brownsville, and Pierce could have bided his time before deserting and rendezvousing with Blaine. Pierce had made it look good during the fighting, emptying his pistol a few times and then hanging back for the most part. As Colonel Barrett's aide, he wasn't expected to be in the front lines.

The only trouble was, once the rout started there were no front lines, and Pierce found himself fleeing for his life from a bunch of Texas devils who screeched like imps out of Hades as they attacked. All Pierce could do then was turn his horse around and ride for his life.

He made it almost a hundred yards before a Texas sharpshooter knocked him out of the saddle with a single well-placed bullet. Pierce died with his face pressed into the sand that thirstily soaked up his blood.

ONE OF THE TEXANS lived through the fight in the back room of the Head of the Boar. So did one of the Mexicans and two of the Frenchmen. Keller locked up the Frenchmen, since it seemed they had less right to be there than either the Texan or the Mexican. He got enough of the story from those two to figure out that the whole thing had been about stealing the gold in that chest. He still didn't know why Blaine had bushwhacked that courier, though he felt sure in his gut that was what had happened.

It took Rip Ford to figure that out, once the colonel got back to town from whipping the Yankees. The canny old Ranger listened to the story Keller told him, then nodded and said, "According to some of the officers we captured out there at Palmito Hill, the war is over. General Lee surrendered to Grant a little more than a month ago at a place called Appomattox. I'm sure the courier was bringing that news to us."

The local sawbones had had to rip up a sheet to make bandages big enough to go around Keller's torso over the knife wound. They were so tight they were uncomfortable, and Keller wasn't in a very good mood. "Blaine found out about it somehow, and he figured you wouldn't go out to fight the Yankees if you knew the war was over."

Ford nodded. "He must have been working with someone in the Union camp, and they plotted the whole thing with those Frenchmen. They wanted me and my men out of town when the robbery took place."

"Why would they want that?" Keller asked.

"Because then the only law they would have to deal with, Sheriff—would be you."

Keller nodded. "I reckon that makes sense, all right."

He was on his third mug of beer and his second plate of beans and tortillas that evening before he looked up abruptly from his food, frowned, and said in offended understanding, "Hey."

# Valuables

*Kristine Scheid*

On June 8, 1861, Mrs. Rose Grenlauer, with the help of her slaves, packed all of her plantation's valuables into two railroad cars and disappeared. Willard knew the exact date because that was the day Tennessee seceded from the Union. It was also the day he got conscripted into the Confederate Army.

Ten months later, he was back in Memphis, such as it was, missing one arm, one wife, and half of his house. The Union Army had burned it just after the Battle of Shiloh, when they occupied the city. General Ulysses S. Grant now used Mrs. Rose Grenlauer's plantation as headquarters for one of his divisions and, it was said, he sat in her husband's library, drinking port and smoking his awful cigars as he made his plans to destroy the South. Colonel Rufus Grenlauer knew nothing of that, of course. He hadn't been home since he joined up right after Jefferson Davis, a friend of the Grenlauers', became president of the Confederacy.

Willard knew all that because he now begged for coins not a block from the Grenlauer estate. The damn Yankee soldiers would give him nothing for his trouble and for all his losses, but the widows and wives, most of whom were still struggling to keep their fancy homes together, usually gave him a scrap or two. Then they'd plead with him to get off the street, worried that the Yankees would somehow hurt him if they found out he was a patriot, as if they could do worse than they'd already done.

Besides, the Yankees already knew he was a patriot. A strapping local man, left sleeve pinned to his shoulder, obviously thinner than a man should be, could be nothing else. That they didn't bother him, that they didn't arrest him, showed that they no longer thought him a threat.

They were wrong.

Someday, he would prove it to them.

And Mrs. Rose Grenlauer would help.

HE DIDN'T KNOW WHEN he starting thinking about Mrs. Rose Grenlauer. Sometimes, he believed it began after he got home and saw her plantation still standing, the bricks, made by hand by the hundreds of slaves her parents had on the estate, untouched by fire or explosions or even gunshots.

His house, the bricks bought at great cost in 1855, when he was gainfully employed as a tugboat captain and which he laid by hand on hot, long summer days, had been knocked askew in a firefight he hadn't been there to see. The wooden porch his wife Selma Leigh had asked him to build just for her and for the children they would now never have, had burned, the fire licking across the plankings and eventually eating the wooden floors she had polished so lovingly after their marriage in December 1856.

The neighbors said she'd tried to defend the place all by herself, using his granddaddy's Revolutionary War musket and a hunting knife Willard had left behind. But in the end, it'd done no good.

The Yanks had captured her, done what they wanted with her, then left her for dead in the middle of the roses she'd planted that very first spring. She'd died three days later, out of her head—"a mercy," said Mrs. Cannon, who'd tended her—apparently injured too severely to live. The sheets she'd lain on had to be burned, they were covered with so much blood.

Willard found this out when he came home, too thin himself, the only thing carrying him was the memory of his pretty wife's face and the cool soothing way her hands would feel on his ruined body. He'd been afraid she wouldn't accept him, not without his arm—not even the army wanted him now, although they were hurting for men—but he knew he'd have to give it one more try.

And he'd been too late. Too late by a month, maybe more. Too late to stop any of it.

Old Mrs. Cannon, she'd said it was a blessing he hadn't been there. He'd have died, too, maybe in the gardenias or at the front of the lawn, trying to protect his wife and his home. His wife would have screamed and he would have been distracted, and the Yanks would have taken advantage, all of them—five, ten, Mrs. Cannon couldn't remember— and then his wife'd had to go through one more horrible thing, watching him die before her very eyes.

Only Mrs. Cannon couldn't have known how it would've worked, not with him home. He'd have had his rifle, and he knew how to use his granddaddy's muzzle loader. He'd have held off five men or ten. He'd have gotten his wife away.

But he hadn't been there. On the day she died, he'd been in a doctor's tent that smelled of old blood and piss, a pile of limbs outside it, and he'd been begging the man in the blood-stained uniform to let him keep his arm, let him keep it despite the bullet that had ripped through it, tearing the flesh and leaving it hanging useless at his side.

They'd gotten him drunk—the last of the army's whiskey, someone had told him later—then made him bite on a stick of wood already chewed raw by other men's teeth. That'd stopped him from biting through his own tongue, but it hadn't stopped him from screaming like he was going to die, probably as his wife'd been screaming, probably while those Yanks were enjoying her and laughing at the victory that they'd so easily won.

Then he'd asked Mrs. Cannon why his house was ruined when none of his neighbors' were, and he'd asked why his wife was dead when almost no women or children died when the Yanks took over the city, and what he'd learned upset him most of all.

His wife, Selma Leigh, had caught the eye of a Yank captain who'd decided that he wanted her and her pretty home all to himself.

*I'm a married woman sir,* she'd said to him, and the Yankee bastard had just laughed.

*Chances are you're a widowed woman,* he'd said back, *and even if you ain't, how's your husband to know what we done if you don't tell him?*

Still, she stuck to her refusal and he'd come with his men one spring afternoon, and taken what he'd wanted. Taken it, and destroyed it, so that when Willard came home, he'd have nothing. No wife, no home, and no memories worth savoring.

Because all he kept thinking was that if he hadn't brought her here, if he'd left Selma Leigh in Atlanta where he'd found her, she'd still be alive now. Alive, and using her dainty hands to grow roses and keep a home, smiling that pretty smile for someone else.

But at least that smile would still be alive. At least someone would see it.

He didn't care if he didn't get to see it, so long as someone did.

Instead, as the perennials bloomed—flowers she'd planted—he laid them on the grave his neighbors had made for her in the backyard, and he promised her, soon as he got rid of them Yankee bastards, he'd find her a proper resting place, just like he'd once promised her a proper home.

HE DIDN'T KNOW WHAT all that had to do with Mrs. Rose Grenlauer or why he started to think of her and her two railroad cars. Sometimes he wondered if he'd been thinking about Rose Grenlauer his entire life. He'd seen her when he was a boy, and she was a young woman, living in the guest cottage while her family's slaves built the most spectacular plantation in Memphis.

Back before the war, the plantation had even had artificial lights, powered by oil squeezed from linseeds, an hour's worth of light taking two days' worth of work to create. The plantation had been filled with marvels and anyone who was anyone in the city'd come to see it. Rose Grenlauer's parents, the Allens, had opened the doors to show off their new home.

He'd sat outside, of course, on the other side of the street. All he'd been able to see was the lovely landscaping, the marvelous lamps placed at the end of the long meandering sidewalk, the brick stairs and the wide white door, opened to admit people who wouldn't even meet Willard's gaze. He'd stood there most of the day, along with other folks who weren't anybody, and finally he'd gotten a chance to see Rose Grenlauer, who'd been Rose Allen then, standing by the door.

She'd worn a white dress trimmed with red to match the bows hanging all over the trees, and her lovely hair had been curled into ringlets. She'd been laughing at something a young man said to her, and then she had looked across the street.

Willard always thought she'd looked at him, but if she had, it would have been the first and only time. He'd seen her after that, had stood outside the house on one other occasion, that of her summer wedding to Rufus Grenlauer. That had been a spectacular event, too; the tents on the lawn, the musicians filling the entire outdoors with sounds Willard had never heard before, the food stacked on tables, and the servants who kept all the bugs away.

The guests had arrived looking more refined than Willard had thought possible—the women in their taffetas, the men in their best suits. Even from across the street he could smell the pomade the men used in their hair, the French perfume the women had sprayed all over themselves, and the flowers—oh, all the flowers—that the Allens had somehow convinced to bloom all over the yard.

He'd vowed then—it was June 1850—that when he married he would provide the same things for his bride: a beautiful home, more flowers than a body could behold, and wealth beyond all her imagining. That was when he'd gotten his job, and in every spare hour worked on the home, first paying for the land, then designing the house itself, and then building it, sometimes with his own hands. When he'd finally found Selma Leigh, he'd had everything he'd dreamed of, except great wealth. But he'd been better off than his parents, better off than his friends, and when the war came, he was able to give more than his service to the cause—he was able to send thousands of dollars—greenbacks—to support Jefferson Davis's new administration.

Like so many others, he'd converted the rest of his wealth into two forms: Confederate bonds and gold, kept in a safe in the house. The safe was gone, of course, gone in the fire that had destroyed half his home. He'd found some bonds, but Memphis was run by the Yankees now, and they didn't recognize what they called Jeff Davis's phony money. So Willard had nothing. No wife, no arm, no pension, and no cash with which to live. He was dependent on the charity of his friends and on the begging he did, as no one would hire him—not looking the way he did, not with his missing arm.

It was a wonder that he survived from day to day.

BUT WILLARD WASN'T A man used to being useless, and for each penny he scrounged, each jibe from a Yankee soldier, each pitiful look from one of the Southern women who used to envy his pretty wife, he grew even more despairing.

He tried finding honest work, but those who didn't stare at him with pity politely refused, saying that he had done enough in service of his country. Others asked him to take a loyalty oath to the United States, something he couldn't bear and something, he knew, that would come back to haunt him when the South won the war.

Poverty, infirmity, loss, none of those were enough to abandon your country, your state, and your dream. He knew that. Others in Memphis knew that as well. He heard them, feeling comfortable around him, talking about ways of fighting back, ways of forcing the Yankees out of Tennessee.

He even went to some meetings, when he could find them, and listened to men too old to serve or women who had no idea what the fighting was like talk about taking on the Yankees who owned his city. But he knew that the Yankees were too powerful. The help couldn't come from the inside. It had to come from outside, and right now, there was too much happening in the South for the armies to concentrate on one city, even if it was on the Mississippi River and other transportation routes.

It was up to the citizens of Memphis to remind the Confederacy of their importance. And, Willard believed, every citizen had a duty to help.

Sometimes, he thought, that was what had focused him on Rose Grenlauer and her two railroad cars full of valuables. He had learned of it from one of the widows who attended the meeting, a bitter woman whose family had sold some of the land to the Allens before they built the plantation.

*Never paid us what it was worth,* she would say. *Even then they were tighter with money than most—that Rose, she's just the worst of them—people dying for a cause, and she runs away with the family silver.*

From that moment, he dreamed of Mrs. Rose Grenlauer, thought of her, wondered if she was still as pretty as the bride he'd seen so briefly on her wedding day, walking underneath a bower of white roses, her veil trailing more than a yard behind her. Was she still a delicate creature of privilege? Or had that year of riding in railroad cars taken some of the blush from her skin?

He wanted to find out. He needed to find out, not just for himself, but for the sake of the Confederacy. Those two railroad cars of hers could be used in the war effort to transport troops and supplies and weapons. And those valuables could buy food and clothing for soldiers or help support the widows and orphans left behind.

Yes, Mrs. Rose Grenlauer had lost her home, but only because she had abandoned it, left it as an obvious place for the enemy to make his headquarters.

Sometimes Willard thought she had been a collaborator with the Union. It seemed so curious to him. She'd left the day that Tennessee seceded. She left her home undefended so that anyone, even that slob of a general Grant, could move inside. She'd taken valuables in railroad cars.

*Maybe,* he'd found himself thinking, *maybe she'd even taken them up North.*

He'd hated that thought the moment he had it: pretty Rose Grenlauer using Southern heritage to fund the Union cause. But he hadn't been able to get it out of his mind. He would stand in his old spot across from the Grenlauer mansion and he'd stare at it, wondering if Grant was there with Mrs. Rose Grenlauer's permission.

The very idea stuck in Willard's craw.

And he knew it was that idea, that one idea, which forced him to take action.

IT'D BEEN HARD. FIRST he'd talked to the servants, the ones who were still in Memphis, the ones who had helped her pack the cars. They spoke of riches beyond his comprehension, silver services that had been in the family for generations, paintings by some of the old masters, jewelry that had more diamonds and emeralds than he'd ever imagined possible.

There was no way to trace the railroad cars, or so he was told, but he knew there had to be. Those cars had to be moved from place to place, whether they were pushed or pulled. It had only been a year. Someone had to remember them. Someone had to know where they were.

He'd stopped begging outside the Grenlauer plantation. Instead, he spent most of his time at the train yards. He did what work he could, voluntarily shoveling coal with his one good arm, dragging parcels from place to place, posting the weekly casualty lists.

Finally they started paying him, without the Yankees' permission of course. When the Yankees came, the train yard workers claimed he was just a bum whom they fed sometimes, and he was happy to keep up the lie. He didn't want his money, what little of it he got, coming out of the Yankees' pockets.

In return for all the work, he got to listen to the gossip. Sometimes he brought up his few stories of train travel during his brief service. Sometimes he brought up legends that he'd heard over the years—ghost trains during the night, things like that—and finally someone told him the story of Rose Grenlauer.

She'd bought the railroad cars with cash, used her own servants to load them, then hired an engineer to take her to an unfinished line where she could live and hide until the war was over.

He'd heard part of that, of course, but not all of it. He figured he could wait until he actually found the engineer, a man who might not come through Memphis again, or he could visit the unfinished lines of track himself.

A year earlier Jefferson Davis had pledged himself to finishing the rail lines, but that hadn't been possible, not with the way the war was going and the South's great need for men. Hiding was easy at the end of one of those unfinished lines—provided, of course, that no battles were being fought around it.

He'd used a map inside the stationhouse, one of the maps that showed every bit of rail ever built, and studied it for days. Some of the unfinished lines were near Shiloh, where he'd lost his arm. Only a few were in areas untouched by the war, and only one was near a small community, where a woman alone, who happened to have gold or other things to trade, could buy something to eat.

It had taken him nearly a month, but he felt he had found her. And now that he had her, it was time to make her do her duty to country.

Everyone else was paying. It was time for Mrs. Rose Grenlauer to pay, too.

OF COURSE, HE HAD no horse and no money to buy one. Stealing one was a capital crime, but, he believed, one he could justify if he had to. Why, he'd simply say that the horse was one he'd found wandering free, probably lost after one of the battles. There were so many lost horses, after all. And if he didn't get caught, he would leave the horse outside the city when he was done.

In the month he'd been searching for Mrs. Rose Grenlauer, he'd managed to buy food. The work had made his remaining arm stronger, and he actually felt like a man for the first time since he'd come home.

It was, he thought, the perfect time.

The horse theft was easy. He took one of the mares from the Grenlauer estate. He recognized the horse. It had been one of Rufus Grenlauer's, left behind by his wife when she took her railroad cars and fled. The Grenlauer horses weren't assigned to any officers, not so as he knew, and he doubted that anyone would know she was missing for at least a day or so.

That got him outside the city into the thin woods and bluffs that lined the Mississippi. He had packed his old saddlebags with food he'd saved and meal for the horse, which he'd also stolen from the Yanks. He was carrying his rifle and several hunting knives, figuring that would be enough.

When he got a few miles outside of Memphis, he doubled back through the woods to the unfinished rail line. He followed it north and cattycorner. Riding jostled him, made his stump ache, but he did it, and was proud of it. Three days over track that was weed-infested and lines that were broken, not by destructive armies, but by time and lack of use.

At times he nearly lost the track for the weeds, his horse reluctant to go through such tangles. Sometimes he doubted the wisdom of his mission—not the idea of making Mrs. Rose Grenlauer do her duty, but the idea of following this line when he had no actual evidence she was along it.

Supposition hadn't served him that well since the war started. As he rode, he was beginning to think it would fail him again.

On the fourth day, he saw rusted shovels and pickaxes abandoned on the side of the track. The wooden rails were gone—probably used as kindling—but some lengths of iron remained. His heart was in his throat as he emerged through a copse of trees and saw the line was blocked.

It looked like it was blocked by more trees. Branches covered the track in front of him, and vines tangled up it. But the branches were haphazard, the vines weaving in and out in a way they'd never do with a living tree.

He needed to know if this was Mrs. Rose Grenlauer's railroad cars and he wasn't sure how to do it, not at first. He hadn't been thinking of a plan on the ride—imagining various scenarios, yes, but not actually planning. Deep down, he never thought he would find her.

He sat on his horse for a long time, staring at the tangle ahead. Nothing moved. He heard no one, saw nothing. Maybe he was mistaken. Maybe he was just seeing an abandoned shed or an old unused car. He would have to find out.

His plan, as it evolved, was simple enough. He was a Confederate soldier, going home, his injury apparent enough. He'd stay with her until he convinced her to accompany him, taking the valuables to Richmond maybe, or Atlanta, somewhere that they could be sold for funds.

He'd always known when he met Mrs. Rose Grenlauer she'd be sweet on him. He'd use that to convince her to give her belongings to the cause.

He rode up, and as he approached the tangle he realized he was seeing box cars. Two of them attached in the middle. Someone had carefully hidden them, but had gotten careless. A lot of the branches had dried and fallen off. Others were so choked by vines that the entire works looked like a jungle from some storybook instead of a forest in Tennessee.

One of the railroad car's doors was open, revealing a small room inside, filled with furniture laid out in a comfortable pattern. He was so intrigued he pulled up right in front and stared in. Upholstered chairs with mahogany legs sat side by side, with a matching table between them, a lamp on it and a book with them. On one side were boxes. On the other, a small bed with a canopy and mosquito netting.

He was just about to dismount when a voice stopped him.

"Who goes?"

He frowned, saw a small woman in a floppy hat and a faded dress holding a rifle on him.

"Willard," he said. "Willard Harrison."

"You put up them arms, Mr. Harrison," she said. He couldn't see her face. It was shaded by the hat.

He put up his arm, keeping the reins draped over his thumb.

"Both of them, Mr. Harrison."

"Beg pardon, ma'am," he said. "I got but one."

She took a step closer. He hadn't remembered her being so small, but then he'd never seen her up close.

"I guess you do." She pushed her hat back and he saw her face. Mrs. Rose Grenlauer all right, thinner than he'd remembered, her hair tumbled around her face like a school girl's. Not the beautiful belle he'd been admiring for years, but a woman who was beginning to look her age. "What're you doing here?"

"Heading home," he said. "To Memphis."

"Then you're headed the wrong way." She didn't sound too friendly.

"I—um—I am?"

"Don't lie to me, Mr. Harrison. You came searching for me, just like them others, hearing snifflings of gold."

"No, ma'am," he lied. "I'm just a soldier on his way home."

"On my husband's mare?" She made a clicking sound with her tongue, and the mare reared. Willard slid off, unable to grab on with his remaining arm.

He landed on his back, and the wind rushed out of him. He couldn't catch his breath, and the sky revolved for a moment. Mrs. Rose Grenlauer came over to him and put a foot on his chest. A foot wearing a man's boot. She levered her rifle at him.

"I remember you," she said. "My father had the servants drive you off more than once."

Willard couldn't defend himself. He didn't have the breath.

"I'm gonna ask again. What'd you come here for?"

He finally got a gulp of air. He managed to squeeze out, "We need your railroad cars, ma'am, and your valuables. Memphis is Yankee-owned now, and the devil Lincoln made

Andrew Jackson military governor of Tennessee. We're losing. We need all the help—"

She jammed him in the chest with her rifle. "You don't need what I got," she said. "I'd tell you to take your horse and get, but it's my horse you got. Guess I'm just gonna have to shoot you."

He scrambled backward and upright faster than he'd known he could move. He grabbed the rifle and twisted it, pulling it away from her. He turned it and leveled it on her, bracing it under his arm, and holding it with his forefinger on the trigger, thumb on the hammer.

"I ain't lying to you, Mrs. Grenlauer," he said. "We need you to do what you can for the cause. The rest of us, we lost everything, but you, you're sitting here till the war's out, sitting on your hoard like what we do don't matter."

She didn't look scared of him. "I'm a woman, Mr. Harrison," she said. "I'm not expected to serve."

"There're others at home, helping with the effort. You could, too."

"I understand there's a Union general sleeping in my house and Yankee soldiers tearing up my yard. There's nothing for me to return to, Mr. Harrison."

"Nothing?" The word screeched out of him. He shoved her with the rifle, pushing her backward with the muzzle. "Nothing? You don't know what nothing is. You and your railroad cars and your fancy husband and your big house that ain't even got a bootmark on the wooden floors. You're here alive and untouched with all your treasures while my wife—"

He stopped, not liking the hysteria in his own voice. What'd his commander said? A man out of control was a man who was going to lose something. A limb, maybe a life.

How well he knew that.

He focused on Mrs. Rose Grenlauer. She no longer looked calm. Her eyes were round and her lower lip trembled. "Yes," she said in a voice that was so soothing and placating it sounded like she was talking to a child. "Yes, you're right, of course, Mr. Harrison. You're absolutely right. I should be helping with the war effort. I should donate all my goods to the cause. I was such a fool not to see it."

Her gaze darted past him, and he whirled. A black man was there, a big dark man in tattered clothes, clothes that Willard recognized as the uniform of the Grenlauer house. The man held a stick.

"Put it down," Willard said. "Put it down."

The black man looked at Mrs. Rose Grenlauer for confirmation. Willard did too, and the black man rushed him. Willard fired before he could even think. The man flew backward and Mrs. Rose Grenlauer screamed. The man landed on his side, blood gushing from a wound in his stomach.

"You idiot!" she said. "You fool!"

And she jumped on him, digging her feet into his side, kicking him, pulling at the gun. He swung his torso, trying to throw her off, trying to knock her away. She was taking his breath away, hurting him, piling into the old wounds, her hands hitting his stump, sending pain where the arm had once been. Reminding him of all the nothing he had, all he'd lost, for a cause she didn't feel she had to fight for.

With a roar, he flung her back. She slid off him and he kicked her away.

"You ignorant piece of trash," she said. "You don't understand what you're asking me to give up. You don't know—"

He shot her. Mostly to shut her up. And it did. She stared at him for a long moment, then fell forward on her face, her eyes open and fixing on the sky.

He was shaking just like he had in his first battle. He glanced over his shoulder, but there was no one to see what he had done. No one except the horse, which was watching him from the side of the railroad car.

"Didn't go like we planned, huh, girl?" he said.

The horse watched him warily.

"She didn't know. She was a traitor to the cause, sitting here on her wealth, hiding out as if what she had was the most important thing in the world."

The horse shifted skittishly from one side to the other.

He sat down, so exhausted he didn't know what to do. He glanced at her, unmoving, and the black man who was just as dead. Of course she would've brought a slave with her. Of course. To protect her and the valuables. Not that it did much good.

A shaky laugh escaped him, and it sounded just a little crazy. Of course it sounded crazy. She was dead and it was because she had pushed him to it, not understanding how things really were, how badly her railroad cars and valuables was needed. She pushed him by mentioning his wife and how he didn't understand sacrifice and—

He shook his head trying to make the thoughts stop. He had to do something. That she was dead didn't really matter, after all. He had the cars and the valuables, and he wasn't going to sit on them, not like she did. He wasn't no traitor. He'd given an arm and a wife to the cause. He wasn't going to stop now.

It would take some planning. But he had time. He could take it nice and slow.

TOOK HIM A DAY to bury them, using one of the rusty old shovels he'd found. He dragged them to the woods and buried them there, away from the railroad cars. That first night, he slept in her bed and knew that wasn't how he'd imagined it. From the first he'd known he'd be in Rose Grenlauer's bed, but he hadn't realized he'd be there alone.

The next day he'd closed the railroad car's doors and covered it again with brambles, hoping it'd stay hidden just long enough for him to do his duty.

That took longer than he thought, too. He couldn't go back to Memphis. That was a Union town now, and the trains, even though they had Southern boys steering, were

Union owned. He had to go farther south till he found his own men, and then he'd have to bring them back.

It took him and the mare three more days to find help, and another day after that to convince the corporal in charge to let three of his men accompany Willard back to the railroad cars. If they liked what they saw, they'd risk sending an engine in to pull everything out.

Four days back to the hiding place—counting the one day he got lost—and he was afraid someone else would have found his treasure, someone else would have stolen it, made all this work for nothing.

This was what was going to redeem him. Wouldn't make the loss of the arm or Selma Leigh worthwhile, but at least he'd help with the cause in a way that Mrs. Rose Grenlauer never did. He would have given everything—the woman he loved, a part of himself, his home, and now bounty that a lesser man would have kept as payment for all that loss. He was giving it back, giving it up, and maybe some day people would remember. They'd say, that Willard Harrison, he wasn't so crazy after all. He was the one that got the money that turned the tide in the war.

The railroad cars were as he left them. The men who'd ridden with him seemed relieved. He knew they didn't really believe him, that they thought they were getting a leave for humoring a former soldier. But when they got there, they got off their horses, tied them to some brambles, and set about opening the railroad cars' doors.

The first car was like he left it, the furniture set up, boxes on the side. The second car he'd never even looked into. It was filled with boxes and crates. One of the men whistled through his teeth as he looked in.

He pulled down the first box, opened it, and swore. Then he pulled down another. The men grabbed boxes in the first car and pulled them down. Willard saw what they did when it was opened. Letters, linens, toys, and books.

"There's supposed to be silver," he said, "and more jewels than anyone else ever had in Memphis."

And there was silver. One serving set and one set of silverware. A pearl necklace and diamond earrings. Gold leaf plates and some baby spoons, also made of gold.

But that was all. Rattles and clothing and portraits of the family, most of them recent and done with that photographic process that was so expensive, but worth nothing for resale.

The men threw things out of the box cars and kicked the boxes and ruined the little furniture grouping and cursed Willard who watched in shocked dismay.

"They'd said," he said. "They'd said there was valuables here."

"There are valuables, you dumb ass," one of the men said to him, face up close, breath smelling of rot. "Some family's mementos. Ain't got no meaning to no one else."

Willard flushed. How to save this? He thought it would be enough to finance food and clothes for an army. He'd thought it might be enough to save the South.

"The railroad cars, at least," he said. "We could use them. Troop transport or—"

"The wheels're gone," the soldier said. "We'd have to repair them first."

Willard looked. Sure enough. She'd disabled the cars so someone who came looking would think they were abandoned a long time. Only she'd never expected someone like Willard. Someone craftier than she was. Smarter. Better.

Someone who'd had a hoard of valuables and lost it to the Yankees.

Something of it must have shown on his face for the soldier who'd been yelling at him stopped, put a hand on his shoulder. "It was a good try. Next time, you make sure you know what the valuables are before you offer them to the army."

Then he whistled to the men, and they rode off, leaving Willard standing alone in a pile of boxes. A pile of memories that didn't matter to no one except Rose and Rufus Grenlauer.

The horse was watching him again, judging him, it seemed. Maybe he was no better than them Yankee bastards, killing and taking what he wanted, then realizing it wasn't worth his effort. Maybe he was no better at all.

He bent down, picked up a packet of letters wrapped in faded ribbon, and placed them back inside the box. He was better. Of course he was. He'd done this for the cause. The soldiers had had no patience, that was all. He'd find what they needed. Then he'd turn it in somewhere else.

Until then, he and the horse, they'd stay here. Where it was safe. He couldn't go back to Memphis. He didn't have a home there or a wife. Or even a dream anymore.

Just a packet of memories of a world gone by. A world he'd known mostly from the outside. Like the visions of a boy who'd stood across the street and tried to stare into a house where he'd never be invited.

A house owned by a pretty woman, with memories of her own.

# The Face

## Ed Gorman

The war was going badly. In the past month more than sixty men had disgraced the Confederacy by deserting, and now the order was to shoot deserters on sight. This was in other camps and other regiments. Fortunately, none of our men had deserted at all.

As a young doctor, I knew even better than our leaders just how hopeless our war had become. The public knew General Lee had been forced to cross the Potomac with ten thousand men who lacked shoes and hats, and who at night had to sleep on the ground without blankets. But I knew—in the first six months in this post—that our men suffered from influenza, diphtheria, smallpox, yellow fever, and even cholera; ravages from which they would never recover; ravages more costly than bullets and the advancing armies of the Yankees. Worse, because toilet and bathing facilities were practically nil, virtually every man suffered from ticks and mites and many suffered from scurvy, their bodies on fire. Occasionally, you would see a man go mad, do crazed dances in the moonlight trying to get the bugs off him. Soon enough he would be dead.

This was the war in the spring and while I have here referred to our troops as "men," in fact they were mostly boys, some as young as thirteen. In the night, freezing and sometimes wounded, they cried out for their mothers, and it was not uncommon to hear one or two of them sob while they prayed aloud.

I tell you this so you will have some idea of how horrible things had become for our beloved Confederacy. But even given the suffering and madness and despair I'd seen for the past two years as a military doctor, nothing had prepared me for the appearance of the Virginia man in our midst.

On the day he was brought in on a buckboard, I was working with some troops, teaching them how to garden. If we did not get vegetables and fruit into our diets soon, all of us would have scurvy. I also appreciated the respite that working in the warm sun gave me from surgery. In the past week alone, I'd amputated three legs, two arms, and numerous hands and fingers. None had gone well, conditions were so filthy.

Every amputation had ended in death except one and this man—boy; he was fourteen—pleaded with me to kill him every time I checked on him. He'd suffered a head wound, and I'd had to relieve the pressure by trepanning into his skull. Beneath the blood and pus in the hole I'd dug, I could see his brain squirming. There was no anesthetic, of course, except whiskey and that provided little comfort against the violence of my bone saw. It was one of those periods when I could not get the tart odor of blood from my nostrils, nor its feel from my skin. Sometimes, standing at the surgery table, my boots would become soaked with it and I would squish around in them all day.

The buckboard was parked in front of the General's tent. The driver jumped down, ground-tied the horses, and went quickly inside.

He returned a few moments later with General Sullivan, the commander. Three men in familiar gray uniforms followed the General.

The entourage walked around to the rear of the wagon. The driver, an enlisted man, pointed to something in the buckboard. The General, a fleshy, bald man of fifty-some years, leaned over the wagon and peered downward.

Quickly, the General's head snapped back and then his whole body followed. It was as if he'd been stung by something coiled and waiting for him in the buckboard.

The General shook his head and said, "I want this man's entire face covered. Especially his face."

"But, General," the driver said. "He's not dead. We shouldn't cover his face."

"You heard what I said!" General Sullivan snapped. And with that, he strutted back into his tent, his men following.

I was curious, of course, about the man in the back of the wagon. I wondered what could have made the General start the way he had. He'd looked almost frightened.

I wasn't to know till later that night.

MY ROUNDS MADE ME late for dinner in the vast tent used for the officers' mess. I always felt badly about the inequity of officers having beef stew while the men had, at best, hardtack and salt pork. Not so bad that I refused to eat it, of course, which made me feel hypocritical on top of being sorry for the enlisted men.

Not once in my time here had I ever dined with General Sullivan. I was told on my first day here that the General, an extremely superstitious man, considered doctors bad luck. Many people feel this way. Befriend a doctor and you'll soon enough find need of his services.

So I was surprised when General Sullivan, carrying a cup of steaming coffee in a huge, battered tin cup, sat down across the table where I ate alone, my usual companions long ago gone back to their duties.

"Good evening, Doctor."

"Good evening, General."

"A little warmer tonight."

"Yes."

He smiled dourly. "Something's got to go our way, I suppose."

I returned his smile. "I suppose." I felt like a child trying to act properly for the sake of an adult. The General frightened me.

The General took out a stogie, clipped off the end, sniffed it, licked it, then put it between his lips and fired it. He did all this with a ritualistic satisfaction that made me think of better times in my home city of Charleston, of my father and uncles handling their smoking in just the same way.

"A man was brought into camp this afternoon," he said.

"Yes," I said. "In a buckboard."

He eyed me suspiciously. "You've seen him up close?"

"No. I just saw him delivered to your tent." I had to he careful of how I put my next statement. I did not want the General to think I was challenging his reasoning. "I'm told he was not taken to any of the hospital tents."

"No, he wasn't." The General wasn't going to help me.

"I'm told he was still under quarantine in a tent of his own."

"Yes."

"May I ask why?"

He blew two plump white perfect rings of smoke toward the ceiling. "Go have a look at him, then join me in my tent."

"You're afraid he may have some contagious disease?"

The General considered the length of his cigar. "Just go have a look at him, Doctor. Then we'll talk."

With that, the General stood up, his familiar brusque self once again, and was gone.

THE GUARD SET DOWN his rifle when he saw me. "Good evenin', Doctor."

"Good evening."

He nodded to the tent behind him. "You seen him yet?"

"No, not yet."

He was young. He shook his head. "Never seen anything like it. Neither has the priest. He's in there with him now." In the chill, crimson dusk I tried to get a look at the guard's face. I couldn't. My only clue to his mood was the tone of his voice—one of great sorrow.

I lifted the tent flap and went in.

A lamp guttered in the far corner of the small tent, casting huge and playful shadows across the walls. A hospital cot took up most of the space. A man's body lay beneath the covers. A sheer cloth had been draped across his face. You could see it billowing with the man's faint breath. Next to the cot stood Father Lynott. He was silver-haired and chunky. His black cassock showed months of dust and grime. Like most of us, he was rarely able to get hot water for necessities.

At first, he didn't seem to hear me. He stood over the cot torturing black rosary beads through his fingers. He stared directly down at the cloth draped on the man's face.

Only when I stood next to him did Father Lynott look up. "Good evening, Father."

"Good evening, Doctor."

"The General wanted me to look at this man."

He stared at me. "You haven't seen him, then?"

"No."

"Nothing can prepare you."

"I'm afraid I don't understand."

He looked at me out of his tired cleric's face. "You'll see soon enough. Why don't you come over to the officers' tent afterward? I'll be there drinking my nightly coffee."

He nodded, glanced down once more at the man on the cot, and then left, dropping the tent flap behind him.

I don't know how long I stood there before I could bring myself to remove the cloth from the man's face. By now, enough people had warned me of what I would see that I was both curious and apprehensive. There is a myth about doctors not being shocked by certain terrible wounds and injuries. Of course we are but we must get past that shock— or, more honestly, put it aside for a time—so that we can help the patient.

Close by, I could hear the feet of the guard in the damp grass, pacing back and forth in front of the tent. A barn owl and then a distant dog joined the sounds the guard made. Even more distant, there was cannon fire, the war never ceasing. The sky would flare silver like summer lightning. Men would suffer and die.

I reached down and took the cloth from the man's face.

"WHAT DO YOU SUPPOSE could have done that to his face, Father?" I asked the priest twenty minutes later.

We were having coffee. I smoked a cigar. The guttering candles smelled sweet and waxy.

"I'm not sure," the priest said.

"Have you ever seen anything like it?"

"Never."

I knew what I was about to say would surprise the priest. "He has no wounds."

"What?"

"I examined him thoroughly. There are no wounds anywhere on his body."

"But his face—"

I drew on my cigar, watched the expelled smoke move like a storm cloud across the flickering candle flame. "That's why I asked you if you'd ever seen anything like it."

"My God," the priest said, as if speaking to himself. "No wounds."

IN THE DREAM I was back on the battlefield on that frosty March morning two years ago, when all my medical training had deserted me. Hundreds of corpses covered the ground where the battle had gone on for two days and two nights. You could see cannons mired in mud, the horses unable to pull them out. You could see the grass littered with dishes and pans and kettles, and a blizzard of playing cards—all exploded across the battlefield when the Union army had made its final advance. But mostly there were the bodies—so young and so many—and many of them with mutilated faces. During this time of the war, both sides had begun to commit atrocities. The Yankees favored disfiguring Confederate dead, and so they moved across the battlefield with Bowie knives that had been fashioned by sharpening them with large files. They put deep gashes in the faces of the young men, tearing out eyes sometimes, even sawing off noses. In the woods that day we'd found a group of our soldiers who'd been mortally wounded but who'd lived for a time after the Yankees had left. Each corpse held in its hand some memento of the loved ones they'd left behind—a photograph, a letter, a lock of blonde hair. Their last sight had been of some homely yet profound endearment from the people they'd loved most.

This was the dream—nightmare, really—and I'd suffered it ever since I'd searched for survivors on that battlefield two years previous.

I was still in this dream-state when I heard the bugle announce the morning. I stumbled from my cot and went down to the creek to wash and shave. The day had begun.

CASUALTIES WERE MANY THAT morning. I stood in the hospital tent watching as one stretcher after another bore man after man to the operating table. Most suffered from wounds inflicted by minie balls, fired from guns that could kill a man nearly a mile away.

By noon, my boots were again soaked with blood dripping from the table.

During the long day, I heard whispers of the man General Sullivan had quarantined from others. Apparently, the man had assumed the celebrity and fascination of a carnival sideshow. From the whispers, I gathered the guards were letting men in for quick looks at him, and then lookers came away shaken and frightened. These stories had the same impact as tales of spectres told around midnight campfires. Except this was daylight and the men—even the youngest of them—hardened soldiers. They should not have been so afraid, but they were.

I couldn't get the sight of the man out of my mind, either. It haunted me no less than the battlefield I'd seen two years earlier.

DURING THE AFTERNOON, I went down to the creek and washed. I then went to the officers' tent and had stew and coffee. My arms were weary from surgery but I knew I would be working long into the night.

The General surprised me once again by joining me. "You've seen the soldier from Virginia?"

"Yes, sir."

"What do you make of him?"

I shrugged. "Shock, I suppose."

"But his face—"

"This is a war, General, and a damned bloody one. Not all men are like you. Not all men have iron constitutions."

He took my words as flattery, of course, as a military man would. I hadn't necessarily meant them that way. Military men could also be grossly vain and egotistical and insensitive beyond belief.

"Meaning what, exactly, Doctor?"

"Meaning that the soldier from Virginia may have become so horrified by what he saw that his face—" I shook my head. "You can see too much, too much death, General, and it can make you go insane."

"Are you saying he's insane?"

I shook my head. "I'm trying to find some explanation for his expression, General."

"You say there's no injury?"

"None that I can find."

"Yet he's not conscious."

"That's why I think of shock."

I was about to explain how shock works on the body—and how it could feasibly effect an expression like the one on the Virginia soldier's face—when a lieutenant rushed up to the General and breathlessly said, "You'd best come, sir. The tent where the soldier's quarantined—there's trouble!"

When we reached there, we found half the camp's soldiers surrounding the tent. Three and four deep, they were, and milling around idly. Not the sort of thing you wanted to see your men doing when there was a war going on. There were duties to perform and none of them were getting done.

A young soldier—thirteen or fourteen at most—stepped from the line and hurled his rifle at the General. The young soldier had tears running down his cheeks. "I don't want to fight anymore, General."

The General slammed the butt of the rifle into the soldier's stomach. "Get hold of yourself, young man. You seem to forget we're fighting to save the Confederacy."

We went on down the line of glowering faces, to where two armed guards struggled to keep soldiers from looking into the tent. I was reminded again of a sideshow—some irresistible spectacle everybody wanted to see.

The soldiers knew enough to open an avenue for the General. He strode inside the tent. The priest sat on a stool next to the cot. He had removed the cloth from the Virginia soldier's face and was staring fixedly at it.

The General pushed the priest aside, took up the cloth used as a covering, and started to drop it across the soldier's face—then stopped abruptly. Even General Sullivan, in his rage, was moved by what he saw. He jerked back momentarily, his eyes unable to lift from the soldier's face. He handed the cloth to the priest. "You cover his face now, Father. And you keep it covered. I hereby forbid any man in this camp to look at this soldier's face ever again. Do you understand?"

Then he stormed from the tent.

The priest reluctantly obliged.

Then he angled his head up to me. "It won't be the same anymore, Doctor."

"What won't?"

"The camp. Every man in here has now seen his face." He nodded back to the soldier on the cot. "They'll never be the same again. I promise you."

IN THE EVENING, I ate stew and biscuits, and sipped at a small glass of wine. I was, as usual, in the officers' tent when the priest came and found me.

For a time, he said nothing beyond his greeting. Simply watched me at my meal, and then stared out the open flap at the camp preparing for evening, the fires in the center of the encampment, the weary men bedding down. Many of them, healed now, would be back in the battle within two days or less.

"I spent an hour with him this afternoon," the priest said.

"The quarantined man?"

"Yes." The priest nodded. "Do you know some of the men have visited him five or six times?"

The way the priest spoke, I sensed he was gloating over the fact that the men were disobeying the General's orders. "Why don't the guards stop them?"

"The guards are in visiting him, too."

"The man says nothing. How can it be a visit?"

"He says nothing with his tongue. He says a great deal with his face." He paused, eyed me levelly. "I need to tell you something. You're the only man in this camp who will believe me." He sounded frantic. I almost felt sorry for him.

"Tell me what?"

"The man—he's not what we think."

"No?"

"No; his face—" He shook his head. "It's God's face."

"I see."

The priest smiled. "I know how I must sound."

"You've seen a great deal of suffering, Father. It wears on a person."

"It's God's face. I had a dream last night. The man's face shows us God's displeasure with the war. That's why the men are so moved when they see the man." He sighed, seeing he was not convincing me. "You say yourself he hasn't been wounded."

"That's true."

"And that all his vital signs seem normal."

"True enough, rather."

"Yet he's in some kind of shock."

"That seems to be his problem, yes."

The priest shook his head. "No, his real problem is that he's become overwhelmed by the suffering he's seen in this war—what both sides have done to the other. All the pain. That's why there's so much sorrow on his face—and that's what the men are responding to. The grief on his face is the same grief they feel in their hearts. God's face."

"Once we get him to a real field hospital—"

And it was then we heard the rifle shots.

The periphery of the encampment was heavily protected, we'd never heard firing this close.

The priest and I ran outside.

General Sullivan stood next to a group of young men with weapons. Several yards ahead, near the edge of the camp, lay three bodies, shadowy in the light of the campfire. One of the fallen men moaned. All three men wore our own gray uniforms.

Sullivan glowered at me. "Deserters."

"But you shot them in the back," I said.

"Perhaps you didn't hear me, Doctor. The men were deserting. They'd packed their belongings and were heading out."

One of the young men who'd done the shooting said, "It was the man's face, sir."

Sullivan wheeled on him. "It was what?"

"The quarantined man, sir. His face. These men said it made them sad, and they had to see families back in Missouri, and that they were just going to leave no matter what."

"Poppycock," Sullivan said. "They left because they were cowards."

I left to take care of the fallen man who was crying out for help.

IN THE MIDDLE OF the night, I heard more guns being fired. I lay on my cot, knowing it wasn't Yankees being fired at. It was our own deserters.

I dressed and went over to the tent where the quarantined man lay. Two young farm boys in ill-fitting gray uniforms stood over him. They might have been mourners standing over a coffin. They said nothing. Just stared at the man.

In the dim lamplight, I knelt down next to him. His vitals still seemed good, his heartbeat especially. I stood up, next to the two boys, and looked down on him myself. There was nothing remarkable about his face. He could have been any of thousands of men serving on either side.

Except for the grief.

This time I felt the tug of it myself, heard in my mind the cries of the dying I'd been unable to save, saw the families and farms and homes destroyed as the war moved across the countryside, heard children crying out for dead parents, and parents sobbing over the bodies of their dead children. It was all there in his face, perfectly reflected, and I thought then of what the priest had said, that this was God's face, God's sorrow and displeasure with us.

The explosion came, then.

While the two soldiers next to me didn't seem to hear it at all, I rushed from the tent to the center of camp.

Several young soldiers stood near the ammunition cache. Someone had set fire to it. Ammunition was exploding everywhere, flares of red and yellow and gas-jet blue against the night. Men everywhere ducked for cover behind wagons and trees and boulders.

Into this scene, seemingly unafraid and looking like the lead actor in a stage production of *King Lear* I'd once seen, strode General Sullivan, still tugging on his heavy uniform jacket.

He went over to two soldiers who stood, seemingly unfazed, before the ammunition cache. Between explosions I could hear him shouting, "Did you set this fire?"

And they nodded.

Sullivan, as much in bafflement as anger, shook his head. He signaled for the guards to come and arrest these men.

As the soldiers were passing by me I heard one of them say to a guard, "After I saw his face, I knew I had to do this. I had to stop the war."

Within an hour, the flames died and the explosions ceased. The night was almost ominously quiet. There were a few hours before dawn, so I tried to sleep some more.

I dreamed of Virginia, green Virginia in the spring, and the creek where I'd fished as a boy, and how the sun had felt on my back and arms and head. There was no surgical table in my dream, nor were my shoes soaked with blood.

Around dawn somebody began shaking me. It was Sullivan's personal lieutenant. "The priest has been shot. Come quickly, Doctor."

I didn't even dress fully, just pulled on my trousers over the legs of my long underwear.

A dozen soldiers stood outside the tent looking confused and defeated and sad. I went inside.

The priest lay in his tent. His cassock had been torn away. A bloody hole made a target-like circle on his stomach.

Above his cot stood General Sullivan, a pistol in his hand.

I knelt next to the cot and examined the priest. His vital signs were faint and growing fainter. He had at most a few minutes to live.

I looked up at the General. "What happened?"

The General nodded for the lieutenant to leave. The man saluted and then went out into the gray dawn.

"I had to shoot him," General Sullivan said.

I stood up. "You had to shoot a priest?"

"He was trying to stop me."

"From what?"

Then I noticed for the first time the knife scabbard on the General's belt. Blood streaked its sides. The hilt of the knife was sticky with blood. So were the General's hands. I thought of how Yankee troops had begun disfiguring the faces of our dead on the battlefield.

He said, "I have a war to fight, Doctor. The men—the way they were reacting to the man's face—" He paused and touched the bloody hilt of the knife. "I took care of him. And the priest came in while I was doing it and went insane. He started hitting me, trying to stop me and—" He looked down at the priest. "I didn't have any choice, Doctor. I hope you believe me."

A few minutes later, the priest died.

I started to leave the tent. General Sullivan put a hand on my shoulder. "I know you don't care very much for me, Doctor, but I hope you understand me at least a little. I can't win a war when men desert and blow up ammunition dumps and start questioning the worthiness of the war itself. I had to do what I did. I hope someday you'll understand."

I went out into the dawn. The air smelled of campfires and coffee. Now the men were busy scurrying around, preparing for war. The way they had been before the man had been brought here in the buckboard.

I went over to the tent where he was kept and asked the guard to let me inside. "The General said nobody's allowed inside, Doctor."

I shoved the boy aside and strode into the tent.

The cloth was still over his face, only now it was soaked with blood. I raised the cloth and looked at him. Even for a doctor, the sight was horrible. The General had ripped out his eyes and sawed off his nose. His checks carried deep gullies where the knife had been dug in deep.

He was dead. The shock of the defacement had killed him.

Sickened, I looked away.

The flap was thrown back then, and there stood General Sullivan. "We're going to bury him now, Doctor."

In minutes, the dead soldier was inside a pine box borne up a hill of long grass waving in a chill wind. The rains came, hard rains, before they'd turned even two shovelfuls of earth.

Then, from a distance over the hill, came the thunder of cannon and the cry of the dying.

The face that reminded us of what we were doing to each other was no more. It had been made ugly, robbed of its sorrowful beauty.

He was buried quickly and without benefit of clergy—the priest himself having been buried an hour earlier—and when the ceremony was finished, we returned to camp and war.

# Matthew in the Morning

## Gary A. Braunbeck

"We are scattered—stunned—the remnant of heart left alive with us, filled with brotherly hate."

—*Mary Chesnut's Civil War Journals*, May 16, 1865

He was found at three-forty in the morning, hanging from a tree less than a half-mile outside of the camp. He had used a set of horse reins to do the deed. So tight had the reins been pulled by his body's drop from the thick limb, so deep had they sunk into the flesh of his neck, that only the bones beneath the fragile skin had prevented his head from being separated from his body.

His name was Luther Wade, Private, Rifleman, 6th Mississippi.

He was found by the camp doctor, who had been unable to sleep, just as he'd been unable to sleep for the last three days. The doctor walked quietly back to camp and enlisted the assistance of a private on watch. They took a wagon and one of the more rested horses and went back to fetch Private Wade. His body was cut down as gingerly as was possible under the circumstances, then laid out in the buckboard and taken back to the field hospital, where the doctor wiped his bleary eyes, shook his head at the pitiful sight, and said, "Damn war can't last much longer now. This boy might have been home in a few months." He didn't want to look on a sight like this. In the last five days he'd amputated seven legs, three arms, and numerous hands and fingers. None of them had gone particularly well because the conditions here were unspeakably filthy. His head was still filled with echoing screams of young men lying on the operating table, begging him to kill them. His boots were caked with gore. His hands, though washed, still felt like they were covered in the blood of brave young men taken too soon from their homes and forced to fight in a war where both sides were doomed no matter who won.

At least there was still some whiskey left for the coffee.

"What do you suppose made him do it, sir?" asked Tyler, the young private whose terrible duty it had been to assist the doctor in retrieving Private Wade's remains and transporting them back to camp. "Ain't we lost enough good men on the battlefield? What kind of a coward goes out in the night like he done and—"

The doctor waved his hand, silencing Tyler. "Be damned careful how you use a word like *coward*, son. Every man has his breaking point. You got no idea what made him do this."

Tyler shrugged. "I didn't mean no offense, sir. It just seems to me that if a man can come away from what we seen at Cold Harbor, then he's just about seen the worst there is."

"Has he now?"

"That's just my opinion, sir."

The doctor gestured at the body. "Did you happen to know him?"

"Luther? Yessir, I did. I mean, we weren't best friends or nothing, but I knew him well enough to play some cards or have a pleasant enough conversation during watch. Ain't nothing he said nor did that would lead me to think he'd ever do a damn fool thing like this, no sir, not a thing at all."

"This late in the war, our beloved Confederacy is full of surprises, right down to its smallest elements," said the doctor, pulling his pipe from his pocket and tamping down what little remained of the sad, bitter tobacco he'd taken from the body of a prisoner who'd died on his table late last night. The Union soldier had known he was going to die from the severity of his wounds, and so had asked the doctor to write a note for his parents. The doctor had obliged the soldier, patiently sitting next to the table while the young man—who could not have been any older than fifteen—dictated a short letter with broken words and incomplete sentences. To show his gratitude for the doctor's help, he offered the pouch of tobacco that was in his pocket. "My father swears this is the damned finest tobacco there is, yessir," he'd said, then died without telling the doctor his last name.

The doctor still had the letter in his pocket. He would carry it with him, he suspected, until the good General Robert E. Lee came to his senses and mustered the courage to admit defeat and sent a messenger to Grant requesting terms of surrender.

The doctor looked at Luther Wade's body. "What's that?"

"Sir?" asked Tyler.

"There's something inside his coat, behind his back— see it there, son?"

"Yessir."

They lifted Wade's body, only half turning him over before the object was revealed.

Wade had pinned an envelope to the back of his uniform. It was addressed, simply, this way:

*To Whoever Finds Me.*

The doctor removed the envelope from Wade's uniform, then wiped off as much of the blood as was still wet enough to be wiped away. Inside, Luther Wade had wrapped the letter in a small piece of torn blanket, perhaps suspecting that rain—or his own blood—might stain the envelope and seep through to the pages within.

The first page had only a few lines on it, giving the names of his parents and asking that the reader please be kind enough to see that the following pages be posted to his parents' address, which was written in a strong, steady, legible hand.

The doctor leaned back against the buckboard, tucked the letter under his arm, and managed to get his pipe going at last. The tobacco tasted like dried manure, but he was going to smoke all of it.

The Union soldier had offered it like it was the most precious thing he possessed; it didn't seem right to simply toss it away because its flavor wasn't to his liking. Might as well have pissed on the poor kid's body, if that were the case.

The doctor puffed away on his pipe, thinking.

"You gonna read the letter, sir?" asked Tyler.

"Yes, Private, I am. And since you were the one who found him, I guess that means you've got something of a right to read it as well, considering the way he addressed the envelope."

"I don't see as how that'd be proper, sir."

The doctor stared at Tyler. "I am not one who believes that killing yourself is necessarily a coward's way out. It is my belief that a body'd have to be in a lot of pain in order to think a death the likes of *this* was preferable to breathing in the air of one more morning. So I am going to read this letter, and then you will read it, and we will at least be able to speak truthfully about Private Wade's reasons for taking his own life when others start in with their half-assed guessing. He might have killed himself, but Luther Wade was a soldier who fought for our beloved Confederacy, and that alone dictates a certain amount of respectfulness at his death. It requires we do what we can to maintain some of his dignity, for there is no man more dignified on this Earth than one of our Confederate boys in his uniform, be he alive or dead, be that death in battle or by his own hand." He offered the letter to Tyler. "Would you care to be the first to read it, Private?"

Tyler looked down at his feet and coughed. "Afraid I don't read too good, sir."

The doctor nodded. "Then cover him up and come on over to my tent. I'll make some coffee for us, and then I will read this letter aloud. Somehow I think it important that his last thoughts be shared with someone."

"Yessir."

"And Private?"

"Sir?"

"Since no one saw us cut down his body nor bring it into camp, I'll ask you to not speak of this for the time being."

"Yessir. Still seems a damned fool thing to do, hanging yourself."

"We're all hanging ourselves, son, from the moment we're born; just takes the rope fifty or sixty years to snap tight, that's all."

To My Dearest Mother and Father:

By now you have undoubtedly heard about the circumstances of my death, and for that I offer my deepest apologies. It was never my intention to disgrace my uniform or the good name of our family, but circumstances have made it necessary that I do not die a hero's death in battle or return home alive and whole.

I must also assume that the papers back home have by now told the sad tale of the battle at Cold Harbor. Though we are not privy to the papers out here, I can tell you this much: No one who wasn't there could begin to capture in words the horror of the slaughter that we took part in. I harbor no great love for the Union Army nor its soldiers, but I must confess to you here that, toward the end of their last charge, it began to turn my stomach, how easy it was to kill them. That dreadful storm of lead and iron seemed more like a volcanic blast than a battle. It did not matter that the Union Army were armed with their new repeating rifles. Our boys had dug in well, creating massive entrenchments in which we were well protected in the earthworks and suffered little from the federal fire. But still, General Grant insisted on a second charge from his soldiers.

It took almost a full day for them to prepare for their second charge, which came a little after four-thirty in the morning. Thousands of Union soldiers crawled out of their entrenchments and marched toward us. It was like shooting cans off a fence. I cannot speak for what happened farther down the line, but where I was, no Union soldier was able to get closer than twenty feet of our earthworks before being cut down—and often cut in half—by our fire. It was deafening, a boiling cauldron from the incessant pattering of shots which raised the dirt in geysers and spitting sands. The men fell and fell and fell. Blood ran thick as mud all around us. It was over in half an hour. The stunned attackers recoiled and sought the protective cover of their trenches, having left thousands upon thousands of their comrades lying on the field. Their dying screams are in my ears still, even as I write this from the relative safety of the field hospital camp.

Oh, my dear parents, I have seen the carnage in front of Marye's Hill at Fredericksburg, and on the old railroad cut which Jackson's men held at the Second Manassas, but I have seen nothing to exceed this. It was not war; it was murder.

Something took place during the battle which I need to confess, but first I must ask you to think back, if you can, to when my beloved brother Matthew and I were children. I promised you, Mother, that I would watch over Matthew during this damn war, and watch over him I did. He was never far from my side. I want you to know this, to know that I tried to be a good and loyal son and brother, one who did everything in his power to keep his word.

I remember, when we were children, the joy I would experience when I awakened to see Matthew in the morning. It never mattered to me that he was so slow-witted and deliberate of speech; a purer and more gentle soul I have never encountered—nor, I suspect, has anyone. Not this side of the angels.

Do you remember how he would always rise before any of us? How he would quietly dress himself and start the coals in the stove so it would be all warmed up when you rose, Mother? Then he would take that big old tin can of his—his "treasure chest," he called it, remember? And he would go outside and look for treasures to place within.

Lord, how I can remember those days when, trapped inside by the rain and unable to go out and play with the other children, Matthew would entertain us with a show of his treasures. "Here is a button from a king's satin shirt. Here is a feather from an angel's wing. Here is a cup once drunk from by our Lord Jesus." How I loved those moments.

Over the last several months, Matthew had taken to singing a song during the long marches to and from our battles. He sang it so much that many of the men learned the words and have been singing it ever since. It goes: Come raise me in your arms, dear brother, And let me see that glorious sun, For I am weary, faint, and dying, How could that battle lost or won; Do you ever think of mother, In that home far in the land? Watching, praying for her children, If I could see that home again!

The men would often sing that line over and over: "If I could see that home again!"

A fragile dream, with blood soaking through your boots, but at least a dream that was still kept alive.

I am sorry for the rambling nature of this. The trip from the battlefield to this new camp is still fresh in my mind. Allow me to tell you something of this journey, which for me will soon reach its end.

I held onto the tailgate of a wagon filled with the wounded, letting it pull me along because my boots had begun to fill with bloody mud. Rain fell in slanted, steely pencilings. There was a constant murmur, the groans of the wounded as the long slow agonized column wound between weeping trees and wet brown fields. I could hear their teeth grinding and even the faint scrabbling of their fingernails against the planks of the springless wagon bed. It was the same road we had followed into battle, only now we were going in the opposite direction and there was no reappearing sun nor crackle of Union gunfire to cause the troops to hasten their steps.

Our faces were grey, the color of ashes. Some had powder burns red on their cheeks and foreheads and running back in singed patches in their hair. Mouths were rimmed with grime from biting cartridges, mostly a long smear down one corner, and hands were blackened with burnt powder off the ramrods. We'd aged three lifetimes when Grant ordered that second, suicidal charge. The captain was calling for us to rally, rally here, rally there, but there wasn't much rally left in any of us, not after that damned battle. There wasn't much left in me, anyhow. I was so empty and cold and tired it was all I could do to hang onto the back of that wagon and let it pull me to where the flag marked the field hospital and the encampment beyond it. I was worried, too, about not having my rifle, but if having it meant that I had to look down at the bearded man in whose chest I'd buried it deep and pull it out of him, then it could damn well stay where I'd left it. Then I happened to look down and Lord if there wasn't one just like it lying in the mud near my feet. I picked it up, stooping and nursing my bad arm, and nearly lost my hold on the wagon. My arm was still seeping from the bullet I'd taken during the last charge.

Exhausted horses and mules refused to pull; demoralized and badly shaken drivers, with straining eyes and perspiring bodies, plied their whips vigorously to no effect; difficult places in the road were choked with blazing wagons set aflame to save their contents from falling into the hands of the enemy.

Hundreds of men dropped from exhaustion. Even more threw away their arms. The demoralization at last began to spread even to the officers, who did nothing to

stop the straggling. Many of them seemed to shut their eyes
to the hourly reduction of their command, and rode in
advance of their brigades in dogged indifference. It was
among the saddest sights I have ever seen. But still there
was, if one looked closely enough in certain eyes, something left of the old spirit which had made the army of our
beloved Confederacy famous throughout the world, and
inscribed its banners with the most dignified and glorious
names of the war.

Still I could hear the echo of tired, broken men
singing: "If I could see that home again!"

Regiment by regiment the columns lurched forward
as the rain grew heavier, rifles sloppily dressed at right
shoulder shift and the men—as well as the too many boys—
stumbling like drunkards or shuffling along like a simple-
ton weighed down with the shame of it all. Soon the wheels
of the wagons and artillery had churned the road into shin-
deep mud. There were halts and countless delays, times
when the men had to trot to keep up, and other times,
more frequently, when they simply stood in the rain, waiting for the man ahead of them to stumble into motion
while the mud and filth grew wetter and thicker and pulled
at their cold feet. The muskets grew heavy. Haversack straps
began cutting into our shoulders, drawing blood. The road
was littered with discarded equipment, empty boots, sabers
and Bowie knives, overcoats, Bibles, playing cards. All that
day as we moved along the column we came upon regiment
after regiment halted by the road, the men leaning on
their rifles or sitting on pieces of debris from the battle that
had found their way to this spot.

As I looked at all the bitter remnants left behind, I
could easily imagine Matthew in the morning, armed with
his treasure chest, gathering these items and saying, "Here
is a playing card from a magician's deck, here is a page
from a Bible once read by a preacher with a voice of gold,
here is a strap from the reins of Traveler, the finest horse
in this war."

I can feel him in the morning, still. His gentleness, his
wonder, his affection, and playfulness. Never has a man
had a more loving brother than I had in Matthew. And

when I think of the way the other children used to tease and mock him, I no longer feel anger; I feel pity—and not for Matthew, for them. In their haste to make him an object of ridicule, they denied themselves the honor of knowing the purest soul they would ever have met. The laughter he could have given to them, the mysteries of this world he could have unveiled to them. They are all the poorer. As we all are now.

And not only in the morning, but now I find that I can see Matthew in the stars at night.

I find, most especially on a night like this, that the thought gives me comfort and courage. I see and feel the Matthew we all knew, he of the slow wits and deliberate speech and tin can of treasures.

Remember him that way; I think he would have wanted you to.

I once asked him why he made up such stories to accompany every new "treasure" he found. I remember he said to me, "We don't know no different, now, do we? How do we know that this feather did not come from a angel's wing? Or this button from the shirt of a king? It's all down here, Luther, buried low in the ground. Mysteries for us to find and wonder about. Someday, maybe someone will find a button from my shirt buried low in the ground, and maybe they will hold it and clean it until it shines and say, This is a button worn by a brave soldier, and as long as I carry it with me, his spirit will protect me from harm."

I know, Father, how you always despaired that Matthew never learned to properly read or write, even when the two of us signed up he was unable to write his entire name and I had to do most of it for him. But I tell you this, dear Father, I tell you this as the son who was always a good student and quick to learn and of whom you were always so proud: I might have been well-educated as far as book-learning went, but I would gladly give all that knowledge back to have been able to see the world for just one day the way my dear brother Matthew saw it. His was a wisdom born not of books and learning, but of wonder and a joy for the details of life that few of us ever know—or if we do know it, it is only as children, and too soon crushed under the weight of adulthood.

And adulthood come fast to a boy on the battlefields of war.

War changes a boy into a man very quickly; and even more quickly does it change even the man.

I ask now, Mother and Father, that you lay aside this letter for a moment and ready yourselves for what I have next to tell you.

Matthew is dead. He died by my own hand. The bearded man I spoke of earlier, the one in whom I left my rifle buried in his chest—that was Matthew. I killed him during the final moments of the second charge at Cold Harbor. I did this with full intention in my heart of ending his life. And though I beg your forgiveness, I cannot say that I am sorry for having killed him.

The Matthew that we knew and loved, the Matthew of the morning treasures, was dead long before I attacked him in the smoke and blood and under the scream of cannon fire.

I began to notice the change in him a few months ago, after a brief but terrible encounter with a Union regiment that left many of our fellow Confederate boys dead. It was the first time Matthew had killed a man. He began to shake as he looked down upon the body of a boy no older than fifteen, then he began to weep; quietly at first, then with greater violence. I held him close and comforted him, not caring a damn about the looks some of our fellow soldiers gave us. I told him that it was all right, he had to do it, but my words did little to soothe the pain of his soul.

"It was so fast," he cried. "He was standing before me just a moment ago, and now he's dead and I killed him, and he'll never see his family again and his mother, she'll be sad for the rest of her life."

The Matthew you knew and loved began to die that moment.

Over the next days, weeks, and months, I saw Matthew's acceptance of death and violence grow from the frightened acceptance of a child to the cold-hearted disregard of a bitter, battle-weary soldier. The light in his eyes dimmed, then died altogether.

He became one of our regiment's fiercest fighters during battle.

He became something of a monster, and I was powerless to stop it. If I could have, I would have stood in the middle of the blood-soaked ground and beseeched God Almighty to stop this war for just a few hours so that I might be able to bring back the Matthew we knew. But God has recently stopped listening to the prayers of the Confederacy. Maybe He never listened at all.

There was one instance, seven nights ago, when a ghost of the old Matthew showed itself to me, and for a moment I thought perhaps he could be saved.

I found him with an injured rabbit cradled in his arms. He was stroking its head gently and singing a soft song in its ear. I remembered then, how he had found that robin when we were children, the one with the broken wing, and how he had nursed it back to health.

I reminded him of that and he smiled at me. For a moment, he was the brother I had always known and loved.

Then he grabbed the rabbit's ears and twisted its head and snapped its neck. "Everything ends up getting buried down low in the dirt," he said. "Death is terrible, and it is the end of all we try to do, so why not help it along?"

I cannot hope to describe to you the coldness in his voice and the emptiness in his eyes.

I knew then that I had failed him.

I knew then that the Matthew I loved was dead.

I knew then that I had to kill this heartless creature who stood before me.

Mother and Father, you would not have wanted him back, not the way he was, not this thing he had become. I know that you must have great disappointment—even hatred—in your hearts for me at the moment, but you know that I have never lied to you.

Our Matthew was already dead.

It was only a matter of choosing the right moment.

The second charge of Grant's men had begun their broke retreat. Smoke lay heavy on the field. Several of our men then climbed from the earthworks and continued firing on the retreating soldiers.

Matthew was among the first to leave the earthworks.

I found him a few dozen feet away, using the butt of his rifle to break open the skulls of Union boys who, though wounded and lying in their own blood, were still not dead.

Matthew was screaming, words I dare not repeat here. Worst of all was the laughter that lay underneath his cries. He continued to beat and kick and stab and kill any wounded man he could find.

All the while his screams mixed with his laughter and landed hard on my ears.

It was the sound of something nailed down and in torment. It was the sound of war's madness at its height of power.

I readied my weapon and charged at him, burying the blade of my rifle deep into his center, driving it with such force that I saw the blade finally come out his back.

He slid down the barrel of my rifle toward me, the gaping wound in his chest making a horrible wet sound, like a starving man slurping a bowl of soup.

I hefted my rifle and lifted his feet from the ground. For a moment the light of a nearby fire illuminated his face, and I saw his eyes.

In them was gratitude.

He had known all along, somehow, that what he had become was unfit to return to the world of families and shops and hard candy and music in the square and littler boys who gather their treasures in the morning.

"Forgive me," I whispered to him.

He smiled, and sang to me: "I remember you, my brother, Sent to me that fatal dart; Brothers fighting against brothers, Well, 'tis well that thus they part."

I let go of my rifle and embraced him as well as I could as he sank to the ground, pulled down by the bloody mud. I stroked his cheek and kissed his brow and told him that we would always love him.

If he understood me, he said nothing. I can only hope that heaven is merciful and allowed him to know; I can only hope that God is understanding and welcomed Matthew into Heaven with open arms, understanding that war had forever ruined the wonder that was my brother.

That is all.

It is a little before two in the morning as I write this. I cannot live with the sins my soul has acquired during this war. I cannot live knowing that I failed my brother, that I was busy killing other men while a monster crept in and took his place. My only comfort is knowing that Matthew was able to reclaim his old self at the very end.

Take me out to the battlefield, let me hear the shells flying by. Let me hear the sound of the cannons, and the cries of the brave men dying. Let me go to this place where I can feel the pain and the coldness and the loneliness that there must be for men such as myself, those who tried, those who failed, those who stood by and did nothing.

Let me take with me all my shame. Let it be buried low with me. Let my body never be found until its flesh is dust. Let the years scatter the pieces of my memory so that someday, perhaps, another child such as Matthew will come upon a trinket that once was mine, and he will wipe away the dirt until that trinket shines, and he will hold it up into the sunlight of a peaceful day and blink against its brightness, and say to himself, "This is part of a medal from an honorable man's chest. I will put it here, with the feather from an angel's wing and the button from the silken shirt of a king."

Maybe they will feel me in the morning, or see me in the stars at night.

I know Matthew will be there.

Good-bye, Mother and Father. I have always loved and respected you both deeply. I shall miss you. I hope someday you will find it in your hearts to forgive your weaker son for what he has done.

May God bless and protect you through all the lonely places that you walk.

With Love, Your Son,
Luther

THE DOCTOR STARED AT the last page in silence for several moments, then placed it atop the others on his table. He shuffled through the pages until he found the very first one, which bore the name and address of Private Luther Wade's parents. This page he set apart from the rest.

"Dear Lord," whispered Private Tyler.

"Indeed," replied the doctor.

He then poured them another cup of coffee, adding to it a generous portion of the remaining whiskey.

Outside, the sun was breaking through the night's gloom. A bird sang sweetly in the distance.

Soldiers coughed and grumbled as they awakened and began preparations to move out.

"That song Private Wade spoke of," said the doctor. "Do you know it, Tyler?"

"Only that part about wishing to see home again."

The doctor nodded, fired up the last bit of tobacco in his pipe—somehow, it didn't taste as bitter now—and puffed away for a moment.

"I know that song well," he said finally to Tyler. The last verse, in particular, I have always found haunting. It goes, 'Brother, take from me a warning, Keep that secret you have won, For it would kill our aged old mother, If she knew what you have done.'"

He then sat very still, staring at Tyler.

After a few moments of silence, Tyler took a deep breath and met the doctor's gaze. "Oh, Lordy, sir, you don't mean—"

"It's *exactly* what I mean," said the doctor firmly, and he picked up the envelope and the remaining pages of Private Wade's letter and tore them all in half, then half again. He rose from his seat and walked outside his tent and tossed the pieces into the nearest fire, then stood and watched until they were burned to black.

When he re-entered his tent, he found Tyler standing over his table, reading the only remaining page from the letter.

"Why did you do that, sir?"

"Because this goddamned stinking war has already caused enough good, decent parents too much grief, that's why. How do you think his mother and father would be able to go on if they knew the truth? Isn't it bad enough that they'll have to live through seeing their beloved Confederacy fall—and we both know it *will*, Tyler—all the while knowing they've lost both their sons? Are you so weak that your conscience cannot abide keeping this a secret so as to spare two grieving parents a burden of pain that no human being could possibly endure? *I* am not that weak, Tyler. For weeks now all I've seen is the pain and agony and pointlessness of death and violence and I've had my *fill*, do you understand me, Private? I could not take away any of these fine soldiers' pain and suffering, I couldn't take it away from their families, I was impotent in the face of war, useless and ineffectual." He snatched away the page with the Wades' address on it. "Well I can spare these two people a *little* of the pain, and that is *precisely* what I am going to do. But you have to help me, Tyler. Are you willing to do that?"

"It don't seem right, sir, I mean—"

"None of this is right, Tyler. It's up to us, as those who will survive this slaughter, to take the necessary steps to *make* it right. I cannot order you to help me, Tyler, I can only ask, and I do so now: as one battle-weary man to another, will you keep the contents of Luther Wade's letter a secret? Will you help me spare his parents that final measure of grief that might very will kill both of them?"

Tyler swallowed once. Very hard. Then nodded his head. "Yessir. And I am a man of my word."

The doctor placed a hand on Tyler's shoulder. "Thank God for that, Tyler. Thank God."

The doctor sat down at his table and found a fresh envelope and piece of stationery, then copied the Wades' address onto the new envelope.

"Sir?" asked Tyler.

"Yes?"

"Private Wade's body."

"Yes?"

"The way it is, I mean . . . how can you explain something like that?"

The doctor paused for a moment, thinking.

"It happened like this, Tyler: This morning Luther Wade asked me to look at a horse that was harnessed to one of the wagons—one of the damaged wagons. As I was examining the horse, Luther Wade was attempting to fix the undercarriage of the wagon. The horse spooked and bucked, pulling the wagon down from the rocks upon which it rested. Luther Wade's neck was caught under the weight of a wheel, nearly severing his head. That is how I will write it in my report and that is how you will tell it."

"Yessir." Then: "Doctor?"

"Yes, Tyler?"

"I'd like to say it's been an honor to spend this evening in the company of a man as fine as yourself."

The doctor smiled. "I'm just a glorified butcher these days, but I thank you for the sentiment, Private. Tell your commanding officer I wish to speak with him before you leave. I want to make sure he knows that you have been of great service to me."

"Thank you, sir.

"Thank *you*, Tyler. Now go. Look down low in the ground for buried treasure."

Tyler smiled, saluted, then left the tent.

The doctor stared at the blank page before him, then, after closing his eyes and humming a bit of a certain song to himself, set pen to page and wrote:

Dear Mr. and Mrs. Wade:

It is my sad duty to inform you of the deaths of your two sons, Luther and Matthew, at the recent battle of Cold Harbor. Both of your sons were good and decent men and

fine soldiers, and both died bravely in defense of our
beloved Confederacy . . .

He paused, then, and listened.

And, perhaps, somewhere deep in his soul where a
weary man holds tight to the remaining dreams of child-
hood, he felt near him the presence of a young boy slow of
wit, deliberate of speech, and pure of spirit.

"Here is a letter about heroes," he whispered. "Here is a
pen once used by Shakespeare. Here is a page from a book
stolen from a secret kingdom where magic never dies."

# Authors' Biographies

**Doug Allyn** is an accomplished author whose short fiction regularly graces year's best collections. His work has appeared in *Once Upon a Crime, Cat Crimes Through Time,* and *The Year's 25 Finest Crime and Mystery Stories,* volumes 3 and 4. His stories of Talifer, the wandering minstrel, have appeared in *Ellery Queen's Mystery Magazine* and *Murder Most Scottish.* His story "The Dancing Bear," a Tallifer tale, won the Edgar Award for short fiction for 1994. His other series character is veterinarian Dr. David Westbrook, whose exploits have recently been collected in the anthology *All Creatures Dark and Dangerous.* He lives with his wife in Montrose, Michigan.

**Edward D. Hoch** makes his living as a writer in a way that very few other people can attest to—he works almost entirely in short fiction. With hundreds of stories, primarily in the mystery and suspense genres, he has created such notable characters as Simon Ark, the two-thousand-year-old detective; Nick Velvet, the professional thief who only steals worthless objects; and the calculating Inspector Leopold, whose appearance in the short story "The Oblong Room" won his creator the Edgar Award for best short story. He lives and writes in Rochester, New York.

Primarily known for making the New England countryside come alive in his novels and short stories, **Brendan DuBois** has written several dozen critically acclaimed short stories, and has had his work appear in several year's best anthologies. One of his latest stories, "The Dark Snow," was nominated for the Edgar Award for best short story of 1996. Recent novels include *Shattered Shell*, the third mystery featuring contemporary magazine writer/sleuth Lewis Cole, and *Resurrection Day*, a techno-thriller extrapolating what might have happened if the Cuban Missile Crisis had turned into a full-fledged war. He lives in Exeter, New Hampshire.

**John Lutz** is one of the most skilled mystery writers working today. His most recent novels are *The Ex* and *Final Seconds*, coauthored with David August. His settings and descriptions always have the ring of authenticity, whether he's writing about the blues scene in New Orleans or the relationships between men and women. His series characters are also in a class by themselves, whether it be the hapless Alo Nudger or the more traditional detective Fred Carver. A favorite contributor to both *Ellery Queen's Mystery Magazine* and *Alfred Hitchcock's Mystery Magazine*, his work has also appeared in numerous anthologies, most recently *Irreconcilable Differences*.

**Avram Davidson** (1923–1993), like many of the authors included here, wrote in several genres during his lifetime. Getting his start in speculative fiction in the 1950s, he wrote several classic stories such as "All the Seas with Oysters," and "Dagon." At the urging of the editor for *Ellery Queen's Mystery Magazine*, he turned to writing mysteries, and he won the Ellery Queen Award as well as the Edgar Allan Poe Award. When he began writing novels, he went back to the form in which he had started—science fiction and fantasy. Notable works include *The Phoenix and the Mirror* and *The Island Under the Earth*.

**Marc Bilgrey**'s fiction has previously appeared in *First Contact, Phantoms of the Night,* and *Cat Crimes Through Time.* A native of Bellvue, Washington, he is a full-time writer.

In her twenty-five years as a writer, editor, and publishing consultant, **Janet Berliner** has worked with such authors as Peter S. Beagle, David Copperfield, Michael Crichton, and Joyce Carol Oates. Among her most recent books are the anthology *David Copperfield's Beyond Imagination,* which she created and edited, and *Children of the Dusk,* the final book of *The Madagasacar Manifesto,* a three-book series coauthored with George Guthridge. Janet divides her time between Las Vegas, where she lives and works, and Grenada, West Indies, where her heart is.

**Billie Sue Mosiman** has published eight suspense novels during her career, garnering an Edgar Award nomination for Night Cruise and a Stoker Award nomination for *Widow.* Always active as a short story writer, her work has appeared in various magazines and anthologies, including *Fathers & Daughters, Monsters in Our Midst,* and *Robert Bloch's Psychos.* She has also co-edited several anthologies, including *Death in Dixie* and a Regional Mystery series. She lives in Midway, Texas, with her husband, Lyle, and near her daughters, granddaughters, and parents.

**John Helfers** is a writer and editor living in Green Bay, Wisconsin. A graduate of the University of Wisconsin–Green Bay, his fiction appears in more than a dozen anthologies, including *Future Net, Once Upon a Crime, First to Fight,* and *Warrior Princesses,* among others. His first anthology project, *Black Cats and Broken Mirrors,* was published in 1998. Recent projects include the mystery anthology *Murder Most Medieval,* as well as a novel in progress.

**Carol Rondou** is an author and graduate of the University of Wisconsin–River Falls. A member of the Society for Creative Anachronism, she also enjoys fencing and researching Colonial American history. Other fiction by her appears in *Black Cats and Broken Mirrors*. She lives in Menasha, Wisconsin.

In 1999 **Kristine Kathryn Rusch** won three Reader's Choice Awards for three different stories in three different magazines in two different genres: mystery and science fiction. That same year, her short fiction was nominated for the Hugo, Nebula, and Locus Awards. Since she had just returned to writing short fiction after quitting her short-fiction editing job at *The Magazine of Fantasy and Science Fiction*, she was quite encouraged by this welcome back to writing. She never quit writing novels, and has sold more than forty-five of them, some under pseudonyms, in mystery, science fiction, fantasy, horror, and romance. Her most recent mystery novel is *Hitler's Angel*. Her most recent fantasy novel is *The Black Queen*.

**Max Allan Collins** is the author of the Shamus Award–winning "Nathan Heller" historical detective series, and the author of such bestselling tie-in novels as *Saving Private Ryan*, *Air Force One*, and *In the Line of Fire*. He has also written comic books, trading cards, and film criticism, and he is the writer/director of three independent feature films and one documentary. He lives in Muscatine, Iowa.

**Matthew V. Clemens** is the coauthor of the bestselling true crime book *Dead Water*, and he contributed a story to the anthology *Private Eyes*. He is the author of numerous magazine and newspaper articles and has collaborated with Max Allan Collins on several previous short stories. He is the publisher of Robin Vincent Books and lives in Davenport, Iowa.

**Bradley H. Sinor** is the author of the novel *Highlander: The Eye of Dawn*. He has seen his work appear in the *Merovingen Nights* anthologies; *Time of the Vampires*; *Merlin, Lord of the Fantastic*; and other places. He lives in Oklahoma with his wife, Sue, and three strange cats who are plotting to take over the world.

In a full-time writing career that has spanned a couple of decades, **James M. Reasoner** has written in virtually every category of commercial fiction. His novel *Texas Wind* is a true cult classic and his gritty crime stories about contemporary Texas are in the first rank of today's suspense fiction. He has written many books in ongoing western series, including the *Faraday, Stagecoach,* and *Abilene* novel series. Recent books include *The Civil War Battles* series, published by Cumberland House, and *The Last Good War* series, published by Forge.

**Kristine Scheid** is a native-born New Yorker who moved west when she was two and has yet to return to the Empire State. She has a history degree from the University of Wisconsin, where she was greatly influenced by Michael Shaara's masterpiece *The Killer Angels*. "Valuables" is her first published story.

**Ed Gorman** is a Midwesterner who was born in Iowa in 1941, grew up in Minneapolis, Minnesota, and Marion, Iowa, and finally settled down in Cedar Rapids, Iowa. While primarily a suspense novelist, he has written half a dozen Western novels and published a collection of Western stories. His novel *Wolf Moon* was a Spur nominee for Best Paperback Original. About his Western novels, *Publisher's Weekly* said, "Gorman writes Westerns for grown-ups," which the author says he took as a high compliment, and was indeed his goal in writing his books. "The Face" won the 1996 Spur Award for best western short fiction.

**Gary A. Braunbeck** is the acclaimed author of the collection *Things Left Behind* (CD Publications), released in 1998 to unanimously excellent reviews and nominated for both the Bram Stoker Award and the International Horror Guild Award for Best Collection. He has written in the fields of horror, science fiction, mystery, suspense, fantasy, and western fiction, with over 120 sales to his credit. His work has recently appeared in *Cat Crimes Through Time, The Best of Cemetery Dance, Once Upon a Crime,* and *Dark Whispers.* He is coauthor (along with Steve Perry) of *Time Was: Isaac Asimov's I-Bots,* a science fiction adventure novel being praised for its depth of characterization. His fiction, to quote *Publisher's Weekly,* ". . . stirs the mind as it chills the marrow."

# Copyrights
# and Permissions

.